S. L. LINNEA
and the first two novels in this spectacular series

BEYOND EDEN

"Army chaplain Jaime Richards once again balances faith with action-oriented purpose in this sequel to *Chasing Eden*, which picks up three years after the previous title left off. . . . Linnea keeps the pressure on and the events racing. She does nail-biting extremely well."
—*Romantic Times BOOKreviews*

"This exciting sequel packs plenty of global action . . . the story line is fast-paced while the heroine is a likable protagonist who struggles with the questions of her faith when she returns to the mortal realm of pain and suffering while immortality is a Garden away. S. L. Linnea provides a deep thought-provoking thriller."
—*Mystery Gazette*

"Having not read *Chasing Eden*, I was concerned about 'catching up'; however, *Beyond Eden* is a stand-alone book . . . I found the writing drawing me into the multiple worlds. Linnea has written not just of Eden and the outside world but also of the scientific experimental community . . . To write such that the reader connects with the characters and feels like she is right there with them, feeling woozy or chewing gum, means you have done a superb job! On a scale of 1 to 5, I give it a 5."
—*Mostly Mystery Reviews*

MORE...

CHASING EDEN

"A roller-coaster adventure . . . reads like a cross between *Jarhead* and *Raiders of the Lost Ark*."
—Agatha Award–winning author
Julia Spencer-Fleming

"Unique, provocative, and engrossing . . . hours of gripping reading." —*New York Times* bestselling author
Cherry Adair

"This novel grabs the reader and races along at breakneck speed. Another thrilling fiction focused around ancient cultures." —*Armchair Interviews*

"Reads like the best of Robert Ludlum, with the realistic military flavor of W. E. B. Griffin, and the adventure of Clive Cussler—this book is impossible to put down."
—Colonel Ian "Red" Natkin, Ret., U.S. Army

"An absolute page-turner. This book has 'you are there' insider details that make you question everything you read in today's headlines. A thrill-a-minute read!"
—*New York Times* bestselling author Christina Dodd

"An intelligent, exciting novel with a tremendously strong feeling of authenticity. The edgy, scary atmosphere comes over vividly—definitely a sweaty-palms read. It is totally original and the ending completely unexpected. I loved it."
—Bestselling author Bill Napier

"S. L. Linnea does a masterful job of keeping the action and surprises coming. The settings are accurate and vivid, and the characters and story lines believable. *Chasing Eden* is a top-notch thriller on all counts." —*Presbyterians Today*

St. Martin's Paperbacks Titles by
S. L. Linnea

Chasing Eden

Beyond Eden

Treasure of Eden

Treasure of EDEN

S. L. Linnea

St. Martin's Paperbacks

This is a work of fiction. All of the characters, organizations, and events portrayed in this novel are either products of the author's imagination or are used fictitiously.

TREASURE OF EDEN

Copyright © 2008 by Sharon Linnéa and B. K. Sherer.

All rights reserved.

For information address St. Martin's Press, 175 Fifth Avenue, New York, NY 10010.

ISBN: 0-312-94216-8
EAN: 978-0-312-94216-8

Printed in the United States of America

St. Martin's Paperbacks edition / October 2008

St. Martin's Paperbacks are published by St. Martin's Press, 175 Fifth Avenue, New York, NY 10010.

10 9 8 7 6 5 4 3 2 1

For Linnéa Juliet Scott

and her beloved horses, Pasha, Dill, and Mia,

all of whom possess a great heart and invincible spirit

For where your treasure is, there will your heart be also.

Matthew 6:21

CONTENTS

—PROLOGUE—

March 30, 1954, 9:46 A.M.
Hills of the Judean wilderness

Omar saw the cave first. With all that would come later, it was a fact of which he'd remind himself daily for the next fifty years.

He and his seventeen-year-old cousin Rashid were tracking a gazelle through the mountains of the Judean desert west of the Dead Sea. The boys were north of Masada, significantly south of Qumran, where the Ta'amireh clan had been finding the valuable Dead Sea jars and scrolls.

It was the heady time that Bedouin boys were allowed out on treasure hunts, despite ongoing hostilities as the fledgling state of Israel came into being. Scroll finds were unlikely, but the Bedouin knew the desert in ways the educated archeologists never would, and their record was good. Besides, the Bedouin collected caves, much like American kids found and claimed swimming holes, for themselves and the use of their clan.

On this day, the cousins were following the tracks of a gazelle that had passed by two days earlier. For thousands of years, the Bedouin had been known as master trackers. Hero tales were told of those scouts who, even in modern times, could identify and track people and animals who had passed through the blowing sands weeks earlier.

And so Omar and Rashid were following the gazelle. They had come through a pass in the mountains Omar didn't recognize. The windstorms of winter often shifted sands significantly enough to alter the landscape. They squeezed through a narrow pass and climbed up onto what seemed to be a plateau.

"What do you think?" Omar asked, raising his goatskin flask to drink. "We've tracked far enough. What does it matter if we sight the animal, anyway? We know what it looks like, a gazelle with a right hind leg that has been broken and mended itself."

Even as he spoke, out of the corner of his eye he saw a swath of blue. Not pale blue, deep vermilion, blindingly bright, glancing off the sandstone of the plateau.

"Seen one gazelle, seen them all," answered Rashid agreeably.

Omar scrambled across fallen rocks and stood staring at the ground. There was a hole, about a foot in diameter, through which the stunning color could be seen. He fell onto his belly to look down. What he saw below was breathtaking.

It was a cave, painted in brilliant tones of blue, yellow, and green. There seemed to be patterns on the walls, circles, and stars and suns.

"What is it?" Rashid asked curiously. Omar rolled over and beckoned his cousin down.

The two boys stared for a moment in silence.

"What do you think it is?" asked Omar.

"A treasure cave, you donkey! *Our* treasure cave!"

"*Ours?* I saw it first!"

"Yes—" Rashid was busy dragging rubble from around the opening, until the hole in the cave's roof was two feet by a foot and a half. "But I was the first one down!" And he lowered his lanky body through the opening, and dropped.

Omar knelt, stunned. The cave floor was a good twenty feet down, and Rashid landed with an "oof" of expelled air. He curled into a ball and rolled, taking the brunt of the fall off his feet.

"What have you done?" Omar demanded. He was the practical one. Rashid often acted first and thought later. Now he was twenty feet down and neither boy had a rope.

Rashid didn't even answer. He sat up and looked around, openmouthed.

"What? What is it?"

"There are shelves," said Rashid. He scrambled to his feet and walked away from the angle of view from up top. "I think I found something!"

Omar was becoming agitated. What should he do? His cousin was stuck in a cave in the middle of nowhere—but they'd finally found something.

And then Omar's wiry cousin was standing directly below him in the shaft of light. "Come on down! You won't believe this place! Look!" He was holding up an ancient clay pitcher with a graceful neck and curved handle.

"How are you going to get up, you fool? If I join you, we'll both die here!"

"Wait; let me see. There's more light. I think we can get out." Rashid disappeared, and reappeared momentarily. "There's another way out," he said. "A side opening into a ravine. We can get out that way. Come on!"

Omar was beside himself. He wanted to see the treasure cave—*his* treasure cave—more than anything in the world. But he was stockier than Rashid, and wasn't sure he could even fit through the hole in the roof. And the drop looked like it had hurt. What if he injured himself?

"Cousin!"

Omar looked down. Rashid was standing below him, the direct sunlight making his white tunic and pants glow with an otherworldly sheen. He stood, feet apart, one elbow akimbo, fist on his waist. In the other, held aloft, there was a jeweled box, maybe ten inches by twelve. There were two gems on the top of the chest, one red, one blue. In the sunlight they were dazzling. Rashid paused for effect, then turned the large box on its side. A green gem sparkled; another side, an iridescent white one.

Omar couldn't stand it. He slung his feet down into the opening, and pushed his chest forward. He'd meant to grasp the roof with his hands and swing himself down, but there was nothing to grab. His hands slipped and his entire weight fell through the roof of the cave.

It was a bad landing. The air was completely knocked out of him. He lay for a minute on his back, waiting for the waves of pain to subside.

And Rashid was standing over him, a happy, gloating look on his face. "Look at this, Cousin; look!" He was hugging the box to himself. "I have it. We're going to be rich, all of us! And I'm going on the Hajj!"

"But it's mine," objected Omar. "If it wasn't for me, you wouldn't even have seen this cave!"

The promise had been made to all the boys that whoever found and brought home treasures of antiquity could accompany the sheikh on the next Hajj, traveling to Mecca and Medina. This was such a huge honor in the life of a Bedouin that once you had made this pilgrimage, even your name was changed. You had a much greater chance of becoming tribal leader.

It was Omar's box.

He lunged to his feet and grabbed for it.

Rashid held it away, laughing. Both boys knew that Rashid was wiry and more agile and could undoubtedly taunt Omar for hours, if he so chose.

But everything Omar had wanted in life, everything he held dear—going on the Hajj, becoming chief, having his choice of wives, being revered—this was his one chance to obtain those things and he knew it. There was nothing outstanding about him. He wasn't dumb, but he wasn't brilliant, either. He wasn't small and agile; he wasn't funny and warm. He was nobody's favorite. That box was his ticket, the thing that would change his life.

Rashid had the box, and he was still taunting, backing up toward the other cave entrance of which he'd spoken. Omar remembered the sun shining from behind Rashid, illuminating him in shadowy relief. He heard rather than saw the cackle of triumph Rashid made.

Nothing in his entire life had ever made Omar as angry as that taunting cackle.

He lunged at Rashid with all his weight, knocked him off balance, and grabbed the box. Then, in a moment of terrible fury, he shoved Rashid backward. And shoved him again.

When Rashid went falling backward out of the cave, the sun was finally fully on his face. So Omar could see the look of distress as Rashid realized he had no balance, he had no cave floor, he was falling.

Omar's breathing stopped. He counted the seconds before he heard Rashid land. There were too many of them. Far too many.

Omar slowly walked to the mouth of the cave and looked down. It was a deep ravine. There were outcroppings of rock all around. But from the mouth of the treasure cave to the ground, there was nothing. It was a forty-foot straight drop.

Rashid lay at the bottom of it. His neck was at a ghastly angle. He did not move. It was clear he was dead.

The horror lodged in Omar's throat. He could make no sound, although his insides were awash in tears.

He went back to the side of the cave, clutched the box to himself, and began to rock, keening. After a while, he crept back to the mouth to look down and plot out the handholds that he could climb down to the floor of the ravine.

There were none.

The next time he looked, he had decided there was a way down, there had to be; he and his cousins had climbed down many a rock face during their lives. He looked at the wall, careful not to let his gaze stray even slightly.

There were slight indentations. If he worked slowly and carefully, he could do it.

He slung his half-empty water bag over his shoulder. Then the problem was how to carry the box. Omar tried everything he could think of, but there was no way to carry the box and leave his hands free for the precarious descent.

He sat in the mouth of the cave, holding the box that was his future. He realized he was like the little monkey who got caught because he would not let go of the treat in the trap. But he would not let it go.

As darkness crept into the cave, he decided he must leave. He tucked the box under one arm. Could he possibly do it? Or would both cousins disappear forever at the bottom of this ravine?

As he lay on his stomach and swung his first leg over, he heard noise from below. Terrified, he scurried back up into the cave and looked down. A single hyena was circling Rashid. Omar yelled at the hyena, but he soon realized Omar was no threat. He slunk off. When he returned, he had brought his pack.

For two ghastly days, Omar quivered in the cave. The hyenas and jackals and scavenger birds came and went, taking Rashid's flesh and bones with them. When Omar looked over, there was nothing left but a hand. Finally something took it. And Rashid was gone.

By the third day, Omar was out of water. He knew he would soon start to hallucinate and then it would be impossible to leave the cave. He had to either die trying the descent or die of not trying.

That was when the good fortune of the box became apparent.

He was thinner than he had been two days earlier. Whether from lack of food or dehydration, the jeweled casket now fit into the waist of his pants, leaving his hands free. He said a prayer and started to slowly descend the sandstone face of the rock. It took him two hours to inch his way down the ravine. Twice he lost his footing and thought he was dead, but somehow another toehold was waiting for him.

When he reached the ground, he bowed down and kissed it, and said the prayer for those who had been spared from death. Then he stood up and realized he had no food and no water and did not know his way out of the ravine. There was very little chance he would make it home alive.

Even as he thought this, he turned around. And ten feet in front of him stood a camel. A camel wearing a tasseled harness. The Bedouin boys knew every camel in a fifty-mile radius and to whom it belonged. Omar had never seen this camel before. It had no saddle, but he didn't care. He mounted it and set off for home.

There was great celebration when he returned with the jeweled box. The men of the clan had a meeting in the big tent, and even sent someone for Khalil Iskander Shahin, called

Kando, the dealer from Bethlehem who acted as the go-between when the Bedouin had something of value for sale.

But before the dealer arrived, the chief's favorite wife, barren for ten years, discovered she was pregnant. She announced unequivocally that it was the good fortune of the box.

Then the men, on the way to market with the clan's woven goat-hair rugs and the bottled sand scenes, had run into a documentary crew who had made a great fuss over filming them and had bought the items for three times their going price.

It was decided they would not sell the box. It was their good fortune.

When they asked Omar what had become of Rashid, he told them his cousin had been offered a ride into Jerusalem and had gone to seek his fortune. He was spoken of often at first, and over the years there was much speculation about Rashid's undoubted good luck; they were sure the augur of the box had gone with him.

It all happened as Omar had hoped. He made his pilgrimage, and was thereafter called Hajj. He became the chief of the clan. He had three wives and many children. And whenever they had guests, he was persuaded to tell the story of the treasure cave.

For many years he did not sleep well.

For many years he did not consider selling the box.

Then came a time he saw no other way.

It was the end of a long day and the CIA Political Officer working with the Geneva Terrorism Task Force was ready to go home, grab some dinner and a Belgian beer. But first he picked up a new file that had been left on his desk earlier in the day.

Frank McMillan was just back from three years as Chief of Station in Tunisia. Three long years. Suffice it to say some of the higher-ups had not been pleased with his performance as Chief of Station of Kuwait City during the early days of Operation Iraqi Freedom. Nor had they been pleased that certain items he'd procured for them had been found to be less than authentic.

Ah, well. Another assignment. A fresh start.

His time in Iraq had piqued his interest in the black-market trade of antiquities. Even though it had nothing to do with his official duties, Frank had one of his assistants tasked to monitor all known venues for newly available items. The folder before Frank was half an inch thick with printouts and Xeroxes of the current crop of antiquities being offered for sale illegally. He opened it and thumbed through the papers under the circular pool of illumination from his desk lamp.

Nothing especially interesting.

Until, tired as he was, one item toward the bottom of the stack caused an intake of breath. He sat up, running his hand through his thick brown hair, feeling his adrenaline surge. He grabbed for his reading glasses, closed the folder, and put the printed paper in the center of his desk. It read:

eBay Item Number: 150 126643 1598
Realistic Jewel Cask Prop From '50s Classic Movie *Jenii*
Starting Bid: $50.00
End Time: Jan-27-07 00:30:00 PST
(3 days, 12 hours)
Shipping Costs: E-mail seller before making bid
Ships to: Worldwide
Item Location: Classic Props Warehouse
Description: This is it, the jeweled treasure box at the heart of the classic film *Jenii,* set in the mountains of the Judean wilderness. This box has been guarded carefully since the 1954 production, no nicks or scratches. Six realistic gems: ruby, carnelian, turquoise, lapis, jade, mother-of-pearl. Cask itself is heavy, measures twelve inches long, ten inches wide, and six inches deep, and comes with a lifetime Certificate of Authenticity. This is a fantastic blue-chip investment piece and was acquired directly from the prop maker. One of a kind. Only time available. Don't miss this once-in-a-lifetime chance to own a piece of film history!
Seller: Classic Props
Feedback: 100% Positive
Member: since Aug-04-01 in United States

Frank put his hands over his face and leaned back in his leather desk chair.

This was it. What he'd spent the last four years waiting for. A clue.

It wasn't a prop, of course. He'd become well versed in the language of the black market and knew the entire listing was code. It was an ancient box found in the Judean wilderness in

1954. Furthermore, in this auction, every dollar bid was $1,000.

He turned his computer back on, went to eBay, and pulled up the auction. He clicked on the photo to enlarge it. It was exquisite. The gold leaf on the outside of the box, the black onyx interior. He moved through the series of photos. Incredible. The hinges, too, were the right kind for Judea of 2,000 years before.

But what had caught his attention were the jewels: ruby, carnelian, turquoise, lapis, jade, mother-of-pearl. This was a rare instance when it was possible that even the canny dealer might not fully understand the significance of what he had.

Frank McMillan was aware that many of his compatriots thought he'd gone to Iraq a pragmatist and returned an obsessed man. He had been dealing there with two powerful men, both of whom believed that the place called Eden actually existed. Both men had died in their quest.

If, by any stretch of the imagination, it was true—if Eden did exist—the implications were staggering. One of his partners, Coleman Satis, claimed his own mother had been born there. She had told him stories of Eden's incredible wealth, of jewels so abundant they were used for home décor. More to the point, she'd told Satis of an advanced society with a wealth of technological and medical advances that would be worth billions to the outside world. And she said they had no army at all. No defense. Anyone with power who found this hidden society could walk in and take over. The ramifications of being that person were enormous.

There was a saying that Satis' mother had passed along to him, a saying that had driven Satis, who was already one of the most powerful men on earth: *Who Rules Eden Rules the World.*

Sounded like a worthy job description, at least to Frank.

Satis' mother had been so persuasive that Coleman Satis— the ultimate pragmatist—had been willing to risk everything, including his life, to find and conquer this place.

Now Satis was dead.

Frank himself wasn't completely convinced it actually

existed. But there were loose ends. Unsolved mysteries. And he was not a man who could tolerate loose ends or the feeling of being thwarted.

He'd come back from Iraq knowing two things. One was that these six jewels—ruby, carnelian, turquoise, lapis, jade, mother-of-pearl—were connected with the mystery. They were the jewels listed in the book of Genesis as jewels plentiful in Eden. He still didn't know how they figured into whatever the hell happened in Iraq, but he knew they did. At the heart of the incident had been a bracelet worn by an Arab girl with those six jewels.

The other thing he knew but could not explain was that a female American Army chaplain, Jaime Lynn Richards, who'd been involved in the secret Eden operation, had disappeared off the face of the earth, from Iraq, for three years. Then she had returned as mysteriously as she'd left, and reassumed her duties, seemingly without anyone in the Department of the Army batting an eye.

Which was impossible. All the Army knew how to do was bat eyes.

The new post-9/11 policy of data sharing between agencies was extremely helpful to Frank on this score. It had enabled him to keep tabs on Jaime Richards since her return, to at least know where she was and what she was up to. Her file said she was five foot seven; from his interview with her four years ago, he knew she had piercing green eyes that saw straight through him, that seemed able to read his thoughts. At least it felt that way at the time. Obviously, she hadn't read them well enough.

Frank pulled out her file and looked at the current photo. Her blond hair was a shade lighter, undoubtedly bleached by the desert sun. She was still in good shape, and had even acquired some pleasing curves. Frank had buffed up in Tunisia; now his biceps and quads were like iron. He laughed softly. Jaime Richards and Frank McMillan, versions 2.0.

According to Frank's information, Richards had missed a promotion board while she was away. At the next board, later this month, her Officer Record Brief—which listed where and when every officer was assigned—claimed that for those three years she was attached to the Office of the Chief of Chaplains in D.C. Frank understood that the Army wouldn't keep her listed as in Iraq—why give someone three years of combat pay when they didn't have to? But there was no explanatory note that she was kidnapped, only that she was on "duty elsewhere." And her personnel microfiche had three single pages labeled "classified" where evaluation reports should be.

What did that mean? In this particular case, what the hell did that mean?

Where had Jaime Richards been? And what did it have to do with Eden and the six jewels?

If there was a chance—the smallest chance—that she'd been in Eden, that she knew about Eden, that she could get there again, Frank had to find out.

From Tunisia, all he'd really been able to do was hear (although several months after the fact) that she'd reappeared and be kept apprised of her location. Now he was back, he was in Geneva, in a situation where he had mobility. He had been waiting for something to turn up, for another ticket into the mystery that was Eden.

This box was it. It had the key jewels, the jewels that to those in the know, signalled "Eden."

Did it have a direct connection to Jaime Richards? There was one way to find out. He'd follow the box, and see who else was following it, too.

He would also keep very close watch on Jaime Richards.

He already had a man on it. His last name was Maynard and he was undercover in Iraq as a Department of the Army civilian working for Army Material Command.

Frank took out his BlackBerry and e-mailed him: *Anything to report?*

The response took only two minutes: *Nothing. She spends most of her time in her office counseling, working in their operations center, or visiting soldiers in the hospital. Although she won't stay put. I spent Christmas Eve dodging mortars because she was climbing frigging guard towers to hang out with the guards. However, no apparent nonmilitary activity.*

*No contact with anyone of interest. She's going on mid-tour
leave tomorrow. Good riddance. Let our guy in Germany sit
outside her place.*

Frank stared at the words. Just stared at them.

The box had appeared, and Richards was on the move.

Was the timing coincidence? Or could the eBay listing and
the chaplain's leave be connected?

Frank's response to Maynard was flagged as urgent: *Wherever she's going, you're going, too. See to it.*

It was all he could do not to add: *you moron.*

Ah. Frank was back, and the hunt was on.

—WEDNESDAY—

Jaime Richards had twenty hours. Twenty hours to fly from Balad, Iraq, to Tallil—make a pickup—and continue on to Ali Ah Salem, Kuwait; Frankfurt, Germany; and deliver her package safely in Switzerland.

She couldn't even count the number of things that could go wrong. She was officially taking her mid-tour leave, and soldiers knew the plane they were on to start the journey out of Iraq could leave today, tomorrow, or, God forbid, a week from today. Or they could get stuck in Kuwait. Last time Jaime's boss had flown out on leave, the emir of Kuwait died, and the whole country—including the airfields—had shut down for three days.

Jaime had twenty hours.

She was packing her bags in the trailer that served as her hooch when she got a call. A COSCOM (Corps Support Command) soldier from one of her subordinate units was critically injured and was being rushed into surgery. It was a classic chaplain's dilemma. She needed to continue packing, there was no way she could miss her flight, and she desperately needed a couple of hours of sleep before the start of her new mission.

But there was a boy, and he was badly hurt.

To her mind, there really was no choice.

She headed for the operating room in the series of large interconnected tents that comprised the hospital, to observe the surgery and pray for the young soldier while the neurosurgeon worked on his damaged skull, which had been split wide open when the Humvee tire he was inflating exploded in his face. The rim had caught him on the forehead, right at the hairline about two inches above his eyes.

"Michael, are you with us?" Once the surgery was complete and Jaime knew she wouldn't get in anyone's way, she stepped up to the patient's side.

He had begun to stir, and squeezed Jaime's hand, on which she wore a disposable purple latex glove. She was amazed that someone could wake up and be aware of his surroundings after having his brain exposed only minutes before.

The young man was lucky to be alive, and even luckier that his skull had taken most of the impact, protecting the brain housed within.

"Doc," she said over her shoulder to a man who was making notes on the patient's clipboard. "That wire mesh you put in his forehead molds perfectly. You can hardly tell this guy had a piece of his skull broken out."

"I told you," he responded. "I'm the best."

She could see him smile beneath his mask but knew that he wasn't kidding.

If I ever need neurosurgery, she thought, *I want someone with that kind of confidence working on me!*

Still in the maroon scrubs she had donned to watch the procedure, she followed the gurney as they wheeled the young man back to the ICU for observation during his first hours of recovery. If they were certain he was stable, they might put him on the next plane for Landstuhl—the military regional medical center—later that morning.

Jaime remembered when she had taken that flight, almost a year before, after being picked up along the highway in southern Iraq. She'd been away for nearly three years. The official story went that she'd had amnesia and spent the time with Iranian goatherds. In fact, although she had spent some time with goats, most of it had been spent in the place known as Eden.

While most people in the world never suspected or believed it, the place that had come to be known as the Garden of Eden still existed. It was hidden—in fact, at any given time only twelve persons, known as Swords, knew the way in and out. At the end of an unusual adventure during her first tour in Iraq, Jaime had been invited to go to Eden, and she'd accepted.

She'd found Eden to be an altruistic society, whose citizens worked to help those in what they called the Terris world. There she'd spent a year in contemplation and gardening, and she was content. Until Clement had invited her to study at the place they called Mountaintop to join those they called the Integrators. The Integrators were citizens of Eden who moved back and forth between the two worlds. They included Messengers, who lived in the Terris world and delivered messages between other Integrators; Operatives, who had received special training in how to intervene in Terris affairs; and the twelve Swords who took people back and forth between the Terris world and Eden during the rare opportunities they called door openings.

Jaime discovered she felt called to be a person of action, and had trained to become an Eden Operative. Though the required training was three years, she'd been sent back a year early on special assignment.

That was nearly a year ago. Now Jaime was back in Iraq, in her Terris job, on assignment as a chaplain with the U.S. Army.

The unit with which Jaime had originally deployed to Iraq had finished their tour while she'd been gone. She'd been stationed in Germany the previous August when one of the chaplains assigned to the 5th COSCOM HQ had become ill and was shipped home. Jaime received the "Tag, you're it!" phone call on a lazy Sunday afternoon while relaxing in her rental home in the little burg of Hochspeyer. In less than two weeks she was back in Iraq.

Jaime checked her watch as she entered the ICU. Twelve forty A.M. She needed to get to the COSCOM Operations Center and clean up a few loose ends before catching her flight to Kuwait. Her original plan was to catch a few hours of sleep before finishing up. But she was now wide awake. Perhaps she should head for the COSCOM, do what she needed to do, then see if sleep was still an option.

Confident her soldier was doing well, Jaime returned to the women's dressing room, which was in truth a storeroom with a curtain hanging over the doorway. She removed her scrubs and donned the new ACU, or Army Combat Uniform, with the gray/green digital pattern. She laced up her desert boots, and pulled her dog tags off a hook hanging above her head. Her brother Joey—Joe, now, but he'd always be Joey to her—had kept them during the three years she had been missing in action. Jaime had retrieved them on her first visit Stateside when she reappeared. She looped them over her head and her blond hair, still obediently in its French braid. As the tags dropped inside her T-shirt, the various trinkets she had added over the years jangled reassuringly. They weren't regulation, but it was comforting to know they were there.

As Jaime left the hospital compound she passed a smokers' pavilion used by the staff on breaks. It was unlit, and she could barely make out the form of a man with a large backpack at his feet, and another one shaped like a teardrop slung across his shoulder, leaning against one of its support pillars. Mortaritaville, as the soldiers called Logistics Support Area Anaconda, was not well lit at night, to make it more difficult for insurgents to find targets for their mortar rounds.

That's odd, she thought. *Why would someone bother to come all the way out here, stand alone in the dark, and not even smoke?*

As Jaime rounded the corner to walk the dark block to her headquarters, she didn't notice the man from the pavilion pick up his backpack, sling it over his shoulders, and follow her down the street.

January 24, 2007, 12:50 A.M.
(3 days, 9 hours, 40 minutes until end of auction)
Judean wilderness west of the Dead Sea
Israel

Hajj al-Asim lay awake on his thick goat-hair mat in the chief's tent. Lying next to him was his third wife, Asad. Although she was usually a heavy sleeper, she had been tossing fitfully all night. He assumed her emotions were embroiled in the upcoming wedding. But then, it was always a difficult transition when your husband took another wife.

The Hajj was not worried about the wedding preparations that had the whole camp in an uproar. That was the women's job, really, although the men certainly would celebrate like there was no tomorrow, as his Western friends might say.

He was not even worried about the dissent shown at the men's meeting hours earlier when he had announced to them that the time had come to sell the box. Not everyone had been happy. The pragmatists, yes. The dreamers, no. *This is how the clan is known,* they said, *If we sell it, who will we be, the clan that* used to *have the box?*

No, the Hajj had a much more pressing concern.

Abihu el-Musaq, the dealer who was selling the box, was a serious man. He had made it clear to the Hajj that their deal was a business arrangement, that once the box went up for sale, if the Hajj reneged on his side of the deal, the consequences would be severe.

The Hajj had under his sleeping rug the printout that showed the item was for sale. The terms of the agreement were in force.

And the box was gone.

It had been stolen.

This put the Hajj in a very delicate position. Of all the dozens—soon, hundreds—of people arriving for the wedding, how could he find the thief, without letting anyone suspect the box had been stolen? For once the dealer knew the box was gone, there would be hell to pay.

The Hajj had to keep it quiet.

He had to find and retrieve the box.

"Rashid," he spoke, as he had thousands of times over the years, "Why did you have to find that damn box? Look what it did to you. Look what it's doing to me."

And he fell asleep yet again with the smirk of his cousin haunting his dreams.

Never again.

After her first assignment as an Eden Operative back in the Terris world, Jaime had quit. She'd returned her First Mission ring, had sent notice that she refused any future assignments. But Clement, the head of the Integrators in Eden—the man who gave Operatives their assignments—knew her a little too well. Instead of an active, frontline assignment, he had offered her an assignment that involved economics research and tracking of world financial issues. Jaime had always had an interest in international affairs, and this was something she could do while on active duty. No one's life was on the line. Why not?

Now, on her mid-tour leave, the assignment was becoming more interesting. Not dangerous, but more interesting. Right up her alley.

Sent an update on the soldier in surgery to his commanders and unit chaplain. Answered all important e-mails. Finished drafting a paper for the Commanding General. Turned on my "out of office" reply . . .

Jaime went over the checklist in her mind. What had she forgotten to do? She couldn't think of anything. If she wanted to grab even a couple hours of sleep—and it was always wise to be rested and alert on assignment—the clock was ticking.

She was at her computer station in the Joint Operations Center. Even though it was the middle of the night, she was far from alone. The night shift staff was currently responding to a convoy crisis. The place looked like a NASA flight center with large screens up front surrounded by an amphitheater of work-stations with computers, phones, headsets, and printers.

She had blocked out the activity around her as she'd spent the last forty-five minutes agonizing over an information paper her commander had asked her to compose. It wasn't that she'd put it off until the last minute—oh, all right, that's exactly what she'd done. The paper was part of a leadership series Brigadier General Culver was putting together for distribution to the COSCOM officers. She asked various members of her command to write up the papers in areas she considered their specialty.

It only made sense for the general to ask a chaplain to write a paper addressing "language and professionalism," urging the officers to watch their language in the workplace.

Poetic justice seemed to be the theme of Jaime's life.

Jaime looked over her draft, feeling she'd done a pretty darn good job of it. (Emphasis on the "darn.") She e-mailed the file to the general, completing her "to do" list.

Just as Jaime was preparing to shut down her computer, she noticed a reply from her commander had already appeared on the screen, which meant she was in her office, even at this late hour.

Does that woman ever sleep?

Jaime looked at her own watch.

Only eighteen hours remained between here and Switzerland.

Still, she had four hours until she had to catch her plane. Instead of heading back to her hooch, she slipped back into the command suite, walking past the aide's alcove, now dark, toward the light from a partially opened door where she could see General Culver looking pensively at the computer screen.

Liz Culver, as she was known to her friends, was about five foot eight, slim, with the build of an athlete and very light brown hair cut short and styled back over her ears. Wasn't there more gray in her hair last week? As she approached the office, Jaime wondered if her commander had found a way to color her hair even in this combat environment.

"Ma'am," Jaime said, knocking on the door frame. "What keeps you here at this hour?"

"Chaplain!" Culver smiled as she stood and motioned her into the room. "Tonight it's a crisis out in Al Asad—a truck crisis . . . nothing you need worry about. I also read your update about our surgery case. When do you think they'll fly him out? I'd like to visit him."

Jaime relaxed, walking to the front of the desk. "They're sending him out early this morning, but he wasn't critical, so he might still be here."

"Either way, it's good to know I had you there."

Somewhat embarrassed, Jaime diverted the conversation. "Ma'am, I also sent you a draft of the point paper. I hope it's what you needed. I'm preparing to head out later this morning."

"On leave, yes. Did I see you are going to Davos, Switzerland? To attend the World Economic Forum? What kind of a break is that?"

"It's become a hobby of mine, and a friend arranged an invite so I could observe some of the proceedings. I'm even scheduled to meet some noted economists. I'm hoping to learn a lot."

"Always trying to change the world."

"Yes, ma'am."

"Well, I do love your enthusiasm, even if I don't share your passion for the topic. On another subject, the command team's replacements will arrive while you are gone, and we'll be just about ready to TOA when you get back."

TOA was a transfer of authority, a process designed to help a new unit prepare to take over the mission of a unit that had been deployed for a year. Culver's unit had just arrived in Iraq when Jaime had resurfaced. The chaplain had liked and admired General Culver since their first brief interactions then, and her positive opinion had been borne out as she'd arrived to work under her here in Balad.

The general's unit was still there only because they'd been

extended a couple months beyond their normal year rotation, and they were more than ready to head home. When Jaime returned from this two-week leave she'd remain in Iraq, working for a different HQ.

"I want to thank you for stepping up to the plate and filling in after Chaplain Roberts became ill. When I got here and you were still MIA, I never in a million years suspected I'd meet you—let alone have you on my staff. It's been a pleasure. I'll make sure Corps treats you right when you slide over to work for them!"

"Thank you, ma'am. Since you may be on your way out the door when I return from leave, would you let me say a prayer for my commander before I go?"

"I'd be grateful," said the general.

The two women sat at the corner of a large conference table in the same room where they'd met under remarkable circumstances only a year ago. The commander folded her hands and bowed her head, and Jaime laid her hands over those of the older woman, asking for patience and courage and to bring her soldiers home safely.

After the "amen," Culver lifted her head and locked eyes with her chaplain. "Thank you," she said. The general and the chaplain walked together to the door, where the senior officer reached out to draw her into a half-hug half-handshake.

"Be safe. Take a warm coat to Davos!"

Jaime turned to make her way back through the darkened command suite and almost collided with a figure waiting quietly in the shadows.

"I see you still haven't lost your touch for ignoring protocol to sneak in and meet with the commander," sneered a voice she recognized all too well. Lieutenant Colonel Ray Jenkins was not the person she wanted to spar with in the middle of the night while exhausted and on a tight schedule.

"Sir." She could muster barely enough respect in her voice to avoid charges of insubordination, but her impatience with this man couldn't be concealed. "I don't know how I can make it any plainer than I already have. As a chaplain serving on the special staff of the CG, I have direct access to the commander."

"Yeah, yeah, same ole bullshit you always give me." He leaned back against the nearest desk and folded his arms across his chest. He wasn't tall, maybe five foot seven at best, but his old-fashioned flattop haircut and gaunt face gave him a severe, overbearing look that made him seem taller than he really was.

"And speaking of bs, did I just hear you're going on leave? What's the plan? To help some little ole ladies make doilies at Bible camp?" He stepped closer so he could lean in and hiss his next question: "More to the point, are you planning to come back this time, or will you disappear to herd goats for another three years?"

Jaime gritted her teeth. Why did this man have to be so difficult? What did she ever do to him?

Well, okay, so she did manage to get herself kidnapped and then disappear for three years while serving in the brigade for which Jenkins was the executive officer. He took a lot of heat for that, and blamed Jaime because he didn't get selected for battalion command. And now he was leading the night crew of the support operations staff for the COSCOM, not what would be considered a plum assignment.

But Jaime refused to let him bait her right now. There was nothing she could do or say that would change his attitude about her, so it was best to just walk away without adding fuel to the fire.

"I'll see you in a few weeks, sir." Jaime gave a half salute in Jenkins' direction as she headed down the hall. Then, smiling, she called back over her shoulder, "I'll be sure and bring you a doily!"

Jaime returned to the operations center to shut off her computer and gather her belongings. Simultaneously, a civilian at an Army Material Command workstation two rows above shut off his computer, picked up a large backpack and another sling, and headed for the door.

January 24, 2007, 5:50 A.M.
(3 days, 4 hours, 40 minutes until end of auction)
Judean wilderness west of the Dead Sea
Israel

"There you are," Tarif said with a smile as he rounded an outcropping and found the young girl sitting by a makeshift pen that held four goats. "Why aren't you down with everyone else, getting ready for the wedding?"

"There's time enough," she said in a dutiful voice that nonetheless conveyed her lack of excitement about the proceedings.

Tarif came over to his cousin, took her hands, and stretched out her arms fully to admire her new dress. She almost gave up her frown at his obvious approval. When he reached out to touch the soft material of the kerchief on her head, she blushed. He knew it wasn't from modesty as much as it was that he understood what she was doing. She was only ten—not old enough quite yet to be expected to cover her head. But it was a wedding, she had a new dress, and she wanted to seem grown-up.

Tarif sat down next to her. "My little Safia. Soon you'll be wearing braids," he said, and his cousin blushed again. He sat down beside her companionably, as he'd done since they were small. He was fifteen now, and soon—when she started wearing braids and a kerchief for real—they'd no longer be allowed to talk together like this. Their times alone were nearly over, and they both knew it.

"When did you get back?" she asked.

"Last night. Just before the men's meeting. It was a long meeting. Lots of arguing." He'd meant it to sound offhand, the fact that he'd attended his first meeting as a grown-up.

She fully caught the implication, and watched his face carefully as he continued.

"The Hajj is selling the box," he went on.

She knelt and leaned in toward him, her large eyes an unexpected blue, dancing with emotion. "Did he say it's because of Ibrahim and Ali?" she asked.

Two of their cousins had illnesses that could only be cured with either surgery or long-term medical care.

"Partly. And partly because we have to move into the future."

"You mean stay in the town," she said.

"I don't know what you have against living in a town," said Tarif.

"Why would I want to live in a box?" answered Safia. "What's to like about it? What's happening to the Jahalin frightens me. I don't want to be stuck in a metal box. I like the open air. I like the goats."

She'd stumbled straight into Tarif's passion. "But we're not going to be warehoused like the Bedouin in the Negev, or forced into little camps like the Jahalin," he said. "I can see what you have against the towns the Bedouin have now. But the reason Bedouin towns are so . . . so stupid is because we don't have any great architects. Not builders, architects. Those are the people who design buildings to look fine. What if we could design a town to look graceful and spacious? What if our houses could look like tents . . . inviting, huge tents with flowing curves and wonderful colors? Only they had heat and air-conditioning and running water? What if you walked into a town and it looked like a magical tent city?"

Safia was staring at him now. "What are you talking about?"

"I want to do it, Safia. I want to be an architect. I want to dream big. I want us to have even better houses than the Israelis!"

The young girl stood up and dusted off her skirt and the pants below it. "You know I believe in you," she said. "I always have. I've always promised to tell you when you sounded crazy. Now, you sound crazy."

He smiled at her, his thick black hair blowing around his face under his kaffiyeh.

Her face was oval and her mouth was wide. "Stay a moment. We may not get to talk again before the wedding," he said. "I hear you're not going back to school."

"No," she said.

"I wish you would."

All Bedouin children in Israel had to attend school now, through the elementary grades. It was Israeli law. Continuing education was offered to them, both boys and girls, through high school, but the attrition rate for girls was enormous. Westerners often said it was because the Bedouin didn't believe women were of enough value to be educated. But the Bedouin girls knew they had to choose. The high school classes were coeducational. Girls could choose to attend, but their status among the eligible Bedouin men would plummet. Girls and boys of marriageable age did not mix freely with the opposite sex; everyone knew that. The girls could do it, some did, and their virtue wasn't questioned—but their values were, and their modesty was.

She looked at the ground. "I want . . ."

"What? What is it that you want?"

"I want . . . to be the first wife of the big tent."

When Tarif knelt down to raise her head, he saw the tear tracks on her face. "That is certainly a worthy goal, and you would make any man a worthy wife," he said. "Why does it make you cry?"

All she said was, "You're so smart. Why must you become an ark . . . an ark . . ."

"Architect," he supplied. "What's wrong with that?"

But she shook her head.

"Come now. We must head for camp. Everyone's awake. The women are cooking and I'm sure they want your help. There will be feasting. Day after tomorrow is the bride's henna night! I'm sure you'll learn some new songs!" he said with a wink. Weddings were the one time even the devout among them were allowed to be bawdy.

"Why does the Hajj need a new wife, anyway?" she asked, slowly disassembling the little goat pen she'd made.

"His first wife died two years ago," Tarif answered. "And his second wife no longer pleases him."

"What about his third wife? And the new one is so young!"

"More luck to him. I'm told the bride is in favor of the match, so we don't need to wail for her."

"He's an old goat," Safia said under her breath, but she knew Tarif could hear her. She knew he was the only one to whom she could possibly say something like that, without fear of it being repeated.

"He is," agreed her handsome cousin. "But tell me, Safia, tell me honestly. Do you think my dreams are too big? Will the djinn, the evil spirits, try to trip me?"

"No," she said softly. "I think your dreams are just the right size for you. I am the one who wants too much."

"I think I know what will cheer you up. Want to come?"

"Suleiman is watching the horses now?"

"Yes. And I believe he's expecting us to stop by. But can you ride in your new outfit?"

"What good is an outfit if it can't sit a horse?" she asked, suddenly excited and alive.

Tarif grabbed a branch off a scrappy shrub and started helping her herd the goats back to camp.

She watched him walk ahead of her, saw how tall he was, how confident, how handsome. And she knew she wanted too much: she not only wanted to be the first wife of the big tent; she wanted the handsomest, strongest, best husband, as well.

She could not have both. It could not be.

The Grand Ziggurat rose from the ground below her like a giant gold-red sandcastle. Jaime couldn't take her eyes off it even as the Army C-23 Sherpa aircraft descended from an altitude of 7,500 feet, flying fast and dodging towers and power lines into the Ali Air Base at Tallil. Nearly four years earlier, during the opening days of Operation Iraqi Freedom, Tallil had been her base. She'd left on a two-day trip to assist a chaplain at Baghdad Airport but had been kidnapped along the way. She hadn't been back to Tallil, to the ancient ruins at Ur, until now.

This was it—the place where her unexpected, life-changing adventure had all begun.

This was also where she'd met Yani, the most arrogant, secretive, competent, handsome—infuriating—Sword who walked the Terris world.

Jaime had no way of knowing it at the time, but Yani was a legend to those from Eden in his role as Sword 23. He was six feet tall, with thick dark brown hair that curled when it was wet, brown eyes that transfixed you, and a natural presence that filled any room. The missions he had completed were impossibly dangerous, the stakes unbearably high, the results life changing for those he helped.

He had been her partner on her last assignment. He'd been the first man since the death of her husband, Paul, with whom she'd fallen in love. Jaime was certain there were many women who had fallen in love with Yani.

But Yani had also fallen in love with her.

It had all started here, with him abducting her among the ruins of Ur.

At the completion of their last assignment, at the same time that Jaime had resigned her Operative status, she'd broken off her relationship with him. She'd left Yani, not because of lies—he was irritatingly straightforward—but because of his complicated truth. And the fact that his truth would always be complicated.

At the time it had seemed to Jaime they had a fundamental difference that made a relationship impossible: Jaime was people focused, while Yani was mission focused. It was who he was. She couldn't live with that.

The question she'd wrestled with daily since then was whether she could live without Yani.

It was a moot point. She had no way of contacting him, and they would certainly never be assigned to work together again. Jaime had removed herself from his rarified universe, and she knew she'd never be invited back in.

She hadn't heard or seen Yani, or anything from or about him, for a year. So how did the memory of him striding across the ruins at Ur still make her breathing ragged in a way that even the combat landing had failed to do?

She had less pleasant memories here, as well. Of nearly being captured in an ambush on the road. Of meeting Frank McMillan, a CIA agent who turned out to be both cunning and dangerous.

The Army C-23 Sherpa aircraft rolled to a stop in front of a soldier wearing a light green flight suit with orange reflector vest. The soldier signaled for the pilot to shut down the engine, which brought a collective sigh of relief from the seven passengers on webbed seating in the hold of the aircraft. The last fifteen minutes of the flight had been like an amusement park ride, only the thrills—and the danger—were real.

Another passenger, a civilian, hunkered way back in the last seat near a pallet of medical supplies. He looked positively green! He had boarded the Sherpa with Richards at Balad, and was dressed in nondescript khakis and a plain navy blue polo shirt over which he wore black Dragon Skin flexible body armor.

He looks familiar. Jaime tried not to stare directly at him. *Does he work in our headquarters, or have I seen him at the hospital?*

The rest of the passengers, all soldiers, having been given the go-ahead from the flight engineer, gladly unhooked their safety belts. Most of them grabbed gear from under the seats and made ready to deplane.

The man in the backseat stood seconds after Jaime did, grabbed his large backpack—and a second one, tear shaped as well. The two packs together stopped Jaime in her tracks.

This was the guy from the smoking pavilion.

Was he following her? It wasn't unheard of for a civilian contractor to travel by Sherpa, but he had run onto the plane at the last minute. If he was following her, knowing she was going on leave, it was likely he'd been expecting her to take the larger, vastly more comfortable C-140 later in the morning with the rest of the leave group. The Sherpa would have thrown him for a loop.

This guy had barely made it onto her plane.

What should she do? This was where she was supposed to pick up her "package," her assignment, before traveling on. But the origin of this package was what the Army would call close-hold. No one's business. Especially not Mr. Sling-Bag.

Maybe she was imagining things. If he went through the terminal and continued on to another destination, she'd know she was overreacting.

Jaime let him deplane first, as she removed her body armor and Kevlar. He was still looking sick to his stomach, but he went down the steps and headed out with the other soldiers across the tarmac for the single-story cement building that served as a terminal.

The other soldiers then moved on about their business.

The nervous contractor waited just outside the entrance to the terminal's passenger holding area, trying in vain to look nonchalant as he watched Jaime deplane.

Oh, shit.

She couldn't believe this was happening. She had no time to deal with Mr. Sling-Bag. But, more than that, she was not psychologically ready to deal with the thought that her current mission might be important enough that she already had a tail.

Furthermore, as an Eden Operative she would normally have all sorts of great devices for communication and for dealing with situations such as this one. Of necessity, she'd left those toys in Germany when she deployed. If something happened to her, or her duffels were searched, she couldn't afford for the equipment to be discovered. Consequently she only had one "drop cloth," which was an Operative's equivalent of a can of Mace. Should she use it now?

This entire thought process occurred as Jaime walked down the steps of the Sherpa. By the time she reached the tarmac, she had made her decision.

The contractor would have identified himself to her if he were on her team. And no one else's team was supposed to know about her pickup.

Instead of turning right and heading straight into the passenger holding area, Jaime turned left and followed a sign for the MCT, or "Movement Control Team." The MCT consisted of a handful of COSCOM soldiers—her people—who coordinated the movement of people and supplies through Tallil. She decided to use a brief visit to her soldiers as an excuse to see if anyone followed her.

She rounded the corner to their office. It was closed, with a sign on the door saying: "Back in 10 minutes."

Now what?

Jaime spied a series of five latrines lined up behind an eight-foot-high wall of concrete slabs known as Texas barriers. She turned and walked down the row of latrines, noting that each stall displayed a green code indicating it was vacant.

She made a quick decision and entered the last one, and waited silently. As she listened for her tail, she pulled a purse pack of tissues from her small duffel and tore it open. In the center of the tissues was another sealed pack. She grabbed and opened it, removing the slightly damp cloth.

After a minute, she heard someone approach. Was it him?

Whoever it was stopped at the first latrine and opened the door—but apparently didn't go in. The footsteps went to the second door, and a pause as the door opened and shut again. Then the third. It had to be him—and he had to be looking for her.

Jaime took the third pause as the opportunity to emerge from her latrine. It was the contractor, and it was clear she'd surprised him. He quickly tried to look as though he were waiting for a stall to become available.

"Hey," Jaime said, holding her latrine door open for him. "You'd better use this one; it's the only one with paper!" She smiled and waited to see how far he'd go not to blow his cover. He approached the open stall door.

As the contractor passed her, Jaime grabbed him from behind, reaching around to put the cloth from inside the Kleenex packet tightly over his nose and mouth. Then she held on as the drug began to work.

As he went limp, she dragged him into the latrine, letting the door fall shut behind them.

She sat him on the seat. He slumped to one side, and she positioned him so that he wouldn't fall forward.

Jaime took one brief moment to look at the contractor in the shadowy light. He was short, maybe five foot four. His hair was cropped, but not an Army cut. He was balding in back. His nose was thin and beaklike, and he wore glasses with black rims. He didn't have his bags on him. The ID on his lanyard identified him as Raymond Maynard, a civilian working for Army Material Command. It made no sense.

Time was short. Jaime quickly exited the latrine. As she did, another soldier was coming up. They nodded briefly as he opened the first door.

She hoped it would be a while before there were five latrine users at a time.

Jaime spotted the contractor's bags on the path by the

Texas barrier. She surreptitiously picked them up and threw them behind the latrines.

She wasn't worried about the health of the contractor. The drug on the cloth was a great improvement over Terris knockout drugs. The man would sleep for forty minutes if no one found him, and then wake up only slightly confused. Even if someone found him, they wouldn't be able to rouse him enough to give any helpful information for another half hour or so.

God willing, Jaime, the package, and the Sherpa would be well on the way to Kuwait by then.

She turned and headed back to the passenger holding area.

Jaime entered the waiting area to find two people: a young soldier sleeping on his duffel and a distinguished-looking woman who appeared to be in her late sixties, vibrant and healthy. She was a little taller than Jaime and had the physique of a lifelong swimmer.

The woman watched with calm curiosity as Jaime approached.

"You've journeyed well?" Jaime held out her hand to shake as she waited for the code phrase that would confirm this woman as the economist she was supposed to meet.

"Exceedingly well." The woman's smile was warm and genuine as she stood and took Jaime's offered hand in a firm grip.

"I'm your final guide," was the chaplain's reply as she returned the smile and shouldered the woman's backpack. Jaime motioned that they should proceed out the door and toward the aircraft. She noted that the woman she knew to be Dr. Andrea Farmer was carrying the Kevlar and protective vest required for the flight, so all things seemed in order for the next phase of their journey: the military hop to Ali Ah Salem Air Base in Kuwait followed by a civilian flight to Frankfurt, Germany.

As the two women crossed the windswept tarmac, a safe enough distance from others to afford some privacy, Dr. Farmer asked lightly, "So we're leaving our unexpected companion behind?"

Jaime continued looking straight ahead, but her shoulders relaxed a bit as she said, "That's certainly my hope."

"Thanks for watching out for me," was the older woman's simple reply. "Do you suppose we're in the clear now?"

I thought we were in the clear before! Jaime thought to herself, but she replied, "We'll be alert, but I think we're traveling alone. Dr. Farmer, are you sure you want to continue?"

"Please, it's Andrea. And if the mission wasn't important, I wouldn't be here. One unexpected companion is certainly not enough to stop me!"

The other passengers had now caught up with them. The two finished the approach in silence. As soon as everyone had stowed their gear and seated themselves, the flight engineer went into his safety briefing. As he explained the requirement for low-altitude flight until they crossed the Kuwait border, Jaime glanced back at the now empty seat where the contractor had been.

Why would anyone care that she was escorting an economist to the World Economic Forum in Davos?

Within two days, this entire mission would be over and Jaime would be on true leave. The first part required her to get Dr. Farmer—Andrea—to her meeting in Davos. Once Jaime was on the ground in Germany, she'd have her "toys," as well as communication with other Operatives. In Davos itself, a whole team of Operatives was already in place. Although Jaime didn't know the entire plan, it occurred to her that the simple fact that a team was required meant whatever meeting Andrea Farmer was planning to attend was probably not on the printed schedule and the situation was likely dangerous.

Still, two days. How hard could it be? As the Sherpa rolled down the runway, Jaime closed her eyes and imagined taking the remainder of her leave to actually relax, maybe in Davos, maybe somewhere else.

She gave only a short glance to the latrine trailer as the plane headed off into the clear sky.

The dollar hit a fourteen-year low against the pound and also weakened versus the euro. J. Aldrich Woodbury rattled his *Wall Street Journal* with irritation and folded it back to examine the financial headlines more closely. It was no surprise. Just ten days earlier the Financial Times Group had unequivocally announced that the euro had displaced the dollar on the bond market. But that didn't make it any less annoying.

A waiter stopped by the businessman's breakfast table with a fresh pot of coffee, but he waved him off. Aldi, as only his family and oldest friends were permitted to call him, was not interested in coffee or croissants.

Breakfast is for wimps. He wasn't interested in the rustic wooden crossbeams and the padded bench seat in the private nook he occupied. He took for granted the solitude he purchased by reserving this dining room, which was normally open only for evening meals, and the waiter whose sole purpose this morning was to see to his needs. And he couldn't be less interested in any of the amenities the Hotel Belvédère, or even the city of Davos for that matter, had to offer.

J. Aldrich Woodbury had one and only one passion. It was currency. Not finances and economics in general. Not the simple massing of wealth into bigger and bigger piles. No, his treasure was currency, the ebb and flow of power in the world financial markets based upon whose currency was strongest, or perceived to be the strongest, and what served as a hard currency backing that system.

And today, Woodbury's attention was on the U.S. dollar.

Dammit! It's dropping quicker than I thought.

For years, the U.S. dollar had been the standard unit of currency for the international markets of gold and oil, and it was the most widely held reserve currency across the globe. But the recent rise of the euro and American blunders in foreign trade and the domestic mortgage market left the dollar falling in actual value as well as global respect and trust.

J. Aldrich Woodbury, banker, financier, and behind-the-scenes advisor to many key policy makers in D.C., had foreseen all this. Given the choice, he would have preferred to keep the dollar in its preeminent position. But that was a dangerous dream that would only lead to personal financial disaster.

So, as he saw it, there were two choices. Either watch the markets closely, and be ready to respond quickly when the bottom dropped out, or give the system a push and ride on top of the wave.

Woodbury did not like waiting, and he refused to let his financial future be decided by others, whereas the fact that he was about to decide the financial futures of millions of ordinary people didn't faze him at all.

He withdrew his BlackBerry from the inside pocket of his black wool suit, and punched a few buttons to look at the closing numbers from the Asian markets.

It's time! He flicked the instrument onto vibrate and returned it to its hiding place. *It's time to take action—no more wait and see.*

He stood, reaching into his pant pocket to find whatever change was rattling with his keys and threw it on the table for the waiter. It was three U.S. quarters.

Spend it quick. He folded the paper under his arm and headed back for his room. *Soon it will be worthless.*

Frank McMillan paced his office, trying not to shout into the phone.

"What do you mean, you lost her in Tallil?"

Maynard's voice was more annoyed than apologetic. "When she got off the plane, I followed her to the latrines. She was waiting for me. She knocked me out with some sort of inhalant."

"So . . . where is she?" Frank's anger was barely controlled.

"I don't know."

"I don't know, she got back on the plane, or I don't know, she stayed in Tallil and went somewhere on the ground from there?"

"I . . . don't . . . know."

Nothing in Maynard's records indicated the man was inept. But by God!

"So you've lost Jaime Richards. After all these months of watching her, she finally moves, and you lose her on her first stop."

"Um, yes, but . . ."

"And now she can ID you."

"Well, yes."

Frank was livid. Jaime Richards was moving, possibly inside Iraq, and he'd lost her.

He wanted to explode, but he still needed information from Maynard.

"Find . . . out . . . if . . . she . . . got . . . on . . . the . . . goddamned . . . plane."

"I tried," said the undercover agent. "But they wouldn't tell me."

"Did you show identification?"

"Yes. Of course!"

Everything Frank McMillan had accomplished that day, everything that was under control, vanished. The fact that a chaplain had realized she had a tail—and had taken him down—was the final proof Frank needed to convince him she was more than a chaplain, proof she was doing something that necessitated knocking someone out.

What if she was heading back to wherever she'd been for the last three years? What if this was his big chance, the one he'd been waiting for?

His teeth were clenched as he said, "You will call me within fifteen minutes and inform me of the location of Jaime Richards."

As Frank spoke, a petite Frenchwoman with thick, straight black hair, who was an associate on the Terrorism Task Force, came into his office carrying papers. Normally he was pleased to see her, as she managed to make office attire look stylish and had a charming accent. Frank had no time for liaisons, but she made the prospect enticing. Today he cursed himself for not closing his door as he finished the conversation. As she handed him a memo, she said, "Richards. Is that the chaplain you've been watching?"

"Jaime Lynn Richards, yes," Frank answered.

"She's probably heading for Davos by now. She's on the invited list for the World Economic Forum. She even has reservations at the Steigenberger Belvédère, where most of the key players stay." The woman gave a small shrug. "Means she must know someone."

Frank looked at her like she'd somehow dropped from heaven. "Sylvie, how long have you known this?"

"Since we got the list," she said offhandedly. "I thought you'd seen it."

"You're an angel," he said.

"You're easily impressed," she answered, as she headed back down the hall.

Enough with the waiting and watching. The pieces were all coming together. After the debacle in Tallil, Frank was done with trusting subordinates to handle Richards. It was time for another meeting, just the two of them.

A meeting Jaime Richards would never forget.

Jaime strode from the terminal into the large building that housed the airport parking garage. She and Dr. Farmer had made it, as scheduled, from Iraq through Kuwait and into Germany. Jaime was now officially on leave from the Army—and she was on her own, to get Andrea Farmer to Davos by nightfall.

It had been an unusually warm winter in Europe, although the air had a refreshing bite to it, and Jaime pulled her jacket closed and zipped it up.

Jaime glanced at the parking lot information she'd just gotten as a text message, which gave her the level, row, and space number of the car that went with the key she had been handed by a gentleman in the greeting area. She was more than pleased to arrive at the designated space to find a titanium gray four-door sedan with heated leather seats and high-end stereo speakers. She opened the trunk and threw in her duffel and Andrea's small suitcase. Then Jaime found and unzipped the black nylon carryall that contained clothing she kept at the ready at her place in Hochspeyer, which had been picked up and placed into the car's trunk for her use. From it, she removed an even smaller satchel. She looked through it quickly as she and Andrea headed for the front seat. Jaime made certain her passport and international driver's license were easily accessible, then got out her trusty handheld, issued to every Eden Operative, and gave a sigh of relief to have her Eden lifeline in her pocket once again.

As Jaime turned on the car, the GPS blinked awake in the dashboard and a pleasant male voice announced it was programmed to guide the car to the Steigenberger Belvédère in Davos.

"Hey, thanks, Rupert," she said, then smiled toward Andrea and explained that she always named her talking GPSs. "I find giving him a name makes it friendlier," she said. "If you don't mind, I'll go ahead and check in." She put the earpiece into her ear.

"Now's the perfect time," Dr. Farmer agreed.

Jaime had flown in and out of Frankfurt before, and had picked up visiting family and friends, so she was used to the yawning concrete levels and circuitous ramps of the parking garage that had to be negotiated just to leave the airport. They whizzed by as she pressed the number 3 and said simply, "Operator."

"Hello, Jaime," came a pleasant voice—this one live, and female. "You and Dr. Farmer had a safe trip, I take it?"

"Incident free, after Tallil," Jaime reported. "So what's up in Davos?"

"The key players are all arriving. In fact, so many of them are either there or scheduled to arrive this evening that we're wondering if the meeting of interest is planned for tonight. If you're in the car now, barring unforeseen circumstances you should be on time. Operative One on this operation, Eddie Williams, is already there. He's a specialist in electronics, and he's been monitoring the communications of those likely to convene the meeting—which the attendees are keeping strictly secret. Nothing yet. Anything you need from us at this point?"

"No, thanks. It's good to be in touch."

"Likewise. Godspeed."

And the connection light disappeared.

The car was warming up as Jaime fed the paid parking receipt to the machine and exited the garage. Now that she was on the ground and nearly on the road, she began to feel the effects of a night without sleep. It was going to be a long trip—and if the whole point was to get the economist there in time for the meeting, which might be as soon as this evening, there would be precious little time for pit stops, let alone rest breaks.

"Dr. Farmer—Andrea," she queried, "do you know how to drive?" It occurred to her that perhaps they might trade off driving and sleeping.

"No, sorry," said the older woman. "Even during my most recent sojourn in the Terris world to get my doctorate I lived on the Stanford campus and always had friends to take me if I needed to travel more widely. I haven't been back in several decades, and I have to say, cars have evolved a lot since then." She smiled at the memory. "The first car I ever rode in was a Model T. Now there was a bumpy ride! It was nothing like this!" She patted the leather seat that was beginning to warm beneath her.

Jaime knew that people who lived in Eden had a much longer life expectancy than their Terris counterparts, but the Model-T reference surprised her, even so. "You first surfaced in the early twentieth century? How many times have you lived here?"

"Only twice. And yes, the first time, when I was very young, was nearly a hundred years ago. Both worlds were very different then. As I mentioned, the only other time I lived here was to get a doctorate from a Terris university so that I could be traceable and taken seriously when I published papers on economic theory."

Jaime stole a glance again at the fit, energetic woman beside her. According to her Terris bio, this important and reclusive (or so it was assumed) economist had received her doctorate in the 1960s. It put her current age at sixty-six, and noted that her hair had been snow-white since birth. Now it was a lovely look for her age—whatever it truly was.

"So can you tell me why, after all these years, you've surfaced for this particular mission?"

Andrea sighed. "It's a long story, one that had its genesis ages ago. . . ."

"A story I could use right now!" Jaime laughed. "If you can't help drive, then I need you to help me stay awake." She had followed the direction signs through the Frankfurt Airport and slid onto the Autobahn, heading south toward Switzerland.

"The reason I'm on this mission," Andrea hesitated for just a beat, "is because I asked—actually, I *pleaded* with Clement to let me come. After long hours of arguing, he finally relented."

"Why was he against it? It seems you'd be the perfect person to send to a meeting at the World Economic Forum. Or is it a problem that your writings make you such a recognizable public figure?"

She was looking out the opposite window when she quietly replied, "His concern was that I'm too close to the topic, too emotionally involved to keep a balanced perspective throughout the mission. In fact, I'm not currently an Eden Operative, but I once was. My first assignment was to infiltrate a secret meeting on Jekyll Island, Georgia, back in 1910. Unfortunately, I was exposed and almost killed before bringing the mission to successful completion."

She fell silent but seemed to be struggling with her thoughts. Jaime didn't interfere. She'd learned through years of counseling that sometimes it was best to let a person talk, or not talk, at their own pace.

"But that wasn't the worst of it." When she resumed, her voice took on a hard, determined edge. "The very thing we'd hoped to prevent happened because I was unable to complete my mission! The men gathered at that meeting wrote the plans for an economic system in your country that may have stunted your economic progress for a century."

"You mean the Federal Reserve System?" interjected Jaime, shifting into sixth, then punching the accelerator to pass a VW that was annoying her greatly. "The U.S. government claims it was set up to protect our financial holdings from disaster. Is it really that bad?"

"Oh, I'm not saying the Federal Reserve Act is the most horrible thing that could have happened. But the public had a right to know and understand the ramifications of the system. Instead, they were purposely kept in the dark. Had they known the whole truth from the beginning, open debate might have led to better choices, a much more balanced system. That's our mission this time as well. Some important financial players are planning a Jekyll Island–style secret meeting at Davos this year, one that could have worldwide financial ramifications."

"And we need to—?"

"According to the e-mails we've intercepted, some powerful leaders in the world of finance are planning to push the world markets in a particular direction, which could affect the livelihoods of millions—driven by the American magnate J. Aldrich Woodbury. We need to discover their plan and expose it. If it's on the level, it will hold up under scrutiny. If not— let's just say this time, we plan to let the world decide."

"When you say 'push the markets in a particular direction,' what are you talking about?"

"We believe they're working together to choose which international currencies to uphold, and which to devalue. If a currency is devalued—whether the dollar, the yen, the euro, whatever—that means the people who trade with that currency will find their investments and their life savings gone, overnight. Even the possessions they have, their houses, cars, whatever, become virtually worthless because only those who own the favored currencies can afford to buy them, and for a fraction of their worth. Entire national economies can collapse—even those belonging to the world's wealthiest countries—if people with the means and the know-how work together to make it happen."

"How exactly is Woodbury planning to pull this off?"

"He hasn't been discussing the details either electronically or by phone. He's insisting on a face-to-face buy-in of the plan. But the stature of the international players with whom he's been in contact is enough to cause grave concern. That's why I have every intention of being there."

"I'm proud to be with you, proud to be an Operative on this mission," said Jaime.

"I'm glad to be with you." She smiled. "Let's get to Davos and bark with the big dogs."

Jaime laughed at Andrea's turn of phrase. "The big dogs have no idea who's on the way," she said, and pushed the pedal to the sedan's carpeted floor.

Abihu el-Musaq lay on a massage table by the pool outside his stone house on the island of Cyprus. He was being worked on by a short, muscular man who used to be a fisherman until he discovered how much money he could make at the local resorts if he became a certified masseur. El-Musaq's pool was designed with an infinity edge on one side, allowing the water to cascade down a level, which gave the illusion that the pool had no end until it merged into the deeper blue that was the sea beyond. Water flowed continually into the pool from two fountains that looked like ancient jars. It was beautiful.

Which always made him angry when he had to leave.

Damn Bedouins.

El-Musaq accepted that there were certain problems and risks that came with the business he'd chosen. Oh, not his legitimate business, which was luxury food imports. But in his other, even more fruitful business in black-market antiquities, he much preferred being the unseen go-between, who never had to leave his beautiful cocoon.

He'd sent a trusted messenger to pick up the item being offered for sale by Hajj al-Asim, the tribal chief in the Israeli desert west of the Dead Sea. The man had returned empty-handed, saying al-Asim wanted to keep it as a good-luck charm for his upcoming wedding, which would be over before the eBay auction ended.

Unacceptable. Completely unacceptable.

The auction bidding was already up to $150,000.00 U.S.—and that was mostly the serious bidders just throwing their hats into the ring. He couldn't let anything go wrong.

He had to have that box.

In his mind, he wasn't displaying prejudice by not trusting the Bedouin. His own grandfather was a Bedouin. One of the few who left for school, discovered there was a real world outside the damn desert, and got a life.

As for trusting them in business dealings, el-Musaq remembered how in the earlier times the Turkish ruler Ahmed al-Jazar had faced outrage because no caravans could cross the desert without being robbed by the Bedouin. So al-Jazar had captured a Bedouin sheikh, and some of his chiefs. Al-Jazar had promised their release only if the tribes promised to leave the caravans alone.

The sheikh said, "It is tradition that we plunder caravans. It has gone on for thousands of years. It's what we do."

So they killed him. And boiled his body

And still his men refused to leave the caravans alone.

The ruler realized he could not win and if he killed the chiefs, the Bedouin would cause even more trouble. He let the men go and ended up having to give them land as a make-good.

It made Abihu el-Musaq crazy to have Bedouin blood in his own veins. He wasn't a thief, of course. He was a businessman. But his particular business meant he had to deal with thieves.

Still, one law of the Bedouin held that if travelers—as opposed to merchant caravans—came their way, they offered protection and hospitality. So Abihu el-Musaq was about to head their way. He'd attend the wedding of the Hajj. He'd leave with the box.

Or he'd see to it that this would be one of the shortest marriages ever recorded.

January 24, 2007, 9:05 P.M.
(2 days, 13 hours, 25 minutes until end of auction)
Judean wilderness west of the Dead Sea
Israel

When all the men had left the tent after feasting, the Hajj's first, son, Farook, returned to him and said quietly, "Your wife Asad waits to speak to you. May she come in?"

Hajj al-Asim gave a deep sigh and turned to go into his private sleeping quarters, but he waved his hand, giving his assent.

Asad entered the room, which was sectioned off by large, handwoven rugs that served as walls. She stood waiting until her husband turned to face her. When he did, he saw she was trembling with rage.

"Why?" he asked, surprised. "What's wrong?"

"Husband, I call on you to right a terrible wrong. While the women were cooking for the feast tonight, someone went into my tent and went through all my things! Our things. Our family's things!"

With a sigh that clearly meant, "Oh, is that all?" the Hajj turned and sat down to take off his shoes. "Was anything taken?"

"Not that I've found," she said. "But this is a great indignity! You must find who did it and they must be punished!"

He removed his second shoe and sat looking up at her. She

was still slim, after five children, and he could see traces of the young woman he'd taken as his third wife. She was still his favorite. For two days more, she was his favorite.

"Wife," he said, "it was done as a protection to you. Something of great worth is missing, and I had to make sure you didn't have it. It wasn't just you—all the members of my household were searched. It was not found. You have been cleared. So, in this instance you are under my protection."

Rather than calming her, his remarks caused the woman's eyes to blaze. "It was you?" she snorted. "You had someone ransack my things as a 'protection'? If you care for me so much, why didn't you simply ask?"

"Now I can prove to everyone you're above suspicion," he said.

She stomped her foot, her nostrils flaring. She was like his favorite pony, high-spirited, stubborn, and needing to be tamed.

"I am your wife!" she said, not shrilly, but in even, measured tones. "I want—the least I want from you is an apology!"

Oh, Asad, he thought, *you are angry with me. You are defiant. You are fortunate that, unlike other chiefs, I do not punish my wives for impertinence, as I have the right to do. In fact, it has always been your defiance that attracted me to you.*

She stomped her foot again.

He smiled. "Come to the mats." She looked at him aghast, as if she was still surprised that her pretty little tantrums provoked this outcome.

"I want your apology!"

"You *demand* from me?"

"I said, I *want* an apology. I'm *owed* one." Now her eyes were filling with tears of anger.

She clearly knew where this was going. But maybe this was her plan. After tonight, she would not expect to come to his mats for a week, at the very least.

"Who is your husband?" he asked. "Who is the Hajj?"

Asad did not answer but looked at the ground, biting her lip.

"Come here. Now."

She could do nothing but obey.

She was a willful little pony. And once again, she would be tamed.

Jaime and Andrea had only made two very brief stops for gas, to use the restroom, buy some fruit, and—in Jaime's case—buy caffeinated soda.

Under normal circumstances, Jaime would seriously enjoy the freedom of being behind the wheel—no convoys, no heavy combat gear, just a turbocharged sedan that handled like a dream in the traffic on the Autobahn. The best part was the six-speed manual transmission. She had always enjoyed the challenge of finding the perfect point between the clutch and the shift, when the next gear moved in so smoothly you could hardly detect the change.

But by nightfall, the effects of the caffeine had ebbed and Jaime was just plain exhausted. She knew she had to get Dr. Farmer to the hotel as quickly as humanly possible. Jaime only hoped she herself could catch a little sleep there before anything happened.

Driving in the dark was not helping.

"Were you aware that I know your great-grandmother?" Dr. Farmer asked.

"No," Jaime said, grateful for the conversation.

"Yes." The older woman smiled. "She told me about the incredible mystery you solved shortly after your arrival in Eden."

Jaime smiled. It was kind of Andrea to do her part to level the playing field of their relationship. The research Jaime had been assigned to do on international finance had led her to a healthy awe of this woman and how astutely she understood the social and spiritual ramifications of economic theory. It was an honor to be accompanying her. Jaime was certain that once the economists gathered in Davos realized that Dr. Farmer was among them, she'd be surrounded and peppered with questions.

Jaime said, "I've really enjoyed reading your papers. Most of the points you make seem crucial. I'd say irrefutable, although obviously there are those who do argue with your conclusions. But the fact is, even if they disagree, you've taken the conversation to a new, and important, level," said Jaime.

"You know, the most important thing I got from my time at Stanford wasn't from the classes or even the brilliant professors. It was the understanding of how many people in the Terris world only think of money in terms of their allotment of it," Andrea commented. "Living from paycheck to paycheck, without ever understanding that their government's financial system determines so much about their daily lives."

"Even stranger is that so many people spend their lives chasing money and never quite catching it. Yet they take no time to get a grasp of the big picture, or even how we were trained to be on this treadmill of consumption." Jaime said. "I know that to be true because, until recently, I was one of them."

"Do you think it's money they're chasing, or the idea of wealth and acquisition that's been sold to them by ad agencies?" Dr. Farmer's question was rhetorical.

"Do you feel individual wealth is wrong, Dr. Farmer?" Jaime asked. Once their conversation turned economic, it felt much more natural for Jaime to use a term of respect.

"My answer to you on that question is much franker than my answer to an economist would be," Andrea said. "Wealth in itself is not bad—depending on what your true treasure is, and where it lies. It won't surprise you when I say that the history of Eden economics changed substantially two thousand years ago when agents in the Terris world returned after spending three years listening to the economic theories of Jesus."

" 'For where your treasure is, there will your heart be also'," Jaime quoted.

"Exactly. As for personal wealth, well, the Bible never says money is the root of all evil."

"The *love* of money, on the other hand . . ." Jaime smiled.

"Causes many problems," agreed the older woman.

"So agents of Eden were present when Jesus was teaching?" Jaime asked.

"Of course. Part of what the Integrators do is pay attention to who is in the Terris world that deserves special attention, who we can learn from, who we can share wisdom with, who should be invited to come into the gardener community."

Jaime knew that those in Eden referred to themselves simply as gardeners.

Andrea continued, "If you look at any history book, you can know that when many important things happened, gardeners were there as facilitators and guides. We can't change human nature, we can't force people to act in courageous and compassionate ways, but we can equip and support those who do."

"So gardeners knew people like Abraham Lincoln?"

"One helped persuade Lincoln to run for office."

"And gardeners were present during the ministry of Jesus. Oh, I would have loved to have been there! And I can only imagine that they might have understood some things differently, or more completely."

"As a matter of fact, a gardener was known to be in Jesus' inner circle. He wasn't one of the twelve who became known as apostles, but he did spend time alone with him. Can you imagine the kinds of conversations they must have had?" Andrea said.

"It reminds me of what Jesus says in the book of John: 'There are so many other things I want to tell you, but you could not bear it.' I'd give anything to hear some of those 'other things'!" Jaime added, "The gardener who was there didn't report back about the content of those talks?"

"The gardener's name was Yacov, and he did talk with some of the other Integrators about what he heard, and what it meant. They urged him to write it all down and send it back into Eden. The other gardeners said economic discussions were part of their conversations—among many other topics," Andrea added, almost wistfully. "Because it's my area of interest, I can only imagine how that information might have impacted Eden economic theory, not to mention theory here in the Terris world. For example, the very purposeful decisions after World War II to make the United States into what we now know to be a toxic consumerist society might never have happened. In fact, the Forum that we're headed for right now might have looked completely different.

"But Yacov was killed—one of those senseless, stupid things. A couple of Roman soldiers found a woman from his village alone at a spring. They attacked her. Yacov came to her defense, and they stabbed him. They probably didn't even mean to kill him. As I said, we can't force people to act in appropriate ways."

Jaime drove, lost in her thoughts. How exciting it could have been to be present at many of the defining moments of history—and probably at many moments that were defining but never made it into the history books. Like when Lincoln had the series of conversations that convinced him to run for office. To hear what Jesus said, and the tone in which he said it. To see him smile. Just to be there.

Wow.

"How are you doing? Are you awake?"

"So far, so good," answered Jaime.

"What will you do once this assignment is successfully completed?" Andrea asked. "I'd ask if you planned to stay in Davos to ski, but I hear they've hardly had any snow this winter!"

"Yes, I've heard the same thing."

"Your great-grandmother tells me she feels you've found your calling as an Operative," Andrea said.

"I'm glad she feels that way," Jaime said truthfully.

The women realized they were getting close to Davos as

they drove into the Gotschnatunnel. They were almost there—Jaime was starting to relax.

Andrea was also in a good mood. She leaned in, and in a confidential friend-to-friend voice she said, "I also hear you've worked with Sword 23. How incredible is that for a young Operative?"

She hadn't expected this reference to Yani. Yani, whom she was working so hard to keep from entering her conscious thought, and who was always close to doing so.

Thus Jaime was sputtering, her blood pressure spiking, her mind suddenly searching for any kind of rational response, when they emerged from the Gotschnatunnel on the south end of Klosters, Switzerland, into a blinding snowstorm.

She had not expected this. And under the snow a layer of ice.

Jaime fought to keep the wheels from spinning as they rounded a curve and headed up a steep incline. There was an inch of snow on the road, and the wheels were not getting good traction. She tried to downshift to give the wheels a better chance to grip. That split second of slowdown was all it took for the car to lose its momentum.

It began to slide backward.

"Shit!" she said, trying desperately to regain forward traction—but the tires wouldn't bite.

Helplessly, she struggled to maintain control of the vehicle as it slowly slid backward toward the curve.

January 24, 2007, 9:38 P.M.
(2 days, 12 hours, 52 minutes until end of auction)
Judean wilderness west of the Dead Sea
Israel

The Hajj had sent Asad back to her tent after their encounter. He had not really suspected her when his dearest treasure had gone missing, and he had honestly wanted to protect her from any accusations should the news ever get out.

Omar sighed. He knew it would not be easy for her to attend his wedding to a younger wife.

He also knew what the women were saying about his upcoming wedding, specifically about his new wife. He expected them to talk. His bride was beautiful, and she was fifteen. He was not beautiful, and he was not fifteen. The fact that she'd agreed to marry him—willingly agreed—had set tongues wagging for many miles.

They were saying she was a gold digger. They were saying he was an old goat.

The men were more charitable.

The first time Hajj al-Asim had noticed the girl looking at him, he'd been sure he was mistaken. He was visiting the camp of her clan; he was doing business with their chief concerning an olive grove. When the Hajj had paced off the property in question, he had gone past the tent of Yasmin and her mother.

Yasmin had been looking at him. Once their eyes locked,

she had modestly looked at the ground. But then she had glanced up again, through thick lashes, to see if he was watching her.

He was.

He came back again to contemplate the olive grove deal. This time he looked for Yasmin. She still sat with her mother, in front of their tent. But this time, when their eyes locked, she smiled before looking away.

The Hajj made many trips to decide whether to purchase the grove.

On his last trip, Yasmin was nowhere to be seen.

"I've been thinking," he said to the clan chief, who was also the girl's uncle. Her father had died in a fall; her stepfather did not have standing as a man with whom to deal. "As you know, my first wife died two years ago. I've been thinking of taking another wife. A favored wife."

"You would do honor to our clan, to any woman," said the chief. The words were scripted, the polite answer to the Hajj of the tribe. "Who pleases you?"

The Hajj couldn't tell if the chief knew exactly whom he had in mind or hadn't any idea. Those words were always spoken with slight hesitation, in case the request would turn out to be problematic.

"Yasmin, daughter of the late tribesman Yusef."

"Yasmin?" It was clear the chief hadn't known. "There are so many girls who would be more suitable."

The Hajj treaded lightly. It was not characteristic for him. But something about this girl touched him, brought out the best part of him. "I would speak with her," he said. "And if she does not wish it, I will choose elsewhere."

"You will speak with her, and if *she* does not wish . . . ?"

The chief was clearly flummoxed.

"When should I return?"

"A week," he said. "You will honor us if you return in a week."

January 24, 2007, 9:40 P.M.
(2 days, 11 hours, 50 minutes until end of auction)
Highway 28
2 Miles northeast of Laret, Switzerland

The sky was pitch-black, the snow swirl cut visibility to near zero, as the sedan continued to slide backward down the mountain road. To make matters worse, Jaime remembered crossing a small bridge just before that final curve. That meant there was no room for error. It was essential to keep the car on the road.

She managed to keep the car straight. Much to her relief it slid backward across the bridge. She knew there was a sharp turn behind it, but before she could see the turn, they hit the curve and skidded toward the guardrail. Reacting too quickly to this danger, she overcorrected, cutting too hard on the steering wheel and sending them directly toward the craggy hillside.

Jaime quickly regained her composure, and this time she pulled the wheel back just enough to help them miss a large rock outcropping. They slid instead into a widened area of the shoulder used for emergency parking. Fortunately, the road flattened out and the auto slowed to a stop inches from the mountain that rose behind it.

"Well, that was exciting," said Andrea with a deadpan expression. "Thank God there's no other traffic! But then, who else would be crazy enough to be out in a blizzard?"

"And who said anything about a blizzard! No snow all season, that's the word I got!"

Jaime rested her forehead on the steering wheel as she caught her breath.

No matter what the conditions, they couldn't stay there; they had to press ahead. She took a deep breath.

At that moment, Jaime would have given anything to be able to fly into Davos. She had been studying for her pilot's license for the past year, but she couldn't accrue flying hours while deployed, and the flight through the mountains would have required an instrument rating. Well, this snowstorm would have nixed the deal, anyway, but maybe if they'd flown they'd already be there.

Enough. Enough wishful thinking.

Jaime lifted her head, ready to attack the hill once again.

"I'm going to back up a little further and get a good running start at this hill," she said to her passenger. "If you're in a praying kind of mood, now would be a good time!"

Jaime started her run, keeping the car in a low gear and getting just enough speed to keep the tires from spinning. She kept steady pressure on the accelerator, and did not back off when she hit the steepest point of the hill. Just as the car reached the peak, the road took a sharp curve, causing the back end of the car to fishtail. But she saw it coming, and maintained control.

Andrea smiled. Her shoulders relaxed.

Disaster avoided. The snowfall was slowing. And while the caffeine was gone, Jaime's new surge of adrenaline would carry them quite a ways. She expelled the breath she realized she'd been holding, and thought how nice it would be if this was the gravest danger they'd face on their sojourn to Davos.

January 24, 2007, 11:32 P.M.
(2 days, 10 hours, 58 minutes until end of auction)
Judean wilderness west of the Dead Sea
Israel

In the still hours of the night before the major celebrations for her wedding started, Yasmin lay awake in her mother's tent, remembering the sound of her father's laugh and then gentle exasperation in her mother's voice as she scolded him for one thing or another. Yasmin didn't know which she missed more—her father or the family life they'd known before he died.

Now, instead, she heard the aggressive staccato of her stepfather's snores, and prayed she'd made the correct choice, that she wasn't leaping off of the *saj* into the fire.

Yasmin vividly remembered the day she turned fourteen. That was the day she knew she was running out of time. Her hair was braided, and she wore a red sash, denoting she had come of age. But her women's cycle as yet came very infrequently. Her mother told her not to worry, it would become regular in time. But Yasmin thanked God that she was maturing slowly. For when the day came that she became pregnant, her life would be over. By tribal law, her stepfather could not marry her. Instead, he would undoubtedly show outrage and disown her. She would either be killed or be cast out, shunned, friendless, and without prospects, to carry and care for a child known as her shame.

Her father had been the younger brother of the chief. Yasmin imagined her mother must have angered the chief in some severe way for the chief to allow the Monster to marry her after his brother's death. Yasmin knew they could not count on the chief for help.

Life in the small tent that was her family's world had become unbearable. The Monster beat her little brother, but not as often as he beat her. From the time her stepfather had married her mother when Yasmin was eleven, he had found fault with everything. He backhanded his stepdaughter casually and had beaten her once or twice a week. The Monster started fondling her, as well. When she turned thirteen, he forced himself on her, although infrequently. He did it only when he thought her mother would not notice.

Yasmin's mother, while not acknowledging any impropriety, stayed close as much as she could. Even when her new husband ordered her off with the sheep, she would try to take Yasmin with her. Sometimes it would be allowed; sometimes it would not.

When Yasmin turned fifteen, she knew her time was nearly up. Her menses were much more regular, as was her stepfather's attention.

Once she thought she was saved. A young man, a distant cousin, had asked for her hand in marriage, but her stepfather had refused, saying the prospective bridegroom had nothing to offer. Yasmin came to understand her stepfather would say this to anyone young, no matter how good his prospects, how good his family.

So when the Hajj himself came to do business with their clan, Yasmin saw her last chance—her only chance—for escape.

Someone as lowly as her stepfather could not dishonor their clan by refusing a marriage offer from the Hajj. It would not be allowed.

Yasmin had not heard good things about the Hajj personally, nor had she heard bad things. She counted on the fact that the talk among the girls would have reached her if the Hajj were also a monster. In any case, she had to escape the brutality of her current life. If she did not, there was no future for her.

There was a meeting of the men in the chief's tent. Her

stepfather was the one who brought her the news. "It seems the Hajj is blind as well as stupid," he said. "He has taken a liking to our own little whore, Yasmin."

Both Yasmin and her mother kept spinning thread, neither one looking up as he spoke.

"It *seems* . . . ," he let the word hang, as if it were an accusation, "the Hajj would come and speak to the little whore in person. It *seems* if she agrees, he will take her to wife."

The Monster towered over Yasmin as he spoke. "So, your promiscuity is obvious to all. You have no shame. You have even ensnared the Hajj!" The back of his hand came down across her face with brutal force. She cried out but then continued spinning.

"Then you will be well rid of her," said Yasmin's mother.

"What did you say?" bellowed the Monster.

"I said we'll be well rid of her," said her mother again. Yasmin saw one single tear run down her mother's cheek as she continued to spin the thread.

To the casual observer, Jaime Richards and Andrea Farmer were two Forum attendees who'd met for a drink in the lounge of the Hotel Belvédère. The two women sat in boxy gray chairs, Jaime nursing a drink that looked very much like a gin and tonic, complete with two lime slices. Andrea was sipping a red wine.

In actuality, Jaime's tonic had no gin and the BlackBerry she seemed to be fiddling with was a communication link to her partner, who was out of sight but nearby.

They had chosen the perfect location. From their seats they could easily see both the bar and any traffic coming into the hotel lobby and up to the front desk. Dr. Andrea Farmer looked chic and comfortable in a floor-length gray knit dress with mock turtleneck and a red wool blazer. Jaime thought the red enhanced the look of Dr. Farmer's beautiful white hair and elegant features, and hoped that when she was even half this woman's age she would look as good.

When she and Dr. Farmer had finally arrived and gone to their shared hotel room, they'd found the door to the adjoining room open and Jaime's partner and the head Operative on this mission, Eddie Williams, anticipating their arrival. Jaime had joined Eddie in his room, closing the connecting door so Andrea could change into evening wear.

"What's the latest?" Jaime had asked. His ebony skin and gelled hair looked dapper above a starched white tux shirt with black tie.

Eddie told her the secret meeting, originally scheduled for that night, had been postponed. Weather-related delays had closed the airports for a few hours, and many guests were arriving late. "Still," he said, "Woodbury is an impatient man. We're looking for it to take place tomorrow morning at the latest. But don't worry. Between you, me, Dr. Farmer, and the other unseen Operatives, Woodbury's crew can't make a move without detection. Not to jinx anything, but this assignment is what I'd call on the cushy end."

Jaime laughed and agreed, "Well, except for the part where Dr. Farmer was nearly killed for discovering a similar meeting—and, from what you told me earlier, these folks seem entirely capable of doing so with us—comparatively speaking, I'd call it a Swiss holiday!"

"Especially for you," he said.

She looked at Op 1, wondering if he was making reference to her relative inexperience. "Especially . . . ?"

Her partner looked flustered. "I mean, you having worked with Sword 23 and all."

"Oh. Well. Not anymore." Were they going to put it on her stupid tombstone? She could envision it: *Here lies some lucky woman who once worked with Sword 23*.

"Obviously not," Eddie said, his humor returning, "If you're stuck here with me!"

"And glad to be! It sounds as if it will be catastrophic for the world economy if Woodbury is able to succeed. Do we have any intelligence on which currency he's going after?"

"An educated guess, following the markets, would be the American dollar."

"But he's American!"

"I don't think this is about patriotism. I think it's about a handful of people becoming very, very rich."

"And millions of the rest of us becoming very, very poor."

"So, let's stop this guy. Why don't you go ahead and get dressed, too?" he said, and he pulled on the jacket that completed his well-cut designer tux. "If you're awake enough, it'd be good to get downstairs to screen the arrivals. If by any chance our man Woodbury turns up in person, I think it's worth the risk to bug him."

"I can help you with that," Jaime said.

"Oh, and—I took the liberty of adding some wardrobe to your collection," said Eddie. As she looked at him with raised eyebrows, he'd said, "I'm the one who picked up your stuff in Hochspeyer. No offense, but anything that can stay in a duffel for three months without wrinkling isn't exactly haute couture. See you down."

Sure enough, Jaime had found a selection of stylish day and evening wear in her size hanging in the closet of the next room.

As she changed and tried to figure out something to do with her hair, the constant references to her working with Sword 23—Yani—kept coming back to her. He was a legend, even to people from Eden. And gardeners were not easily impressed. What would they think if they knew she was the woman for whom he gave up being a Sword? The woman for whom he became a lowly Operative for whom emotional attachments were allowed—and then she'd opted out of their relationship? She sighed. Everyone still called him Sword 23. Apparently the title was like that of President of the United States—even after you vacated the position, you kept the title out of respect.

So what would they do if they found out she was the one who made Sword 23 not a Sword anymore and then she dumped him?

Tar and feathers? Run out of town on a rail? If only they knew.

Twenty minutes later, she and Andrea had taken up their spots in the lobby, Jaime in a black cocktail dress with spaghetti straps, accented by a diamond brooch with matching earrings.

What a difference a day makes! she couldn't help think.

Sitting with Andrea for ten minutes, Jaime had learned

more about key players at the conference than she would have
discovered in months of personal research. With each name
mentioned by Andrea, a picture and bio would appear on the
screen of Jaime's handheld, often with cartoons and graffiti
added by the unseen Op 1. Jaime had quickly discovered that
her Operative partner for this mission was brilliant with anything electronic. However, since very few projects challenged
him, he tended to let off steam with practical jokes.

Oblivious to Eddie's antics, Andrea continued in her role
as teacher, talking about the G8, debt relief for Africa, and
other topics related to the hotel guests who passed by.

Jaime took a sip of her drink and turned to look through the
coffered windows that offered a view of the lobby. At that moment, some sort of buzz electrified the air itself, as photographers from all corners of the room began to converge near the
front doors. Others in the lobby stood up out of curiosity, to
see what was causing the stir.

Jaime looked at Andrea, who gave a slight shrug. She
glanced at her handheld, where Eddie had messaged; *Probably one of the celebs*. She turned it to Andrea, who read the
text and nodded.

Jaime looked down to see that Eddie had added; *Or Donald
Trump*. She rolled her eyes.

Andrea watched the continued frenzy as the door at the front of the hotel opened automatically and another line of paparazzi backed in. They were followed by a couple of private security men, then a four-man entourage, currently in their Sunday best.

It turned out Eddie's guess was correct. After the entourage, a handsome young man, six feet at least, came striding inside. Thick black hair with a natural wave swept his collar. Andrea could see rather than hear the reporters yelling questions, photographers coaxing, "Shepard, over here! Look to your right!" Andrea herself immediately recognized the rock icon who answered the cacophony calmly, with some polite, "I'm tired, pleased to talk with you tomorrow" brush-off, and disappeared down a hallway as hotel staffers stepped up to prevent the reporters and photographers from following.

The older woman couldn't help but notice that this particular celebrity had caught even Jaime's attention. But when the younger woman saw Andrea looking at her, she smiled and looked away. "Guess Eddie called it," Jaime said. "Are you familiar with his theories?"

"Yes." Andrea smiled. "He's an unlikely message bearer, but the discussion he's bringing to the table deserves hearing out. For so long, discussions of economics have centered on wealth accumulation without regard to sustainability—of the planet, of communities, of human happiness. I know he's made himself an expert on many of these issues, but I'd like more specifics and more information. I'm always leery of someone who uses his popularity to get a place at the table."

"Add to watch list?" Jaime said.

"If for no other reason than that he's not only younger but considerably better looking than the others on the list!"

Jaime laughed at the unexpected answer, and then continued with what Andrea might have described as a small, private smile, tapping her stylus in response to the unnecessary wealth of materials, including "hunk" photos, that Eddie was providing of Shepard on Jaime's screen. She shook her head and rolled her eyes.

Andrea returned to the business at hand, pointing out two Chinese power brokers arguing in a corner.

"The one on the left," she said, "is Yin Zhen Su. The other is Ran Li. Yin is a newcomer, on the top ten list of movers in the Chinese financial world, made his money in information technologies."

Jaime looked up from her data screen to observe the two men in the flesh. "But what's with the other guy? He looks put out."

"Ran represents *old* money," replied Andrea with a bit of a sneer. "He is from a dynasty that is China's equivalent to the Rockefellers. His family stuck it out after the establishment of the People's Republic of China and made themselves billions under Mao. He is very conservative and has no respect for 'new money' like Yin."

"Okay, so no respect, but should we add him to the watch list?"

"Definitely. He's cutthroat in his business dealings, and holds a grudge against the West based upon major losses by his family holdings in Hong Kong."

While they were studying Ran Li, two men walked past. The first was a tall, handsome Spaniard, with dark hair and eyes and a bronze complexion, wearing a flashy silk suit. The other man could be categorized as "mousy," short, with a high forehead, overly large ears, beady eyes, and very bushy eyebrows. While everyone else seemed to have loosened their ties and jackets after a long day, his traditional black wool suit with white starched shirt and maroon tie was still totally buttoned, totally in place. As he passed, he gave a very slight, almost imperceptible nod in the direction of Ran Li, who returned the nod.

Andrea surprised Jaime by grasping her arm.

"That's him," Andrea said.

"Him?" Jaime responded.

She was quivering. "Jameson Aldrich Woodbury. The man who's convening this dangerous meeting."

Frank McMillan glared at the young man in the Swiss Army uniform who respectfully handed back his passport and Agency identification. He shouldn't be hard on the soldier, he knew. After all, he was the one standing outside in the snow. But he was rank and file, a foot soldier, and Frank had an inborn contempt for him, as such.

The snow was letting up as Frank headed into Davos. He'd heard rumors that next year's World Economic Forum would move to a different location, in part because the Swiss Army was tired of the expense and hassle of guarding the world's economic leaders.

More than anyone else, Frank and his compatriots on the Terrorism Task Force knew that half the people in Davos this night were Forum participants and the other half were there to watch the first half. Whether Swiss Army, private security, terrorists, or members of the worldwide intelligence community, it was like convening a big game of "I Spy."

And that didn't even count the damn protesters, who caused the most damage and got the most press. The Swiss Army was supposed to turn back protesters—people protesting globalization were rumored to have the biggest presence this year—and let them go wreak havoc in Geneva instead. Since there was only one road into town from the north and one to the south and one train station, it was a manageable situation.

But, instead of tailing terrorists or economists or businessmen or politicians, or even his fellow spies, Frank was following an Army chaplain.

An Army chaplain who very possibly held the key to wealth and riches far beyond anything dreamed of by the billionaires at the conference. The ultimate treasure that was Eden.

Go figure.

He'd tried to capture this woman once, four years earlier.

This time, he vowed she would not get away.

January 24, 2007, 11:57 P.M.
(2 days, 9 hours, 33 minutes until end of auction)
Steigenberger Hotel Belvédère lounge
Davos, Switzerland

"Jam-e-son Al-drich Wood-bu-ry." Andrea was speaking more to herself than to Jaime, as she pronounced every syllable of his name separately. "He's grandnephew of Nelson Aldrich and CEO of a consortium of American banks."

Seeing this man in person was more disturbing than she had imagined it would be. Her thoughts raced back to a time almost a century before, when she was a much younger woman, and in mortal peril.

It had been November 1910 when a barefoot Andrea raced through the plantation oaks surrounding the Club House mansion on Jekyll Island, Georgia. Behind her, a cacophony of male voices were crying out.

"Stop her, someone!"

"Who is it?"

"It's one of the chambermaids. The white-haired one."

"Don't let her escape!"

She had been discovered, eavesdropping from the balcony of the Club House turret room. That damn eclipse! It had drawn the men out to the yard and into perfect position to see her spying from above.

Trapped! All she could do was flee. Andrea had dropped down onto the Club House roof and run into the night. She was heading for the resort's dock in hopes of finding a boat, any boat, she could borrow for her escape.

The young woman was thankful on behalf of her bare feet that there was virtually no underbrush. The darkness caused by the eclipsed moon made it a challenge to negotiate the trees, but her eyesight was excellent, and in spite of occasionally running into hanging moss, she managed to keep her pace and avoid any major collisions.

She could hear someone behind her but didn't dare even glance to see if he was gaining ground.

Mustn't get caught . . .

Upon reaching the riverbank, she found she had miscalculated and was farther downstream from the dock than expected. Dodging driftwood, grimacing as her feet pounded pebbles and shells, she headed upstream along the bank. Her lungs were protesting from the effort. She was in good shape, but she was not prepared for this.

Finally, the full length of the pier loomed out of the darkness. Her heart fell. No boats. Not a kayak or canoe or rowboat. Nothing!

Andrea looked back to see a tall man, with starched white shirt and suspenders and, most important, a shotgun, clear the trees where she had emerged moments before.

Without hesitation, she stepped on the dock and ran out toward the water, knowing there was no place to go but—

"Stop or I'll shoot," she heard from somewhere behind her.

Andrea did not miss a stride but continued her sprint full speed toward the end of the pier and dove as far out into the water as her momentum would take her. Muffled behind her was the blast of a shotgun. She felt searing pain as she kicked down beneath the surface.

So cold. So dark.

These were her last thoughts before the water engulfed her and she drifted away.

January 24, 2007, 11:59 P.M.
(2 days, 9 hours, 31 minutes until end of auction)
Steigenberger Hotel Belvédère lounge
Davos, Switzerland

So he was here. Jaime didn't as much as glance his way, but her body was tensed, ready for action.

"Eddie says it's likely Woodbury's organizing the secret meeting."

"I'm ninety-nine percent certain he is. His presence here certainly isn't for anything but his own gain. Woodbury never comes to these meetings, has absolutely no interest in creating an even playing field where those with the power and influence use that power to help others. He is a financial power broker who wants to influence international currency flow.

"Lately, he's been a publicly vocal advocate for continuing the dollar as the only viable choice for global currency reserve, yet private e-mail traffic between Woodbury and Ran implies a different agenda."

"So who's the hot-looking Spaniard with him? He is Spanish, right? His accent sounds Castilian."

"That's interesting," said Andrea as she followed the man with her eyes, never moving her head. He and his companion took possession of two nearby chairs and a glass coffee table by a large stone fireplace. They seemed to be having a friendly but energetic debate.

"I'll have you know," Andrea pretended to chide Jaime,

"that very impressive and dignified man is the financial advisor to the prime minister of Spain."

"Hmm, so probably a little out of my league."

"Give me five minutes," came Eddie's voice in her ear, "and I'll hack his phone number for you off the Internet."

"Op 1, thanks, but forget setting me up." Jaime spoke to her invisible partner. "What I really need is a diversion so I can access Woodbury unnoticed."

"One diversion coming up!"

Jaime breathed slowly, calming her nerves as she palmed the communication disk she hoped to plant on J. Aldrich Woodbury. She stared through the window into the lobby, noting a large mural behind the reservation desk.

"I wonder who that man is whose face is so prominent on the mural?" She hadn't realized she had said this out loud when someone beside her in the black pants and vest of a Belvédère waiter spoke.

"It's Ernst Ludwig Kirchner, a famous German expressionist artist who lived here in Davos for many years." The waiter's English was heavily accented but very understandable.

Jaime looked up to say "*vielen Dank*" to the man, and found the impish smile of her partner, Eddie. He winked, and asked, "Do you ladies need anything else to drink?"

"*Nein, danke,* we're fine," answered Andrea as Jaime recovered from her surprise.

"Then, I'll just see if the fire needs tending."

Eddie slipped over to the hearth and set aside the grate. Then he picked up a log waiting to be added to the fire and threw it on top, a little too forcefully. Sparks began to fly as one of the burning logs came spurting out, rolling onto the floor. The two men who were seated by the fireplace scrambled over their padded chairs, frantically brushing off flying embers and hustling to avoid getting caught by the glowing log. As they stumbled away from the danger, calling the waiter an oaf and an idiot, Jaime slipped up behind them and with one slick move slipped the disk under Woodbury's collar.

She returned quickly to her seat and picked up her drink.

"I'm impressed," said Andrea. "Did they teach you how to pick pockets at Mountaintop, too?"

Mountaintop was the Operative training center inside Eden. Jaime blushed, and looked back over toward the fireplace to see Eddie sweeping up the mess and apologizing profusely to the two men who had regained their seats. But she noticed Woodbury wasn't looking at the waiter at all. His gaze was directed in her direction.

Have I been made? Does he know what I just did?

But he wasn't looking at Jaime. His eyes seemed locked on Andrea, and he had a very puzzled look.

Jaime stared down into her drink as if it were missing a slice of lime.

"Andrea, is there any reason Woodbury should know you? Are there pictures of you in any of your textbooks?"

"None. But there might be something else. My hair."

Now she had Jaime's interest piqued.

"Your hair?"

"You see, my hair has been this color since I was a teenager."

"And . . . ?"

"Well, I am embarrassed to admit this, but the reason I failed to complete my first mission was I was discovered. Caught snooping, and recognized due to my unique hair color."

"Still, why would he . . . ?" Jaime suddenly had a very weird idea. "Hey, you said he was grandnephew to Nelson Aldrich. Suppose they passed down the legend of the mysterious white-haired woman who died in the river. Maybe he thinks you're a ghost!" She chuckled.

"Or an omen . . ." Andrea was very serious.

"Well, before he decides to come over and see if you're spectral or real, let's get going. We've done what we needed to do."

As they headed toward the lobby, Jaime couldn't help but notice Woodbury's watchful gaze following them all the way out the door.

—THURSDAY—

It was the family legend, whispered among the men when they had consumed enough brandy and cigars. The story of a mysterious white-haired woman who had appeared at the scene of a legendary secret meeting. The tale of a spy who had disappeared in the waters of the Jekyll River.

Woodbury was not a superstitious man. In fact, he prided himself on his ability to gather facts and make decisions based upon those facts without involving extraneous emotion.

But seeing that very striking woman on the eve of an incredibly important meeting . . . a meeting whose significance could eclipse that of Jekyll Island. Even J. Aldrich Woodbury found that a bit unnerving.

Omens? Then he shook his head and snorted. *Don't waste my time!*

Woodbury's granduncle had engineered one of the biggest coups in modern financial history when he established a federal reserve system that cushioned banks from the inevitable ebbs and flows of markets. It had been a smart move then—for the banks, that was—but Nelson Aldrich knew it was eventually destined to crash.

Omen or no omen, J. Aldrich Woodbury had engineered the next great coup, turning the world's reserve system on its head!

The banker stood in white undershirt and boxers, observing his reflection in the bathroom mirror as he carefully scraped the last of the shaving cream off his neck with a straight razor. He leaned in close to the glass and felt with his hand to make sure he had not missed a hair.

Woodbury despised the unshaven look so many young men seemed to sport these days. If one of his male employees was unfortunate enough to walk into his office with the hint of a five o'clock shadow, he would be fired on the spot. If it meant shaving twice a day, so be it!

Woodbury was reaching for a towel when his assistant, a young woman named Nicole Barron, suddenly appeared over his shoulder in the mirror. Woodbury, a closet sexist, had never before hired a woman to work as his executive assistant, but Barron was the daughter of one of his Harvard classmates and had just graduated from Harvard Business School herself. As a favor to his classmate, the banker had agreed to take the young graduate on as an assistant, which for the most part translated as "valet."

But the young woman had no reason to complain. She was getting paid good money and, if she did well, her references would allow her to work anywhere she wanted.

Contrary to his first impression, the banker had to admit Nicole had promise. Her looks were certainly deceiving. At just over five feet, with long silky black hair and almond eyes that added a slightly Asian flavor to her countenance, she was often dismissed by clients and competitors as being harmless. She'd told him she was half Chinese, a quarter Mexican, and a quarter Irish, Russian, and French. A walking international consortium. Her drive, her energy, and her willingness to go for the throat when closing a deal made her very dangerous in negotiations.

"Your newspapers, sir." Nicole waved three large papers and stepped back to let her boss pass but continued her update at a slightly higher decibel as he disappeared into the bedroom to finish dressing.

"Our tickets are confirmed on the train for Geneva tomorrow with the follow-on flight to Boston. All arrangements finalized for Strela Alp at noon today. Every guest has now confirmed their attendance. I'll get the key from the manager and have it open by eleven thirty. Will you be needing anything else before then?"

Woodbury walked back into the sitting room tucking in his shirt. He noted for the first time that the young woman was not wearing a business suit but instead seemed dressed for outdoor activities.

He paused, frowned, then replied, "No, just make sure the room is ready. Keep your BlackBerry handy."

With a quick nod, the assistant disappeared out the door.

It's possible I was wrong. Barron may not have what it takes to succeed.

Having decided the fate of his assistant's career, the banking magnate threw a tie around his neck and returned to the bathroom mirror to make sure the knot was perfect.

January 25, 2007, 8:30 A.M.
(2 days, 2 hours, 0 minutes until end of auction)
Highway A5
6 miles southwest of Larnaca, Cyprus

Abihu el-Musaq watched the countryside through dark tinted windows. Mountains of rock covered by pine, cypress, and dwarf oak flew by as the stretch limo wound its way along the southern coast of Cyprus toward the Larnaca International Airport.

If el-Musaq absolutely had to travel, this was the only way to go. Plush seats, thick windows tinted so you could look out, but others could not look in. Yes, he liked to watch things, but secretly, in such a way that he would not be watched by others.

Maybe it was because el-Musaq was a fat little man in a world where fashion models of both genders were tall and slim. Perhaps more to the point was that the features of his face were oddly proportioned. He wasn't what you would call ugly, just unusual looking. The width of his eyes was slightly greater than normal, and they were not precisely aligned, so when people looked at him they rarely smiled, but they did often stare, as if trying to figure out what was wrong.

So, el-Musaq preferred to live and work where he could watch others, but they could not watch him. He treasured his privacy above all else. He had a telescope on his rooftop that enabled him to spy on bathers at the beach. He had placed hidden cameras around the house so that he could observe the maid and the cook at work. And he always traveled in his limo with deeply tinted glass.

But now he was heading for the airport, forced to leave his cocoon and fly to Israel and to the damn Bedouin camp. Forced to leave his place of privacy and watching others. Why? Because some idiot sheikh had decided he did not want to give up the prized possession he had promised to sell. Because the dolt did not understand the implications for both of them if the sale did not go through.

Abihu el-Musaq fully understood the implications, and he was not willing to give up *his* life for a jeweled box that some oversexed old goat was hoarding. He would make the Hajj understand the seriousness of the consequences, and return with the box.

He had checked the bids one last time before leaving home. They were now down to three serious bidders. And yes, serious was the key word. In previous auctions all three bidders had proven they were willing to go to the max for an item they coveted, and they were serious in the action they would take if the deal did not follow through.

The Afghan poppy dealer. *What could he possibly want with the box? Claim some religious significance?* He held the current high bid, but past history would indicate he might fall away at the close of bidding.

Now the Canadian woman, there was a tough bidder. She must have an incredible collection of artifacts in her personal museum. But she was not the danger; her husband was. Rumor was he had torn a man limb from limb who had displeased his wife.

And finally, the Brit. What was he, some sort of archeologist? More rumors . . . that he was the picture of the perfect English gentleman. But it was said he was the most ruthless of the bunch. It would be extremely dangerous to cross him!

So, how best to convince the Hajj to give up the item? A trade, maybe. You want something from someone, be prepared to offer something they wanted just as much, or more. In this case, the trick would be to steal something of equal or greater value than the box and then offer it back to the Hajj in return.

But el-Musaq would need some accomplices for this plan. He would stop in Bethlehem and add some people to his entourage. His family was indebted to him for the constant flow of money he sent their way. And besides, he would be less conspicuous traveling with others.

The Hajj had only met el-Musaq's trusted messenger, and so el-Musaq himself should be able to join the marriage celebration without anyone being wise to his purpose.

The car was now slowing as it approached the outskirts of Larnaca. Content with his plan, the little man settled back into his seat to watch pedestrians along the road. A woman was carrying a child on her hip, and a couple were holding hands as they strolled down a path and a young boy skipped along behind them.

I see you. El-Musaq smiled a secret smile.

Jaime sat with Dr. Farmer in the sunshine that filtered down between massive cumulus clouds as they lounged on the outdoor terrace of a mountain restaurant. They were surrounded by skiers and hikers who had stopped for lunch before continuing their day of winter sport in the mountains above Davos. The two women were dressed warmly, with hiking boots, layered sweaters, and light parkas.

This was it. As calm as Jaime tried to seem outwardly, her adrenaline was pumping.

As Jaime picked through what was left of her lunch, (her *pommes frites* were cold, but who cared?) she listened over earphones and watched what appeared to be a video iPod. The video feed she reviewed was not a recorded program, however, but was live and provided by the tiny camera planted by Eddie in a basement room two floors below them. Andrea had her own set of earphones plugged into the same device.

The call from Eddie had come about six that morning. He told Jaime he'd tapped into a phone conversation between Woodbury's assistant and Ran Li. It was terse but just what they needed.

"Noon. Strela Alp. Wood door to basement. Knock twice."

Strela Alp was a restaurant on the mountain above Davos.

The only way to reach it was to ride the Schatzalp Bahn, a kind of mountain tram, from Davos Platz straight up the mountain, followed by a ten-minute walk up a winding path.

This *had* to be the location and time of the meeting they were waiting for.

Eddie had wasted no time. In what they both knew to be a highly dangerous operation, he'd broken into the meeting room in the early-morning hours and planted a small video device to observe the proceedings. He'd then set up an observation point and recording equipment in a small barn behind the restaurant.

Jaime and Andrea arrived at eleven thirty. On her way up the outdoor staircase, Jaime noted that near the foot of the steps there was an old wooden door in the wall. It looked like a walk-out basement but seemed old and unused. It also fit the description from the phone call Eddie had heard. This must be the place.

They'd settled onto the terrace above and ordered lunch. The table provided a suitable vantage point from which to watch as hikers and skiers trudged up the snowy path and mounted the stairs to the terrace.

As they waited, watching the live feed from the as-yet empty room, Jaime put a chilly hand into the pocket of her jacket and felt a crinkle of paper. She'd nearly forgotten. The message light on the telephone in her room had been blinking when she awoke. But when she'd called for her message, it was to discover someone had left her a written note, which she picked up at the front desk.

Jaime Richards, is that you? it asked. *Thought I saw you in town. The hotel wouldn't give me your room number, but said I could leave you a note. It's been too long. Are you free for dinner?—Mark*

It was from an old friend of hers, whom she'd met through her late husband, Paul. Mark and Paul had shared many of the same passions, including working for a lasting peace between Israel and Palestine. In fact, they'd met on a fact-finding trip. Hearing from Mark brought back so many old memories. Paul and Jaime had gone on several working vacations with Mark and his wife, Ondine, and had spent as much time as they could at their home in the French Antilles as Ondine fought, and finally succumbed to, pancreatic cancer. And now Paul was dead, as well. Those days had been a different season of Jaime's life, a different time. The four of them had been so young, so hopeful.

The four of them had been alive.

Just touching the note brought back so many complicated feelings.

It brought her back to the world before Yani.

Was she free for dinner?

Jaime sighed and thought, *Let's start by seeing if I live through lunch.*

The first sign of activity was when a young snowboarder wearing very close-fitting black ski pants, a red windbreaker, and Oakley sunglasses came whizzing down the hill above them and stopped at the base of the restaurant. At first Jaime thought it was a young teen, but as the woman stepped off the board, shook the snow off her boots, and removed her cap, long dark hair fell to the middle of her back. This was no child.

Jaime waited for the snowboarder to ascend the steps to the restaurant terrace, but she never appeared. Instead, the young woman appeared over the video feed in the basement room below.

She can't be more than twenty-five. Jaime wondered how someone so young could be a financial power broker. But her confusion disappeared when the woman set to work moving chairs around, pulling a dusty cover off of a couch, and cleaning off a coffee table. She disappeared up some inner stairs and reappeared with a tray with bottles of Belgian beer—of this they were certain because Eddie zoomed in to check the labels.

"Leffe Brun," Jaime heard him comment over her earpiece. "That's good stuff!"

"Eddie, do we have an ID on her?" Jaime replied.

The response took only a moment. "Name, Nicole Barron. Woodbury's current assistant."

The tables around Jaime and Andrea began to fill with customers, but every once in a while someone would come up the walkway, approach the front of the restaurant, and never appear at the top of the steps. Usually these people were dressed more like businessmen and -women than hikers.

Andrea provided commentary for Jaime and Eddie as the crowd in the basement room grew.

Ran Li had brought two other Asians with him. "I think they're Chinese stock traders," whispered Andrea. "And that petite woman on the rocker, fur-lined ski jacket and coffee-colored skin . . . don't let that angelic smile fool you. She is the Leona Helmsley of India, a multi-billionaire who operates in real estate investment and is about as cutthroat as they come.

"The handsome man sitting on the arm of the couch is a banker from Argentina. His home base is Bariloche, tourism capital of the country, and he manages one of the largest state-owned banks. He's slowly built its portfolio since the crash of 2001, which was not easy in what has been, historically, a very uneven economy."

Precisely at noon, Woodbury appeared. Jaime and Andrea had not seen him come up the walk, so he must have been waiting inside the restaurant somewhere. His sudden appearance was dramatic, startling everyone.

"Reports first. Then time line," he began, taking charge. "Ran, what do you bring to the table?"

"Five of the top ten institutions, all family owned, will join with my own."

"Ipsa?"

The petite Indian spoke with authority. "In spite of differences in our political associations, I have gathered allies in both India and Pakistan who see the personal advantage in joining this venture. A total of eight banks will buy in."

"Excellent. Matias?"

The Argentinean spoke hesitantly at first. "The political leadership of Argentina can and will have nothing to do with such a venture . . . but of course I have still convinced four very large investors to join us."

One of the Chinese stockbrokers said nothing but held up both hands, displaying nine fingers.

Woodbury nodded with satisfaction. "I myself have twenty-two very capable large-scale investors joining me from the U.S. and Canada. With this support I believe we can achieve our goals."

He pulled out a calculator, punched in a few numbers, thought for a moment, then scribbled some numbers on a piece of paper. He passed this around for all to see.

"This is my estimate of the minimum amount it will take to move the market." Jaime couldn't see the paper but noted that eyebrows raised as each person in the circle observed the figures on the paper.

"Slowly, carefully, over the next year, everyone in this cabal will purchase Chinese yuan, as well as shares in the Chinese gold market. Also, add as much gold and silver bullion from the London market as you can without causing suspicion. Be careful not to drive up the prices.

"At the same time, I want you to purchase large quantities of U.S. dollars. Be very public about these purchases, and don't worry about market fluctuations.

"Then, one year from now, on a specific Friday afternoon to be named later, everyone will sell all their dollar holdings and purchase more yuan with those sales, driving up the yuan at the moment the dollar is crashing, and setting it up as the new candidate for a world reserve."

"And if someone jumps the gun and sells out early?" The Argentinean banker did not sound as if he had great trust in his fellow conspirators.

Woodbury moved his gaze methodically about the room, locking eyes with each participant as he slowly spoke.

"The stakes in this game are extremely high. The potential rewards are staggering. So must be the consequences of betrayal. If anyone leaks this plan, if anyone cuts and runs early, they're dead." The matter-of-fact way in which he spoke the last two words brought a chill to the room greater than any caused by the Alpine snow outside the door.

As she listened, Jaime was struck by the profound calm Woodbury demonstrated when plotting to ruin the economy of his own nation. She squinted as the sun popped in and out

of the clouds, and noticed how people all around were taking
great advantage of the fresh powder with skis, snowboards,
and snowshoes.

*What a shame to take a breathtakingly beautiful place like
this and make it the scene of such a nasty plan.*

Could they really do this? she mouthed, looking over to get
Andrea's professional opinion. But Andrea wasn't there. Jaime
looked around the deck to see if she was in sight, maybe
stretching her legs, or asking the waiter for water. Just as Jaime
was about to go check the restroom she heard Eddie over her
earphone.

"What's she doing down there?"

Jaime had a sinking feeling in her stomach as she turned
back to check the video feed. Right there, standing in the doorway of the basement room, was Andrea. Each of the members
of the meeting was staring with shock in her direction.

"What's she doing?"

"I'm on it!" Jaime was grabbing her things and throwing
them into her backpack. "I've turned off the video feed, but
keep me tuned into the audio."

Jaime threw twenty Swiss francs on the table and ran down
the steps to the ground level. She looked frantically around,
noting the long sloping hill they had mounted to come to the
restaurant, and knowing there was no way they could delay
the group long enough to get back to the train ahead of them.

Leaning against the outer wall of the restaurant was an as-
sortment of skis, poles, and sleds. Her gaze fell on one particular piece of equipment; she hesitated just for a moment, then
grabbed it to make ready for their escape.

Andrea knew she'd made a rash decision. But she'd waited almost a hundred years for this.

"How dare you!" She was seething with righteous anger as she faced J. Aldrich Woodbury across the room. "How dare you treat the financial holdings of millions of people with such abandon!"

Woodbury was standing now, no longer in shock, his own anger building as he took a few threatening steps in her direction. "Who are you? And who let you in here?"

Andrea did not back down. "Who I am is unimportant. That you will not succeed in this venture is!"

"And how do you think *you* are going to stop us?"

"I've already stopped you. Your plan can't survive when exposed to the light, and a video feed of this meeting is already on its way to every major television network." A good bluff never hurt anything. A video feed, yes. Every major network—not quite yet.

The rest of the room exploded in an uproar.

"A video feed?"

"I'll be ruined!"

"This can't be happening."

The participants were all standing and screaming at one another.

"Wait!" Woodbury shushed them. "That hair. I saw you at the Hotel Belvédère. But you can't be; there's no way—"

Here she was, standing in a room surrounded by very angry people, many of whom probably wanted to hurt her. But Andrea had no fear for her own life. Now, however, she realized that her outburst might jeopardize her home, give someone a clue to information they should not have about Eden. She started to back toward the door.

She needed a diversion.

"Yes, I was at the hotel. We've been watching you for some time."

"Who is we?" His voice was heavy with danger.

Andrea opened her mouth to attempt an answer and felt a rush of wind as the door opened behind her and someone jerked her backward into the sun. Jaime slammed the door shut and wedged two ski poles between the ground and the door to block it from opening outward.

"I have her," she was speaking into her microphone. "I've wedged the door shut. What's happening inside? . . ."

"People arguing, yelling at each other," she repeated for Andrea. "Woodbury is furiously giving orders to that young assistant. Oh, excellent, Op 1 just cut the lights on them!"

The wooden door in front of them rattled as someone pushed against it.

"Let's go. This won't hold very long."

Andrea could tell Jaime was put out. "I don't know what came over me!" Andrea apologized.

"Not now; we've gotta move. We can't outrun them, so I've borrowed this toboggan." Jaime pointed to a long, flat sled made of bent bamboo with a bright red pad and steering ropes tied to the front end. "Have you ever ridden one?"

"This is my first time to see snow!"

"Well, now you have another first. Sit down here at the back and once I jump on stretch your legs around my waist, but keep them on the sled."

"Once you jump—?" The sled lurched as Jaime pushed it

while running beside it. She had pointed it down the hill toward the train station and it quickly picked up speed as she jumped on. She plunked down in front of Andrea, who was desperately trying to keep her legs out of the way.

Jaime wedged her feet against the front curve of the sled, and grabbed the steering rope.

"How do you steer this thing?" Andrea spoke loudly into Jaime's ear to be heard over the rushing wind.

"Steer?" Jaime laughed, then cocked her head and was suddenly quiet. "Op 1 says someone's following us. Can you see anyone?"

Andrea looked back to find Woodbury's dark-haired assistant, Nicole Barron, now 100 meters behind them. She seemed to be sliding but did not have skis.

"Yes, the young woman who was with Woodbury looks like she's surfing down the hill!"

"We've got to make it to the train station ahead of her! Lean with me as I pull on the rope. And when I say, let your heels drag off the sled just a bit so we can slow down to make this curve."

Andrea could see their path narrowed and curved sharply to the left, then another switchback to the right.

"Okay, lean left and drag." As they leaned, Jaime pulled hard on the left-hand rope and put her boots out into the snow along with Andrea's. The back end of the toboggan flipped around nicely, but the momentum kept them sliding sideways down the hill. They came to a stop on the level below but were now facing backward down the path.

"Is this the way it's supposed to be?" Andrea was bewildered.

"Arrgggh." Jaime jumped off, quickly pulled the sled around 180 degrees, and ran beside it again.

As they picked up momentum once again, a German couple walking their briard along the path had to dive into a snowbank to keep from getting run over.

"*Entschuldigung!*" Jaime yelled as they flew past. The man lost hold of his dog's leash. The briard bounded after them, his owner calling from up the hill.

"Are we still being followed?"

The narrow path was bumpy, and Andrea found it harder to turn and look.

"We've picked up a very hairy, four-legged pursuer. The woman on the board is trying to negotiate the carnage we left behind us."

Jaime saw a large snow-covered jungle gym that she recognized as part of the children's play area outside the train entrance. "We've got to slow now." They were heading straight at the playground, and dragging their feet once again for friction. It looked like they would not stop in time, and Andrea closed her eyes as Jaime jerked hard on one rope and they skidded sideways up against the jungle gym.

The large dog, bounding along in pursuit, was unprepared for the sudden stop and came barreling onto Jaime's lap. Thrilled with the capture of his prey, he began licking her in the face.

"Love ya, big boy, but not now!" She pushed him off her lap and leaned down to help Andrea stand up.

"Come on; I think the train is boarding!"

Leaving the toboggan, they hurried to join the queue of skiers and hikers entering the train station. Swiping their rail passes to enter the turnstile, they stepped quickly down steep cement stairs, passing up two train cars to enter the front one, pushing as far into the middle as the crowd would permit.

Jaime looked back over the press of people to watch the entrance. Just as the car doors were preparing to close, she saw a short woman carrying a snowboard burst through the turnstile and dive into the last car.

"I think Barron made it on the train. We need to position ourselves so we can push out in front of the crowd and use them as a buffer to slip away before she catches up."

Andrea followed as Jaime cut a path through the standing passengers, wading between ski poles and snowshoes until they reached the exit door. At that moment the train lurched and began to slowly make its way down the mountain.

All they could do was wait. As they rolled past snow-covered evergreens toward the station below Andrea reflected on the events of the past hour. She knew she was responsible for their predicament, and was trying to find the words to express her regret.

Before she could say anything, Jaime spoke up.

"I have no idea why Clement was concerned about your ability to remain objective on this mission!"

At first Andrea looked chagrined, until she saw the glint in the young woman's eye and realized she was making a joke.

"I can't believe I did that!" Andrea shook her head in disbelief.

"I can't believe it, either!" Jaime was laughing now. "That took guts! And the look on his face!"

"It was reckless of me, and I do apologize."

"Apology accepted. And while I don't think it was the best choice for how to kill their plan, I think you have effectively done so. But now let's think about how to ditch our friend back there. I can't think of anything she or her cronies would ask that we'd want to answer. We obviously can't go back to the hotel. Well, first things first. Let's get lost."

Andrea knew continued self-recrimination didn't help anything, but it would kill her if she was responsible for Jaime's capture. Andrea also didn't have the full training Operatives received to withstand torture. She prayed they wouldn't be caught.

They couldn't be.

At the end of the four-minute trip, the *Bahn* gently lowered into its berth at the bottom of the hill. The moment the doors opened, the crowd pushed the two women out into a narrow stairway. Jaime pushed Andrea ahead of her and snuck a look back. The snowboarder was buried in a crowd of about thirty to forty people behind them.

"Can you jog?" Jaime asked as they came through the turnstile and out the door.

"I can move out smartly!"

"That'll do."

They were in a short alleyway that dumped out onto Davos' main street. As they reached the curb Jaime looked around purposefully. "We need a crowd where we can disappear," she said under her breath. Then, "Perfect!"

To their right was the entrance to a casino, barely a half block away. At the curb by the front entrance was a stretch limousine around which a large crowd had gathered. In the center of the crowd was the rock star Shepard, talking to reporters and signing autographs.

"Do you trust me?" said Jaime as she tugged Andrea in the direction of the mob.

"What are we doing? We'll draw more attention to ourselves in this media circus!"

But Jaime didn't lead her into the crowd surrounding the musician. Instead, Jaime towed Andrea over to the street side of his limo, opened the back door, and slid inside, pulling the astonished woman down to the floor of the limo with her.

"What are you doing?" Andrea asked again. "When they realize we're here, they'll remove us—which will draw *a lot* of attention!"

"I'm buying time," said Jaime to the perplexed older woman.

Soon they heard the voice of the driver over the din of the crowd: "Sorry, no more autographs. Shepard, it's time to go."

The crowd outside parted reluctantly with—Jaime assumed—some help from the burly security detail.

Then the back door to the limo was opened and a handsome young man plopped into the seat opposite Jaime's position. Andrea had not had much experience with the Terris celebrity culture, but she could tell this man had an aura about him. Part confidence, part charisma, part the glow of adulation? Whatever it was, it fit easily into his bemused expression as he found the two women hiding on the floor of his limousine.

At that same moment, the surlier of the two bodyguards poked his head in the door and looked very startled at the unexpected company in the car with his boss.

"What are you doing? Out! Now! I'm sorry, sir!" the bodyguard said as he began to signal his companion.

Andrea's blood pounded through her veins. What now?

Shepard cut him off with a quick wave of his hand.

"It's okay. Tell Serge to move on."

Andrea was certain she could not be any more surprised

until the bodyguard closed the door and the musician smiled at Jaime.

"So. Does this mean you're free for dinner?"

"It's been too long, Mark," said Jaime. "And it's great to see you."

The limousine began to crawl ahead through the noon traffic. As it did, Andrea saw Nicole Barron in the midst of the crowd, scanning every direction. She was holding a cell phone, obviously giving someone information that was not being well received. Even though the limousine windows were darkly tinted, Andrea stayed low on the floor as they drove past her.

"It's been way too long," Mark said. "And I'm assuming, from the fact that you and your lovely companion are hiding out of sight on the floor of my car, you've got some interesting explanation!"

He reached across and shook hands with Andrea. "I'm Mark Shepard, by the way."

"Well, I *could* use the teensiest bit of help." admitted Jaime.

He smiled and leaned back. "That's my Jaime. Okay, let's have it."

"Some very unfriendly people are following us, and we need to slip away unseen. Can we ride with you for a bit, then have you drop us off?"

"So, is that all I am to you, a convenient ride?"

"You've got me pegged."

Shepard grinned. "Always happy to play the knight in the white limo. Although I do fully intend to collect a dinner in exchange. Where do you need to go?"

"Getting out of here is a good start, thanks. And give me a minute."

Mark pushed a button and instructed the driver and security man in the front seat as Jaime took out her handheld and began texting updates with Eddie. Then she looked up at Andrea. "We've got backups waiting to spirit you away to a local safe house. Mark, can you help get us to the pickup spot? Then perhaps create a slight diversion?"

"A diversion? What kind? My boys and I have an entire playbook."

"That's my Mark!" Jaime teased him back.

"So we need to drop off your friend. Once she's safely squared away, must you disappear, too? Or do you have time for a catch-up?"

Jaime leaned back against the sidewall of seats.

"I can't really be seen here for a while, either. So—what kinds of getaways do you have outlined in that playbook of yours?"

Frank McMillan was standing in the hallway of the Congress Centre outside the current session of the World Economic Forum with several of his coworkers from the Terrorism Task Force when his cell phone vibrated.

"McMillan," he said.

"What goes up must come down," answered the male voice.

"Talk to me."

"I waited for Farmer and Richards at the top of the *Bahn.* They arrived in a hurry, and I was able to join them in the first car for the ride down. Only had time to plant a device on one of them, but did accomplish that."

"Which one?"

How could this idiot think he was interested in Farmer? He'd never said anything about Farmer!

"Richards, of course."

Frank felt his shoulders relax as his blood pressure began to drop. Finally someone had done something right. Finally.

"And, Chief?" his operative continued. "You might want to pick up the signal yourself. She's still on the move."

"Well done," said Frank, and he touched the earpiece that turned off the phone.

Shepard was true to his word. He and "his boys" did indeed have a playbook of rehearsed diversion techniques, which had allowed Jaime to take Andrea out of his limousine and into an unmarked Operative car without anyone realizing the musician hadn't been alone on his drive.

They'd then driven on—east on Talstrasse, past the sports complex, then back west on Promenade, giving Jaime enough time to take off her white jacket with blue scarf and replace them with a black coat, red scarf, and red ski cap. She tucked her blond hair up inside and put on a pair of sunglasses. A typical Davos look—which didn't reveal much about her at all.

Shortly after they passed the Congress Centre, Jaime hopped out of the limo just above the Central Sporthotel. She did her best to blend in with the foot traffic, and took the stairs down into the Sporthotel complex. She had ten minutes to kill, and she spent several of them chatting with the man with the horse-drawn carriage at the hotel door. They were magnificent white steeds (technically "gray," she knew, as the only horses that are "white" are rare albinos) with matching red plumes.

Standing in one spot gave her the opportunity to surreptitiously check to see if anyone was following her—but it seemed she was alone.

When precisely four minutes remained, Jaime bid the carriage driver farewell, turned right, and walked two short blocks back down to Talstrasse. She reached the agreed-upon spot, and had been waiting for less than two minutes when a Peugeot pulled up. Jaime hesitated because the car before her was a two-door sedan with intertwined silver and green streamers flowing jauntily across the side. But the driver put on the right turn indicator, then the left, then sat idling. It was the sign she'd been told to watch for.

She opened the curbside door, hoping she'd recognize Shepard's driver. Instead, she was surprised to find Mark, alone, in the driver's seat. "Your coach, milady," he said simply.

Jaime climbed in, moved her own white jacket and blue scarf from the seat, and closed the door. Mark leaned across, kissed her cheek in welcome, and drove on, continuing east.

"You can do this?" Jaime asked.

He laughed. "What, drive?"

"No, go out by yourself."

He was wearing a black cap and sunglasses. "I do it all the time. People look for the trappings of Shepard, not so much the person."

"Where are we headed? Sorry to ask, but I've got to check in and let my crew know where I'll be, in case they need me."

"We're heading for a small restaurant in Laret, which isn't far. The proprietors know me. They have a back room with a separate entrance, so no one will even know we're there."

Jaime typed this into her handheld. It was only seconds before Eddie's reply flashed across the screen: *We've successfully removed your package from play. You're off duty. Man, you don't let grass grow, do you? Have fun discussing economics!*

And on the screen flashed a photo of Shepard wearing a radio mic, singing in a stadium above hordes of screaming fans.

"You good?" asked Mark.

"Laret it is," she replied. "And what kind of car is this? It's not exactly what I expected."

"It's the new HDi hybrid. Not technically on the market

until 2010, but they asked if I'd show it around. Gets sixty-nine miles per gallon, using electricity and diesel."

"Why am I not surprised?"

Mark smiled, and skirted around a cluster of people who paid no attention to the unmarked sedan at all. "So," he said, "are you going to tell me what you're doing here? What all this hubbub is about?"

"You're a fine one to ask me about hubbub!"

"Hey! I wasn't hiding in some bloke's limo with Andrea Farmer!"

"Touché. Although—wait, how did you know who she was? I never introduced you."

"Dr. Farmer was probably the most buzzed-about participant of the year; give me some credit. She's known by her hair—plus I saw you with her last night in the lobby bar. Wasn't hard to get background. So why were you with her?"

Jaime did a mental calculation of what information would come out concerning their day's activities, and realized if Eddie had distributed the footage, it would probably be in tomorrow's papers, if it wasn't already on CNN.

"Woodbury had hatched a scheme to manipulate international currency. He'd brought in high-stakes players. Dr. Farmer was able to expose the plan. Needless to say, there are some very powerful folks with whom she's not very popular at the moment."

"You were here with a famous reclusive economist foiling a plan by J. Aldrich Woodbury?"

"That's about the size of it."

He shook his head. "Okay. I admit that wasn't my first guess."

"How about you? I was sorry I couldn't hear your presentation. I was off with Dr. Farmer . . . not that I could have gotten in, anyway."

The lanky musician beeped his way through another knot of pedestrians and expelled a long breath. "Aw, Jaime," he said. "I know that most of the people in that room were there because I'm a freaking musician. Probably most of them weren't even listening to what I said—or, if they were, it was with disdain, or perhaps sympathy, for the well-meaning rocker who likes to dabble in economics.

"But what I'm talking about—what *we're* talking about, it's not just me!—is so damn important. Worldwide economic theory needs to stem from an entirely new premise, and before it's too late! The whole idea that markets should not be regulated, that they're always self-correcting, made sense in a time when the goal was to get every individual more, more, more! But now that we've run smack into the fact that the Earth does not have unlimited exploitable resources—the fact that a global consumer culture will spell the death of humanity sooner rather than later has got to be put into the mix.

"They're all talking about bringing the second- and third-world countries up to par with the first-world countries in manufacturing and per capita income. But supposing China does catch up to us. If the Chinese owned and drove automobiles at the rate we Americans do, the amount of carbon dioxide emitted would multiply fifty times over. The planet would be dead within a decade.

"We've got to stop thinking more is better! Instead of bringing China and India up to par with the U.S., we've got to say, *Enough!* to ourselves. Instead of letting the markets go on unchecked, exacerbating the growing rift between haves and have-nots, we've got to begin to find a sustainable middle ground for all of us."

His voice had risen, and he looked chagrined. "I'm sorry. You just heard my stump speech. As you can tell, I tend to get emotionally involved in this. It's not always helpful."

Jaime smiled. "How can you not get emotionally involved, when the fate of Earth and of several billion people is at stake? Especially when our own country is at the epicenter of the problem, refusing to regulate markets or even sign the Kyoto Protocol because it would keep corporations from earning unchecked profits? Why not kill our grandchildren to sustain a fossil fuel–based economy?"

To say that Mark looked at her with surprise was an understatement.

She continued, "Even those who worship at the altar of Adam Smith, if they actually read Smith's theories, will see that he talked about unregulated markets in the context of a community-based economy."

"Good God, Jaime, you've read Adam Smith?"

"He is the theorist at the base of the self-correcting market models. We are at the World Economic Forum. Give me some credit," she said.

This time he laughed. "Paul would be proud of you."

"And Ondine would definitely be so very proud of you."

Somehow those simple sentiments were enough to make them both lapse into silence as they drove north out of Davos.

January 25, 2007, 1:40 P.M.
(1 day, 20 hours, 50 minutes until end of auction)
Bayt Lahm, West Bank, Israel

"You will do as I say, woman!"

Abihu el-Musaq shook with anger as he gestured at the furniture in his mother's apartment. "All of this, the rent, the clothes, the furniture, all of this have I given to you. And this is how you show your gratitude? By refusing to accompany me to a wedding?"

"But Abihu, they are so primitive. I do not want to wear the burqa or sleep on the floor."

"You did so when you were young."

"Yes, and I swore I never would again."

They had been arguing since he had arrived a few hours before. When el-Musaq surprised his mother with this sudden visit, she was not particularly happy to see him on her doorstep. Then when he asked for one simple little favor, to accompany him to the Bedouin camp, she responded with whining and excuses. "I have other plans . . . ," then . . . "I have nothing to wear" . . . and finally . . . "I am too old for this."

"Enough!" The man waved away all her excuses. "It's only for a few days. I have a job, you will help me, or I will cut you off from all future income. You can make your way as a whore on the street for all I care."

The older woman looked at the burqa her son now held out to her. As she took it, silent tears slid down her cheeks.

"So, are you still military?" Mark asked Jaime as they headed away from the craziness of Davos.

"Yes. In fact, right now I'm on my mid-tour leave."

"Mid-tour leave?"

"It's the two weeks you get in the midst of your deployment in Iraq, to allegedly give you some touch with reality, or at least a little breathing room."

"Wait—you're deployed to Iraq?"

"I was there yesterday morning."

"In Iraq. Yesterday morning."

In response to her nod, he said, "So now that you've temporarily derailed Woodbury's life and plans, what are you up to next? How long do you have?"

"I—I don't know, really. I've been so focused on getting here with Dr. Farmer that I hadn't really planned past that. I really didn't expect to be done so quickly." As she spoke, she wondered briefly just who had Andrea, where they were taking her, and how they'd get her back for the appropriate door opening into Eden.

Mark was quiet for a minute; then he said, "Jaime. Instead of going to lunch, let's go to my place, in France, for a few days. I'd love for you to see it, how we're working toward making it a sustainable community. I don't think you and Paul ever saw the manor we restored there, did you? It's the first place Ondine and I bought together. Now, though I get back to Chicago whenever I can, Lac-Argent feels like home to me. Let me show it to you. And let me pamper you, if only for a few short days."

If this was anyone but Mark, she thought, *I'd assume an offer like that has to come with a catch. There'd have to be a clause about selling my soul in there somewhere.*

"Jaime. Come on. I haven't seen you since Paul's funeral. And we swore we'd keep in touch."

"But wait—you're at the World Economic Forum, convincing people to rethink the current market model of economics. How could I take you away from that?"

"I've already made my presentation. I've had private meetings with the people who top my list. What would I miss? The Google party?"

"I've heard it's a hot ticket. And—I know the password," she teased. It was a local joke, because *everyone* knew the password.

"Seriously. Even if I went, what are the odds of having a meaningful conversation with anyone in the press of a thousand people?"

"But—"

"Kiddo. I'm coming off a world tour with the band. I just presented on a panel at the World Economic Forum and had a series of private meetings with hard-asses who have no intention of giving up their chance to make mega-bucks, no matter what the cost to future generations. Just what does it take to earn a few days off? I'm beat. Not as beat as you, I'm sure, but come on. Let's give each other a break."

"Oh, man, Mark, that sounds so good. Where in France is Lac-Argent? And how would we get there?"

"It's in the north. In the Champagne region. And to get there . . . well, this is embarrassing, for someone who is preaching environmental responsibility . . . but we'd take my plane from Zurich to Reims."

"Why is that embarrassing?"

"That monstrosity of a stretch limo wasn't mine. The private plane, and all its wicked fuel consumption, is. I just haven't figured out another way to travel that makes sense . . . given my current circumstances."

Jaime said, "Actually, I'm working on getting my pilot's license, and I'd love to fly to France with you."

"So you'll come?"

She laughed. "Let's just say you had me at Champagne."

This has to be a dream, Jaime thought. *Any second now, I'm going to be awakened by a phone call to my hooch in Anaconda, giving me news I don't want to hear. This can't possibly be real.*

The last few hours had been magical. They'd arrived at the airport in Zurich to find one of Shepard's assistants waiting with a bag lunch, which they'd eaten in the hangar while the plane was being fueled. While on the road, Shepard had asked what size clothes Jaime wore, and the assistant also handed Jaime a small suitcase packed with a comfortable pantsuit, a dark skirt, two sweaters, a gray sweatshirt that said *Zurich,* underwear, toiletries, makeup, a pair of jeans, and three different autumnal colors of Henleys in a soft combed cotton. She found it ironic that more men had shopped for her in the last twenty-four hours than had in the previous thirty years.

No one at Shepard's manor house in France had known to expect him, but a single call had set well-oiled cogs in motion. They'd arrived with enough remaining daylight for Mark to give her a walking tour of the land surrounding the twelfth-century manor house. They'd strolled the vineyards, the farmland, and visited the sheep meadow and the horse pasture. He'd shown her the state-of-the-art recording studio in one of the outbuildings, which not only helped him record close to home but also brought a steady stream of income to the village.

Mark's eyes lit up as he promised to show her around the village and the surrounding countryside the next day. "It's easier for this corner of the country to decide to become sustainable, because there's so much open land and agriculture to begin with. But as far as supplying our own renewable energy sources, that's worked out for an unexpected reason. Like everywhere else in the world, local families have trouble keeping their children 'down on the farm,' in such a 'boring' place as this—unless there's something radical and subversive they can be a part of. We have a whole young generation here, actively working at making this a model of a sustainable community."

He'd given her a wink and continued, "Of course, it also helps that most of them help run the studio and mix it up with some of the top bands in the world."

His cook/housekeeper, Mrs. Halpern, had been happily flustered to show up and whip up a succulent meal of trout amandine and local root vegetables for them.

It was as they ate in the kitchen at the farm table by the stone hearth, chatting with Mrs. Halpern and catching up on the local news, that Jaime let herself think—for the first time in a long time—a world without Yani could still, possibly, hold some delight.

Then Mark had invited Jaime upstairs into the half of the house that constituted his private quarters. He'd shown her to a guest room, told her to choose from one of the swimsuits in the drawer and meet him in the bathroom of his suite. The bathroom itself had an ancient working fireplace, and a Jacuzzi by a large window, overlooking the countryside. They sat, in the warm bubbling water, sipping wine and watching the moon rise over the small river that ran through the backyard.

It was all so overwhelmingly unexpected that Jaime had gone for the only way she could think of to tease him. "Okay, so how many women can I assume have come through here, if you stock a choice of swimsuits?"

He looked discomfited, like he would have expected that

from anyone but her, and she felt bad that she'd given in to her own insecurities and acted like . . . well, like an insecure woman in a hot tub with a great-looking guy who undoubtedly had his choice of partners.

"Jaime, I . . . ," he started.

"I'm sorry, Mark. Really. You don't have to explain anything to me."

"There was a time, in my younger days, when it was exciting to cut a swath through a sea of beautiful girls, I won't lie," he said. "The boys and I . . . we had our fun. By the time I met Ondine, though, I'd had my fill of adoring fans, sixty percent of whom thought that a one-night stand meant you were committing to them and forty percent of whom had nasty diseases. It's not that much fun to have to throw a well-meaning young thing out of your room every morning, especially when you have a raging hangover.

"When I met Ondine, I was ready to put that behind me."

"She was special," Jaime said softly. "Again, Mark, I'm sorry."

"No, I haven't really talked about this . . . but, after she died, I decided no one would blame me if I had a few lost months of indulgence. You know, to bury the pain. So I tried to. And I couldn't. I had a few nights of groupie sex, but it was . . . awful. Seriously awful. I couldn't feel *anything* for those girls. It scared the hell out of me."

"But it's understandable, given what you'd been through. You know that, right?"

"The good news is, it made me realize I couldn't go back in time. Nor did I want to. Since then, I've tried to keep up my rock star image . . . but the fact is, I've had a couple of semi-serious relationships, but that's it. I can't say not *any* sex, otherwise. But . . . it's been a while.

"Oh, shit, Jaime. That sounds like a come-on if ever I've said one. But it wasn't meant to be."

Jaime took another sip of the Shiraz. "Mark, relax; it's me. Your old friend. You can say what you want. I'll keep it safe."

"Thanks," he said. "I've needed an old friend for a while."

"Me, too," she said.

"So, do you want to talk about Iraq?"

"Hell, no. I mean, not right now. This is all too wonderful. What I really need is to have my head in a totally different place for a little while—if that's all right."

And then, he'd done the last thing she'd expected. He'd started humming. She didn't recognize the tune, but it was simple and melodic, and the rich timbre of his voice was obvious. Jaime leaned her head against his shoulder and enjoyed feeling the song rumbling inside him.

He put his hand on top of her head, and stroked her hair, gently.

"Old friend," he said.

"Old friend," she replied. And she thought, *If only Yani could see me now.*

They'd relaxed for a while before he picked up his watch. "Oops, it's time," he said.

"Time?"

"Our masseuse and masseur await."

"You're joking."

"I said I wanted to pamper you," he said. "Let me do this, Jaime. I've owed you so much for so long. And I've always felt guilty toward you . . ."

"Guilty? Toward me? Why? I can't think of one reason!"

"What you—and Paul—did for me, for Ondine and me . . . during her final illness. The strength and support you gave us. It's what made it all bearable. And I swore I'd be there for you after Paul was killed. But then—Jaime, it was so hard. Losing such a friend of my heart, so soon after losing my wife. Losing Paul just about did me in. I didn't feel like I had anything left to give to you. But I've always felt bad. Like I let Paul down. Like I let you down."

Jaime held the soft nap of the towel around her with one hand, and with the other gently stroked Mark's face. "It must have been tough for you. Paul was so special. I should have realized what his death did to you. But I was overwhelmed by loss, too. We both did what we needed to do to get through. No recriminations on either side, okay?"

The stubble on his chin felt rough, and intimate.

"No recriminations." He pulled her to him in a gentle hug. "Thanks for that. Meanwhile, we have this local couple who must have graduated from therapeutic massage school at the top of their class."

"That's great. Because I happen to have an opening in my schedule just now."

He grinned. "Then let me show you the way."

January 25, 2007, 10:05 P.M.
(1 day, 12 hours, 25 minutes until end of auction)
Judean wilderness west of the Dead Sea
Israel

The Hajj had asked three well-known jewelers in Tel Aviv to show him their finest work, that he might choose a gift for his new bride. Two of the jewelers had already met with the Hajj to show him their wares. The jewels they'd brought were breathtaking, each in its own way.

The Hajj knew that without money from the sale of the box he would not have the purchase price for any of them.

But he very much wanted to give a gift, a special gift, to Yasmin. He wanted to somehow let her know that he valued her, thought her special—his own precious jewel.

When he had gone back to her camp to meet with her, a week after speaking to her uncle, the chief, about marriage, she had surprised him yet again.

Her mother and aunts had been there, all heavily veiled, and she had been veiled herself. Yet her eyes above the veil had been the eyes that had first captured him.

In Bedouin culture, marriages were arranged, the deals made, the bride-price agreed upon, by the men. It was not unheard of that a prospective groom meet with his intended and her family before the bargain was made. What made it unusual was that the Hajj had wanted to speak with *her,* to make sure she favored the match. Traditionally, if the girl's father or guardian agreed, that was enough.

When Yasmin's uncle brought the Hajj into the clan's big tent to meet her, the female relatives had formed a half circle around her. Her mother sat closest. The Hajj sat down in front of Yasmin, a good three feet away. He had studied her face briefly, although her eyes were on the ground. "I have come to ask if you would like to marry me," he said, not loudly, but firmly enough that everyone gathered could hear.

"*Inshallah,* and if it pleases you," she answered, not looking up.

"I promise your mother and stepfather a good bride-price," he said. "You will be cared for all the days of your life." And then, before anyone could fully grasp what was happening, he leaned forward and said, for her ears only, "And this is really what you wish?"

Then the girl took a risk and also leaned forward. In reply, also in a quick, soft voice, she had said, "My cloth of honor will not be stained."

The brutal, unexpected honesty of that remark sent him reeling. In any normal circumstance, such an admission would be enough to not only cancel the engagement but also besmirch the honor of every male relative she had. Yet the way Yasmin had said it, the gentle pleading in her voice, the flash of her eyes as she looked up at Omar—it was as if she could trust him, and him alone, to save her. Her very life was dependent on his kindness. If he repeated out loud what she'd told him, she would be killed. For some reason, she had chosen him, risked everything to trust him.

She had treated him as a good, kind man. As her savior.

In that moment, he knew he would die to keep her secret, to defend her honor.

"Then it shall be," he said, again loud enough to be heard by all.

Her mother and the other aunties bowed and retired from the tent, taking the prospective bride along with them.

The Hajj then settled in to talk to the chief, and so it would be known that the girl Yasmin had brought the highest bride-price of any girl in the clan.

Jaime lay under a crisp, cool sheet on one of the massage tables in the room next to the Jacuzzi. The room had well-tended indoor plants, a small sauna, a heated tile floor, and dual massage tables. She felt as far from a combat zone as she could possibly be.

Which didn't mean her emotions weren't in turmoil—and now not solely because of Yani. The memories Mark had brought up were both painful and exquisite. She well remembered the June when she and Paul—who were dating at the time—had joined Mark and Ondine at their place in the French Antilles. Ondine had been battling pancreatic cancer for over six months. She'd just been in New York for tests to see how the latest rounds of therapies had done. Paul and Jaime had joined her on Mark's private jet for the trip down to the islands, Paul on a two-week break between the school year and summer classes, Jaime on a two-week vacation.

They were hopeful of good news, and had spent the first full day relaxing, swimming, and listening to some of Mark's new music. Mark and Paul had met shortly after Mark's band had released its first album, and Mark had joined him on a trip sponsored by an organization working for peace and justice in the Middle East. The two young men had hit it off immediately, and had become friends. Paul was impressed by Mark's talent but never by his fame. Mark was impressed by Paul's passion and understanding of international issues. As the years passed, Mark was grateful to have someone who didn't treat him like a rock star. Paul was equally glad to have someone who didn't treat him like the Reverend Doctor Professor Atwood.

The two couples were in the spacious living room, all done in whites, with vast windows open to the ocean breezes, when the call came. Ondine talked for a while before hanging up.

"What news?" asked Mark, and she smiled a tremulous smile.

"Not good, I'm afraid. The cancer's back, more virulent than ever. He says I have a month, maybe two."

For half a minute, there was complete silence.

"We'll fly back with you tomorrow," Paul said gently.

"No," she said firmly. "No." Ondine had always been tall and graceful, with dark brown hair in a fashionable short cut and large brown eyes.

She continued, "I've told the doctors I'm not coming back. If two months is all I have left, I have no intention spending it feeling sick and weak from the 'cure.' I'm going to grab on to life with both hands while I can, and go home with a smile on my face."

"But, Ondine—" Mark's voice was plaintive.

"And no more of that holistic crap, either. I'm eating the good stuff," she said.

Jaime hugged her first. The four of them had prayed together for strength, and love, and fun. Then it seemed clear that Mark and his wife needed some time alone.

Paul headed outside to the beach. "Richards," he said, and Jaime followed him out.

When Jaime joined him on the beach, she was surprised to find him wiping a tear from his cheek. "Oh, Paul," she'd said, "this is so hard."

Paul stood gazing out across the oranges and pinks of the sunset behind the endless waters, where egrets swooped and danced, heedless of the affairs of humans. "Richards . . ."

"I'm here."

"I don't . . . you know I've said I never expect to marry. I need to be free to go anywhere and not worry about whether or not I'm in harm's way. I can never give a wife a stable nine-to-five life, and kids."

Jaime was quiet. She'd heard this speech often before, and didn't know why she was hearing it again. She knew that's what Paul thought, who he was. She'd come to terms.

"The thing is . . . what this makes me realize . . . is that the only thing more dangerous than something awful, like losing your wife . . . is not having her because you never had the courage to marry her in the first place."

She hadn't seen that one coming. The sand beneath her feet suddenly felt uncertain, like it could shift at any moment.

But he didn't say anything else.

Jaime was fine with the way things were. She loved her career. She had just been promoted. Paul had always seemed like a knight-errant to her. Could she love a knight-errant who had a wife—even if she was the wife?

Did she want to marry Paul? Did she want to marry anybody?

"Richards?"

"Atwood, are you saying you want to get married?"

"What do you think? I wouldn't change. . . . There's still a chance something could happen to me. . . ."

"Uh, Paul, you're talking to someone who's in the Army?"

"I know; I know. The thing is I've always thought something could happen to one of us. But now I see that even if it does, I want to have you before I lose you."

"That's probably one of the more cheerful proposals on record."

"God, I'm sorry; I'm doing this all wrong. What do you think? Or am I a fool even to ask?"

"Is this your way of saying you love me?" She didn't mean to goad him, but she was trying to buy time.

"It's my way of saying that life is all about love and Ondine is right, we've got to grab it with both hands, while we can."

Now that the moment was here, could she do this? Could she marry Paul Atwood? She'd fallen in love with him when she was his student, but now they were out in the world. Was this for real? Was it forever? Why was love so ethereal? She wanted it to be something you could test, and prove, and hold in your hands.

But if Paul had been the one to say he had two months to live, it would kill her. He was her world.

"All right," she finally said, quietly. "I want to have you while I've got you, too."

They told Mark and Ondine after dinner, sitting on the veranda. Mark clapped Paul on the back, and Ondine leapt to her feet.

"But this is marvelous! You're engaged! When is the wedding?"

"We hadn't gotten that far," replied Paul.

"How about . . . let's see. A week from this weekend. Not Friday, that's the Fourth of July. But how about Saturday the fifth? Or Sunday the sixth?"

"Wait a minute . . . you mean next week?" Jaime asked.

"Yes! Why don't you get married here? I always wished we'd had this place when Mark and I were wed. It's perfect! Either the local chapel, or down on the beach!"

"Ondine, that's so nice of you . . . such an overwhelmingly kind offer . . . ," Paul sputtered.

"I'm . . . not exactly a barefoot on the beach with flowers in my hair kind of person," Jaime said, surprised.

"Did you want a military wedding, with the swords and everything?"

"No. No. But—"

She turned to Paul. "Would you be sorry not to have a wedding back home, so the rest of the faculty and your students could come?"

The look on Paul's face was comical. "*My* students? You mean miss having a shivaree?" he asked, tongue in cheek.

Ondine said, "Paul. I've known you since I've known Mark. I love you to pieces. I also know you're completely capable of still being engaged when you're seventy-three. Which would mean I'd miss the wedding. So if you're serious about marrying this extraordinary woman, why don't we go for it?"

Paul, Jaime, and Mark sat, blindsided by Ondine's energy and passion.

"We'd need to start right away. But we could do this. I'd help you plan everything. You'd start by calling your family and friends and seeing how many of them could get here during the next week. We'd send the plane to pick them up. Couldn't we, *mon ami*?" Ondine asked her husband.

"Well, yes, I suppose. You're sure . . . this wouldn't be too much for you?"

"Oh, for God's sake, I've had enough of the three of you sitting around watching me die, and it's only been since dinner. Give me something else to focus on. Something about the future. About life. Let Mark and me give you a wedding."

"I suppose," said Paul.

"I suppose," said Jaime.

"Great! Then let me get my list of caterers!"

"I think this calls for brandy and cigars," said Mark, and Paul agreed immediately.

It was later that night, when the house was quiet and Paul was asleep, that Jaime had come down, alone, to stand by the wall of windows that faced out over the ocean. She'd been standing there for a minute before she realized Mark was in the room, sitting on the sofa.

"Richards," he said, and she'd turned and gone over to him.

Even in the moonlight, she could tell he'd been crying. "Mark . . . the wedding . . . if this is all too much for you, just say the word, and I can explain to Ondine . . . it would cost a fortune, just to bring in our families and close friends."

Mark motioned her to sit, and she sank onto the edge of the sectional that was at a right angle to his.

He had a glass in his hands—scotch—but he wasn't drunk.

"The thing is . . . ," he started. "The thing is, none of this means anything." He gestured with the drink in his hand. "The house. The jet. None of it. It's times like this that you see money means nothing. Ondine is my only treasure. She's about to be snatched away, and there's not a damn thing I can do about it. All the money in the world wouldn't help. It means nothing."

"I know," Jaime had responded softly. "You're right."

"So all I can do . . . if she wanted to go to the moon in the time she has left, I'd somehow get her on a goddamned rocket. If it makes her happy to throw you two a wedding, Jaime, the expense of picking people up is not a concern. If you and Paul are willing to get married—this quickly—please, let her go for it."

Jaime took Mark's hand, and he didn't pull back.

But he looked at her then and she could tell he'd switched gears. "Paul is one of my best friends. I know you love him. Do you truly want to marry him, Jaime? Will you be good to him?"

"Yes," Jaime answered. "And yes, I will." As she said it, she knew it was true.

So Jaime and Paul got married, barefoot on the beach, Jaime with flowers in her hair, with two dozen friends and family members in attendance. One of Paul's colleagues officiated. Mark Shepard sang. It was a glorious day. Ondine was glowing.

A month later, she was dead.

Three months later, Paul was dead, the victim of a suicide bomber on the Pedestrian Mall in Jerusalem.

Nine and a half years had passed. And now Jaime lay on a massage table in Mark's manor house with Mark on the nearby table. And her emotions were in turmoil, yet again.

Long leaded windows looked out over the landing of the main staircase in the manor. The rich tones of the carved wood gave the room that housed the landing a warm glow. Mark had shown Jaime how he'd lovingly restored the house, which had been run-down and falling apart when he'd bought it. He'd kept many original details, while updating it with modern wiring and green sources of energy.

The result was that what was once a large, imposing manor house now felt welcoming and homey. From the window, she could see past the gardens and trees to where the stone bell tower still rose above the village's tenth-century stone church.

"Hey."

She turned around to find Mark, in long flannel pajama bottoms and a *Think Green, Think Global* T-shirt. "Great nightgown." He grinned.

She had to smile. Whatever little elf had shopped for her in Zurich had bought a satiny white sheath nightgown, with a diaphanous white robe to be worn over it. Her shoulder-length blond hair fell free. Iraq seemed a million miles away.

"Could I interest you in a nightcap by the fire?"

"Sure. Has Mrs. Halpern gone home?"

"Yes. No one here tonight but us. Well, us and Derrick, my

security man. Where I am, there's always a security man." He shrugged. "Is your guest room comfortable? That used to be our wing—Ondine's and mine. I, well, switched things around. Redid the rooms."

"It's great, thanks. The shower was heavenly. Warm water and everything. I've learned not to take anything for granted."

He took her hand and led her down the hallway toward his rooms, past the door to the bathroom suite where they'd had their Jacuzzi and the next room, where they'd had their massages. Behind double arched wooden doors, they entered a spacious living room. At the far end was another tall set of wooden doors, which sat slightly ajar. She guessed it must lead to his bedroom beyond. A large stone hearth opened off the same chimney as the walk-in fireplace downstairs. A cheerful fire was roaring. No lights were on; instead small votive candles dotted the room. Lush classical music emanated from an unseen source.

"Dear God. You have no idea how much I've needed this," Jaime whispered.

"You and me both," he answered.

He sat down on a white rug in front of the fire, and Jaime sat beside him. Whatever the rug was made of, it was soft and luxurious. Mark opened his arms, and Jaime let herself lean back against him. His chest was rugged and well muscled. It was clear he worked out.

He put his arms around her, and leaned against an armchair, watching the flames dart through the logs before them.

"It's all so beautiful. What you've done with the house," she said.

He didn't answer. She sat slightly forward and turned her head to look at him.

"It's you that's beautiful," he said. He closed his eyes. "You're so lovely, and I'm dying to kiss you, but I'm terrified."

"Terrified?" she asked quietly.

"I need you so much. I need you to be the friend of my heart. I would never do anything to jeopardize that. If I came on to you romantically, but it wasn't right, and I lost you . . . or even if things became awkward . . . I couldn't stand it. So tell me if it isn't right, Jaime. Please, tell me."

She studied his face in the firelight, the confusion, the yearning. She put her hand behind his head, and she kissed him.

Well, she began the kiss. When he joined in, it was like the fire had jumped from the grate to encompass them both. The electricity in his touch ignited her body again and again.

The sheer outer robe came off, as did his shirt. He was so sturdy, and handsome, romantic, talented, bighearted . . .

He was her Mark.

The straps of her nightgown had fallen from her shoulders long ago. It felt natural for him to lay her on the soft rug and follow a line of kisses, from her mouth to her neck, slipping the top of her nightgown down to her waist. He caressed her breasts, kissing them, taking each nipple into his mouth, causing a bolt of lightning to shoot through her body, all the way down to her toes. She gasped, and stretched beneath him.

Silent tears began to run down her cheeks. Mark looked up and saw them, glinting in the firelight. And then they both heard it—a bell tone. Mark looked up at the fireplace where a small red button was flashing.

"Bloody hell," he said.

"What?" she asked.

"Apparently there's a phone call—or something that needs seeing to—that the staff has judged important enough to call me at this inopportune moment. Damn! I'm sorry, Jaime. Let me take care of it and tell them to turn off the system. The world can turn for one night without me."

"It's probably Larry Page from Google, who just heard you left town before the bash."

Mark grinned, stroked her hair, and said, "Anyway, I was just thinking that the only thing that would make this any more perfect would be if we had a bottle of local champagne. And fortunately, I happen to have one, chilled, in just the next room. I'll grab it on my way back."

"Sounds great."

"May this be the beginning of a long, and very perfect, night," he said.

Before he stood, Mark leaned across and kissed the tracks of her tears. "Don't cry," he whispered. "He would be happy for us. I know he would."

Jaime smiled at him and nodded. And as he momentarily left the room, she put the backs of her hands up to wipe the moisture from her face. What was killing her—*killing* her—at this moment was that the tears were not for Paul.

They were because the fine, handsome, talented, wonderful man who was kissing her was not Yani.

She was lying on her stomach on the soft white tufted rug when he returned. She'd brought a small pillow down from the sofa, and was watching the hypnotic dance of the fire, losing herself in the music.

"So sorry to disturb this romantic moment," came an unexpected male voice.

Jaime sat bolt upright, grabbing at the top of her nightgown, holding it against her chest. It was not Mark Shepard returning with champagne.

It was the barrel of a gun, pointed directly at her, held in front of a man who stood in the shadows.

"Who are you? What do you want?" she sputtered. It sounded like bad movie dialogue, but this had nothing to do with what she was expecting. She had been off duty. She'd turned off the ever-watchful part of her brain.

"I'm an old friend."

"Of Shepard's? I don't understand."

"No, Jaime Lynn Richards. Chaplain. Major. An old friend of yours. We have some unfinished business. I hate loose ends; don't you?"

"An old friend of mine?"

She was completely confused. How did this guy know who

she was? All her Operative "toys" were back in her room. This couldn't be happening.

But wait—Mark. And Derrick, the security guy.

"Help!" she yelled. "Intruder! Help!"

The gun didn't waver. The man didn't get angry, or tell her to stop.

"Sorry, waste of time," he said. "Come on now. We've got a lot to talk about."

As he moved into the light, her mouth dropped open with amazement. "Yep. Frank McMillan. CIA. Sorry I don't have any Vanilla Diet Cokes. I know they're a favorite of yours."

Frank McMillan?

Dear God, dear God, dear God! He was the rogue CIA agent who'd been in on her kidnapping during her first tour in Iraq. According to Yani, Frank was the one who'd wantonly killed half a dozen of his own guards, just for the hell of it.

Why was he here?

"Let me explain what's going to happen. You're going to stand up, and come with me. We're not going to go far. We're going to have a little chat. If you're cooperative, I'm sure I'll be in a good mood. If you're not, well, I get to hurt you, which means I'll be in an even better mood. Let's get going."

Jaime was running scenarios in which she could disarm him. It was made considerably harder by the fact that the satin sheath she still wore was so figure hugging and tight.

"Here's the thing. You try to take my gun, you get shot. In fact, at any point, you're not completely cooperative, you get shot. Not killed, shot. I'm a pro at this. I know just where the bullet should hit to kill you, slowly. Very slowly. Your old friend Adara? My handiwork. Dead woman walking. So. You want I should shoot you now, or you want to stay in one piece for a few more minutes?"

Dear God, how could someone so brazenly brag about killing someone slowly, let alone someone as smart and kind as Jaime's friend—and Yani's sister—Adara? But Adara had thwarted Frank; she'd escaped, even though mortally wounded, and gotten important information to Jaime and Yani.

Jaime knew better than to taunt Frank with this information. The safety was off his gun. He pointed it toward the side of her abdomen.

Jaime stood up. She pulled the straps back up onto her shoulders, and reached down for the robe.

"Don't need it," he said. "Walk."

Jaime turned around, and walked.

Frank McMillan forced her across the side lawn at gunpoint. They left the estate—with no sign of Mark or Derrick the security man—and crossed the old, cobbled street toward the medieval church. She'd seen a car, which she assumed to be Frank's, parked under the row of trees that delineated Shepard's property. The town beyond was completely dark.

She knew if she made a sound, he would shoot her.

It was clear that, although the church was still in use, the bell tower was not. The only approach was through the ancient cemetery. They wove through simple headstones until they reached the entrance. Weathered planks had been nailed across the rotting door. They had recently been removed.

Frank shoved the door open just wide enough for him and Jaime to enter, pushing her through first.

With a sweep of his flashlight, he illuminated the old stone stairs that led up in a square pattern, following the outer wall of the tower. There were no windows on the first floor, or on the second. He took her up to the third. The stairs ended. There were still no windows. An old wooden ladder led up from that floor to what was once a trapdoor to the belfry.

On this third level, Frank was already set up.

A canvas bag was thrown against one wall, a lantern on the

floor opposite it. Frank turned on the lantern. The room flickered into stark relief of light and shadow.

A large wooden post was fixed into the center of the floor and ran up into the ceiling. It was about a foot wide, had been squared. Two-thirds of the way up, there was an old iron ring attached to each of the sides.

Frank McMillan stood, looking at her. He looked healthier and more robust than she remembered him. He had a better haircut; that much was certain. She knew he was remorseless and dangerous. She had no clue what he wanted from her.

"What did you do with Shepard, and the others?" she asked.

"Since when is this your interview?" he asked. It was as if he found her continued presence of mind amusing. But she'd been trained to remain calm in situations such as this—to show neither fear nor insolence.

"Here's the thing," he said.

There was nothing she hated more than Frank McMillan's "here's the thing"s.

"Usually, we'd sit down, I'd explain what information I need from you, and we'd enjoy a nice talk. However, since I don't want to worry about you trying to bolt down the stairs—I'd rather not shoot you first thing—I'm going to restrain you from the get-go. One less thing to worry about."

Jaime stood, trying to remain impassive.

"Do you recognize what the post is in front of you?"

"No." Although she could hazard a guess.

"In the Middle Ages, the Church—indeed, many scientists—thought demons were responsible for a whole slew of things. Mental illness, infertility, uppity behavior in women. This is a demon-removal post. You bring the miscreant up here, and beat him or her until you get the submissive, non-demonic behavior you seek.

"But don't worry. I'm fully expecting satisfying answers from you without resorting to any medieval remedies. Right wrist, please."

He'd gotten a pair of metal handcuffs from the duffel. She held out her wrist and he snapped one on. Then he ran the cuff through the metal ring on the post in front of her. "Other wrist," he said. She complied, and he pulled her left arm up and snapped the other cuff around her wrist, several inches above her head. The position wasn't immediately uncomfortable, but it soon would be.

"There. Now we can concentrate on more important topics. Because I'm in a generous mood, let's start with answering your question. Mr. Shepard and his security man are fine. In fact, it was Mr. Shepard who handed you over to me. You could have stood there and hollered all night. They had no intention of helping you. In fact, they'd worked hard on keeping you occupied, and your guard down, until I arrived. So. No use in looking for help from that quarter."

Jaime knew she wasn't supposed to contradict her captor, but everything in her posture betrayed the fact that she couldn't believe that Mark would ever do anything to assist someone like Frank.

"You're looking doubtful," Frank said, almost happily. "Let's see, how did the plan go? Lunch in Laret—then, wait! Change of plans. Fly with him to a remote location, where he can have you disarmed and waiting until the nice CIA agent has time to arrive. Ring any bells?"

Jaime closed her eyes. It couldn't be true. It couldn't.

"Oh, it took a bit of persuading. It took threatening terrible harm to something Shepard obviously values more than he values you. Ah, well. Everyone has their price. Now. On to the night's business. I assume you know why I'm here?"

After his first statement, it was hard for her to track what he was asking. The idea that Mark had brought her here, romanced her, brought up his ties to Paul, kissed her—all to turn her over to a trained, demented CIA agent? She had seen many betrayals in her time, but she had never felt one so deep in her gut.

Frank nudged her.

"What?" she said.

"Why I'm here. Your guess."

"You had something to do with the plot in Davos?"

"Davos? Plot? Which one?"

She kept her voice neutral. "Then I guess I don't know."

"Take a look at this." He held a color picture in front of her. It showed a rectangular box with a gem on each side and two on the top.

"Mean anything to you?"

"I've never seen it."

"The gems. Ruby, lapis, emerald, mother-of-pearl, carnelian, bdellium. An odd combination of six stones. As fate would have it, the six are mentioned in the book of Genesis as those found plentiful in Eden. Ringing any bells yet?"

The blood had all left her hands and upper arms now, and the muscles in her shoulders were beginning to burn.

"No. Sorry. It looks like a nice box. But I've never seen it before."

"Jaime, Jaime, Jaime. Back to your friend Adara. I believe she owned a bracelet encircled by those very same jewels."

She knew he brought up Adara to upset her, throw her off balance. As much as she loved Adara, as furious as she was at Adara's murder, she couldn't take the bait. She couldn't go there.

"I believe these gems are tied in to the location of the spot called Eden. I lost two close comrades who were looking for the location. It pisses me off to lose comrades, especially when the mission is incomplete. But I think you can help me find the missing puzzle pieces. I believe you know about Eden. I think you know the importance of those six jewels, and their link to this secret place. I even think . . . you've been there."

Jaime's expression remained completely impassive.

"Let's start with some easier questions. After we last spoke, at Ali Air Base in Iraq, you disappeared for nearly three years. Where were you?"

"Someone kidnapped me. I was badly injured in the process. A family of goat herders kept me safe and nursed me back to health. When I began to regain my memory, they took me to a highway where I could be found by American troops."

"Goat herders."

"Yes. The type of goats we had was called Talli."

"And your kidnapper, what happened to him?"

"Somehow I think he was killed. But I don't remember it, and it wasn't my doing."

Frank took two paces back, toward his bag. "Okay. To re-cap. So far tonight, I've given vague threats; you've given your cover story. It's time to move on."

His voice had turned into a kind of growl. "Not to keep beating a dead horse, so to speak, but your friend Adara bravely—and foolishly, as it turned out—refused to give my comrade and me the information we sought. I was forced to resort to drugging her, which worked very well. I'm sure you'll become quite the Chatty Cathy, too, once you're properly doped. But lots of extraneous talk comes with the territory. I don't have time for that. It's my theory that you're a normal person. A nice girl. A chaplain, for God's sake. True, nice girls don't usually drop civilian contractors. Nice girls don't leave Iraq just when jeweled boxes go up for auction. Still, I don't believe you realize the game you're playing is dreadfully real."

He walked up to her, and ran something hard across her bare shoulder blades, where the nightgown was backless.

"It's my guess that when you realize it's real, not a fun game of spies, you'll be much more forthcoming. So. Let's restart the conversation." Now he brought the back of a large black whip up to where she could see it in her peripheral vision.

"Here is your part of the conversation: 'I know what's in Eden. This is how you get there. . . . ' "

It made it easier for Jaime that she didn't know how to get there. No matter what he did to her. That was what Swords were for, why only the Swords knew how to get in and out.

Jaime took a breath. At the Operative training center at Mountaintop, she'd been taught to withstand torture. She'd been trained to protect her mind, to compartmentalize pain. She had to get there, to that place, before he started hurting her.

But first, she had to stop thinking about Mark, about the horrible thing he'd done to her. She had to stop wondering why he had, what atrocity Frank had threatened. She had to get a grip.

"How you get to Eden is . . . ," Frank coaxed.

Jaime fell back on the script, and the familiarity of it comforted her. "You're seeking information I don't have, Mr. McMillan. You can do to me whatever you want, but the fact is, you think there's a place called Eden, and you think I know how to get there. I don't. I'm sorry. I don't want you to hurt me, but even if you do, it won't change the fact that I can't give you the information you seek."

"This is the fun part," he said, and she could hear the smirk in his voice. "This is the part where we find out what happens when the pain becomes real."

—FRIDAY—

The first stroke hit Jaime so hard that it not only tore the skin of her upper back and bit into her muscle; it knocked the wind out of her as well.

She knew she was at the critical point. There comes a time in torture, when the pain has been severe long enough, that your mind takes a vacation on its own. Until then, she had to lead it to safety. So she did as she'd practiced so many times, and removed her conscious mind from her body.

She took it to a safe place in a cave in Iran, where colorful soft pillows, in blues, reds, and golds, surrounded her. She could hear the bleats of the goats in her herd outside; she even knew which mother and which kid she heard loudest.

The second blow hit below the first one, and wrapped nearly all the way around her torso. She knew, in the part of her brain that was watching the proceedings, that she screamed with each stroke, that the nerve receptors from her torn muscles were sending messages to her brain, where the neurons were firing at the pain center like mad. The wise woman at the gate of her brain's pain receptors willingly accepted the messages, acknowledged there was pain, the pain was caused by injury, and replied it would be seen to. For now, it would have to be accepted.

In the cave, there were flowers. For some reason, she could smell tuberose. There was no tuberose in Iran, but she loved tuberose, and its scent enveloped her.

"I'm sorry," said Frank. "I'm ruining the front of your nightgown." And he put the handle of the whip under the thin spaghetti strap on her right shoulder and snapped it. He did the same to the left strap. The top front of her gown fell to her waist.

She heard music then, wonderful, Middle Eastern music, the kind you couldn't help dancing to. It surrounded her in her cave, and brought the spicy smell of ginger with it.

The observer part of her knew he'd exposed her breasts to humiliate her, but he'd done it too late. Her mind and her spirit were no longer present in that body. They were concerned for it, and grateful to it, but no longer involved with it.

The third blow was higher, and tore the soft skin of her right breast as it wove around. Her body instinctively leaned in closer to the pole for protection.

"Eden is in Iraq, is that right?" Frank's voice was conversational. "It won't kill you to say. It's easy. So easy. It's in Iraq. Where? Southern Iraq? Say the word, I stop."

"You're doing so well. I'm proud of you," said the kindly goatherd as he lit a fire in the cave, but as he spoke, she realized it wasn't the goatherd's voice at all. He stepped aside, and Yani walked into her cave. His eyes shone with concern for her. "You've learned well," he said. "I'm proud."

Yani wasn't supposed to be in this cave, this safe place in her mind she'd prepared for such a night as this. But, as the fourth stroke hit her, down low, across her lower back, she let him in. She let him touch her face.

"I'm sorry for what I said to you," she said to Yani, through her tears.

"What?" asked Frank.

"I'm sorry," Jaime repeated, and reedited her comment for Frank. "I'm sorry I don't know how to help you."

In the safety of her cave, she fell to the ground, and curled up. She couldn't help that tears were streaking her face. She felt Yani stroking her hair, and she was peaceful.

In the tower, as Frank brought the whip back for the next blow, his personal cell phone kicked to life. He stopped for a moment, annoyed, and then recognized the ring tone.

"Sorry, honey," he said. "I've got to take this."

And he scooted down the stone steps before hitting the button to connect.

The observer part of her sounded the alert, and Jaime snapped back to consciousness. Frank might only be gone a few minutes. She had to work fast.

Thank God he had only used one pair of cuffs. She'd been afraid he was going to cuff each hand separately to opposite sides of the pole, which would have made escape much harder. And thank God that she was military—even when she wasn't wearing her usual French braid, she ended up sticking bobby pins into her hair to hold it back somewhere.

Jaime could barely reach her head with her thumbs, but she did finally, and was able to reach a bobby pin. Unfortunately, it had the little plastic nubs on each end, and she couldn't reach her mouth to pull them off. She'd felt one more bobby pin, so she took a chance and dropped the first one.

With the second one, she had success. One end of it had no plastic nub.

The height of the iron ring put her arms at an odd angle, but failure was not an option. She worked her hand positions until one hand could reach the cuff on the other wrist. The lantern didn't throw much light, but she could see the small hole that could spring the cuffs if she could fit the bobby pin in.

She'd gotten really good at this at Mountaintop. She'd

never been in exactly this position, and her muscles had never been screaming with this much pain, but she'd taken off dozens of pairs of handcuffs. . . . *Steady.* . . . *Concentrate.* . . .

When the cuff sprang open and her arm was released, she collapsed onto the floor, nearly weeping with relief. But she didn't have time for relief. She wasn't out yet.

If Frank had taken the stairs to a level below her, she had only one choice . . . to go up and see if there was any escape route at all out of this place.

Jaime took a chance and spent twenty seconds springing the second handcuff, since wearing it even on one wrist would undoubtedly slow her down. She left them on the floor and went to the ladder in the corner.

She hadn't expected her back and shoulders where the whip had torn her flesh to protest the climb so severely. But she had to get out. Had to. Pain would be dealt with later. She forced her arms to cooperate as she climbed through to the next floor.

There were windows. A series of small, rectangular holes cut through the blocks of stone. She thought she could possibly squeeze through one.

But to where?

She peered out. In the darkness, she could see the church roof about a story and a half below. But the bad news was, the church roof was tiled and it was slanted. If she landed on the wrong spot, she could slip off and fall to severe injury.

Although she still heard Frank's voice in conversation below, she knew she didn't have time to delay. She'd have to go, and she'd have to do it now. It was either risk further injury by falling from the church roof or invite drawn-out death at the hands of Frank.

She'd risk the roof.

Jaime looked out again, gauging where the top ridge of the roof was. It seemed to be below the center rectangle. She was going to try to angle herself feetfirst.

Fortunately, the window was close enough to the floor that she could climb into it and turn herself slightly.

The rock bit into her raw back and she bit her lip. It hurt like hell.

There was no way for her to look behind her. She lowered her legs out, and caught herself by her hands. Fortunately, the whip hadn't bitten into her arms, but her shoulder muscles objected mightily as she tried to keep control and lower herself as much as she could before she dropped.

Then she let go.

She did a slight turn as she fell, and was able to catch hold of the ridge of the roof as she landed. The roof had clay tiles, and she cried out in pain as her exposed breasts scraped against them. She knew she'd gained some cuts and abrasions, but the pain of the hard landing itself was what caused her to lie for a moment on her stomach, gasping language she wouldn't want to have to explain to General Culver, and catching her breath.

When she finally looked to the side, she found, to her great relief, that the church was built in a clearing between the stream and the road. The road curved up around a hillside and came up and around the side of the church. She half-crawled, half-climbed across the roof to the far edge, from which it was a doable drop to the rock wall that ran along the cobbled road.

She was out.

Now what?

She held the top of her nightgown against her, although it was sticky with blood. She ran barefoot across the road and through the trees on the edge of Shepard's property. She let herself sit for a moment behind Frank's car.

He hadn't locked it. She opened the door silently and looked inside, searching for anything that might help her in her own escape. But the car was clean. Nothing in it at all—and no keys, of course. Most likely a recent rental.

Jaime tried to think clearly. She needed to get as far away from Frank, from this place, as possible. But she also needed to get her Operative handheld and some clothing.

Dare she go back to the manor?

The ground floor was still dark; front windows lining the second floor—including her bedroom—were dark. Mark's rooms on the second floor faced the back, and she couldn't tell if they were lit or not.

If she could get her handheld, she could summon help.

She decided to try getting back in and out of her room as quickly as possible.

Jaime stayed in the shadow of the shrubs that lined the long drive as she approached the manor. She tried the side door that led to the housekeeper's apartments—and to the back staircase—but the door was locked.

Frank had brought her down the center stairs, and there had been no one there to witness their descent. She might have to try it.

She hurried along the cobbled courtyard to the front door. She snuck a peek through the window on the right side of the door. The entry room, from which the stairs commenced, was vacant. There was a small automatic night-light still burning.

Jaime held her breath as she put her hand on the doorknob. It turned, and the door opened, silently. No alarms, no voices, no security guy. Nothing. She stepped into the welcome hall. As she took her hand off the outer knob to close the door from inside, she noticed that the outer handle was sticky—most likely with her blood.

Oh, well. All the bad guys knew she was here, and likely knew she was bleeding. If it helped leave a trail for the authorities, more the better.

From there, she didn't hesitate. She hurried to the bottom of the stairs, crept up as quickly as possible, and hurried down the corridor that led to her room.

The small suitcase with the new clothes purchased for her sat open. The fact that Mark Shepard had gone to so much trouble to lure her here hurt as much as her torn skin. She pulled off the bloody nightgown and left it in a heap on the floor. Her back was so sticky—she'd give anything to take a shower. But the sound of water running through the pipes made the idea too risky. Instead, she pulled on bikini briefs and held up the jeans. They were low riders, and she thought they'd fall below where she'd been whipped. Gingerly, she pulled them on, and found she'd been correct. Now what? She perused the tops, knowing she couldn't choose anything that would be tight enough to touch her back or sides.

Jaime took the Zurich sweatshirt, which looked roomy, and pulled it over her head. She relaxed slightly, as it didn't actually touch her except on the top of her shoulders and arms. She'd been wearing boots up at the hillside restaurant with Andrea. She didn't really need or want them, but they seemed a better choice than bare feet.

Jaime then grabbed her purse, and made sure her handheld was where she'd left it before slipping to the front window. She stood behind a side curtain to look out. Everything was quiet.

Time to go.

She silently pulled open the door to her room and scanned the dark hall. Nothing. This time, she turned the opposite way, went through the old wooden door to the servant stairs, and hurried down through the silent dark. The stairs ended in an old-fashioned keeping room, with a mudroom and outer door to the left.

Jaime took a deep breath and exited into the night air.

January 26, 2007, 12:32 A.M.
(1 day, 9 hours, 58 minutes until end of auction)
Judean wilderness west of the Dead Sea
Israel

Yasmin heard her father's voice calling her from outside the tent. She sat up at once, surprised and happy, and ran to the door. Her father stood, tall and handsome beneath the full moon. He held in one hand a dress, of blues and greens, covered with coins and precious jewels that shimmered in the moonlight.

"For you, my little one," he said. "My gift to you. A wedding dress."

Yasmin felt her chest fill with hope and happiness. She opened her arms to run to him. She couldn't move. The tent flap was open—she could feel the desert breeze. There was nothing by her feet to trip her, and yet she couldn't move.

"Father," she called.

"Don't you want it?" he asked, and he began to fade away.

"Father, yes, yes! Don't go!" Yasmin called. She felt something warm on her neck, and batted it away with her hands. But it remained.

She opened her eyes, and she was still in her tent on her mats in the dark. And the Monster was next to her, his breath hot on her face.

"No!" she said, and she began to struggle.

"Shut up, you little whore," he said, and he was holding her so she couldn't move, and climbing on top of her.

And then from the darkness beyond came another voice.

"No," said her mother. Her voice was quiet but like steel. "No. Not the night before her henna night. No."

The Monster looked up, ready to say something dismissive to his wife, to cow her.

But she spoke again. "You will never touch my daughter again. You will never again beat my son. Because if you do, I will go to the council. I will tell them what you do. Not only in this tent, but beyond. I will tell everything."

"You wouldn't dare," he said. "You would be called a liar. You would end up forsaken and alone."

"Even if they thought that of me, perhaps they would not believe that my daughter, the wife of the Hajj, is a liar also. Perhaps they would not believe that my son, the nephew of the chief, is a liar. But even if they did, we would be better off alone."

"You wouldn't dare."

"Touch either of them again and you will see what I dare," she said. "Now go to bed." And Yasmin's mother turned away.

Yasmin waited a moment, hardly daring to breathe.

Finally the Monster rolled off of her, and moved heavily to his mat.

And Yasmin lay in the dark, and tried to think of nothing but the colors of the wedding dress her father would bring her, if he could.

Jaime lay on her stomach in the midst of Shepard's vineyard. *Op kidnapped, injured, escaped,* she'd texted. *Need help.*

"And probably therapy," she muttered under her breath. "Shepard, damn you anyway."

The reply was instantaneous. *Go onto frequency J,* it said.

Frequency J was the highest-priority frequency, with the highest security feed. Everything said or texted would be scrambled in such a way that it could only be decoded by another J-frequency communication device.

"Jaime, are you all right? What on earth is going on?" She recognized the male voice as that of C4, one of the seven Operative Coordinators overseeing different regions of the Terris world.

"I'm injured, but it's not life threatening," she said softly. "I was kidnapped from the home of a friend—well, I thought he was a friend—by Frank McMillan, the CIA guy who worked against Adara and me in Iraq in '03," she said.

"You're injured?"

"Yes. Painful, but non–life threatening. I'm out now. But he's still here somewhere."

"We've got you on the scanner; we're arranging for pickup right now. Where were you when you were kidnapped?"

"At the home of Mark Shepard. McMillan claims they worked together to procure me."

"Why?"

"McMillan wanted information. He showed me a photo of some sort of antique box that had the Six Sisters. He wanted to know about it. He's still hunting for information about Eden."

"Where is he now?"

Jaime raised her head and looked toward the tower. She thought she saw the shadow of a figure moving through the graveyard.

"He's about two hundred yards away from where I'm hidden. He's looking for me. He's got a car parked here at Shepard's estate, but he's across the street in the old churchyard."

"Okay. Stay down. Back with instructions in a moment."

The night was clear and very, very cold. Jaime noticed the cold because she hadn't put on the white ski parka she'd been wearing on her adventure with Andrea. Partly because it would have pushed the sweatshirt down onto her injured back but mostly because it sported a wide stripe of reflective tape.

To her surprise, the next voice she heard was a female voice.

"Jaime. This is TC2. C4 has given me your information." TC2 was one of two Terris Coordinators who oversaw all the Operative missions and reported directly to Clement, the head of Operatives in Eden. Her call had been bumped up, and quickly.

"Jaime. Describe your injuries to me. Do you need to be treated by a physician?"

"McMillan gave me four strokes across my back with a whip before I escaped. Hurts like anything, but I'm okay."

"By 'okay' do you mean you can continue to work? Be honest with me."

"What do you need?" Jaime asked.

"I need you to follow Frank McMillan. Get as much information as you can about what he knows and where he's going. Do you have any means by which to do this?"

"I don't have any locator devices. I had one in Davos, but I used it on Woodbury."

"You don't have access to a car?"

"No."

As she said that, she saw Frank's lantern turn on in the churchyard. Apparently he'd given up looking for her and was headed back to the estate. His lantern disappeared around the front of the church as he walked to the road that wound up toward Mark's.

"How important is this?" Jaime couldn't believe she was asking.

"Vital. He's stumbled onto the current critical."

The "current critical" was the most important mission going at any given time.

"Let me see what I can do."

It was a split-second decision that would either work brilliantly or be a fatal error. Jaime stayed as low as she could and hurried to Frank's BMW. She hesitated because she knew opening the door would likely turn on the dome light.

But she did it. She pulled open the driver's side door, and pulled the small lever on the floor that popped the trunk. Then she shut the door as quietly and quickly as possible. She ran to the back of the vehicle, climbed into the trunk, and pulled it closed.

Jaime landed on her back, and it was all she could do not to scream. Instead, she fought to regulate her breathing and wait until the waves of pain subsided.

Through the small gap between the pull-down armrest and the backseat, she could see that the interior light had dimmed and gone out.

It was only then, in the dark, that she had a moment to think. What if Frank went back into the manor house for a few hours? What then?

What if he decided to throw his duffel into the trunk?

As she heard his footfalls approach, she frantically typed in: *OS* (observe silence).

Where are you? came the texted question.

I'm in his trunk, she replied. *He's getting in.*

The door behind the driver's seat opened and he threw something inside. Probably his duffel. Thank God.

Then he opened the driver's side door and sat down heavily.

"She's gone and I can't take the time to find her," he said into his phone.

He put the key into the ignition and screeched into reverse before heading off into the night.

January 26, 2007, 1:24 A.M.
(1 day, 8 hours, 6 minutes until end of auction)
Autobahn A4
10 kilometres northeast of Château-Thierry, France

The BMW M5 sedan flew like an angry wraith along the highway toward Paris, its driver expertly controlling the machine while his mind focused elsewhere.

For a fleeting moment Frank McMillan had been pissed off when he realized Richards had escaped. But he quickly let that go and moved on. It only wasted energy to dwell on mistakes when the information he sought was now his.

Instead, Frank savored his memory of the encounter. As if in slow-motion replay, he could picture the very tip of the whip making its first contact with Jaime Richards' skin. He remembered that instant, the involuntary flinch, the split second before that lovely scream, and her bare back bowed as every muscle constricted in a vain attempt to escape the source of pain.

Then came McMillan's favorite moment, when the first drops of blood welled up in the open wound left by the whip. There was more blood to follow, but that first hint of red drew him in like a tiger to its prey.

Frank savored that memory, and the beast inside him roused at the thought of finishing the job he had begun in the tower.

But first, back to the mission at hand. Upon reaching the

Autobahn, McMillan had kicked the BMW engine into "M Drive," allowing him to make full use of the 500 hp engine. His heads-up display now read 250 kph, and while he knew the auto could go even faster, he would look for a smoother spot in the road before opening it up completely. The French did not manage their highways with the same care as the Germans.

"Brutish" was how one reviewer had labeled this car. Brutish, maybe, but Frank wasn't interested in style. Performance mattered. Performance, and the challenge of controlling a touchy gear system. In the right hands, this car had the power to leave any competitor in the dust. And his were the right hands.

"Tel Aviv," the driver spoke to the voice-actuated Bluetooth phone system. In response, it dialed one of his CIA connections in Israel. The operative picked up the line on its second ring.

Without introduction, Frank went straight to the point: "Okay, tell me. Who's selling the box?"

"A Bedouin tribal leader named al-Asim," replied the agent speaking from his office in Tel Aviv. "They live out in Judea, south of Qumran. There's a big wedding there in a few days."

"I'll need a cover. Have a concept for me by the time I call back from the airport in two hours."

"Frank," complained the agent. "You ask too much. I don't have time for this! Look, I'm working a big project for my boss right now. He wouldn't be happy if he knew the time I've already spent—"

"I will say this once, and once only." The menace in McMillan's voice was palpable. "I have not forgotten your screwup in New Orleans. One word from me and you're out." He could feel the agent squirm on the other end of the line. Frank knew he had him by the short hairs. "My cover. Two hours."

"All right."

Frank smiled at the note of defeated resignation in the man's voice as he hung up.

Pathetic, and clueless. Don't you know you're only in the game as long as you are useful to me?

Frank McMillan had learned early in his career that the

game was best played by gathering data, or, better, dirt, on all his associates. Peers, subordinates, superiors, no one was exempt. He had learned this the hard way when another agent had threatened to use one of his missteps against him. Of course he had to kill her, but he would always be grateful to her for introducing him to the game.

Now, after twenty-plus years, Frank's collection of information was formidable. After the debacle with the Dagger of Ur a few years before, most station chiefs would have been fired. Instead, his knowledge of the darker past of several of his superiors enabled him to skate by, sliding to another assignment.

The nervous director forced to be the bearer of the news that McMillan was being transferred to Tunisia had asked oh, so politely that Frank just lay low for a while and let it all blow over. They would "get him back in the game" soon. Well, of course the man had reason to bend over backward to keep Frank happy. A picture, as they say . . . worth a thousand words.

McMillan had hated Tunisia, the isolation. But he had bided his time, and now he was back in the game, using all his resources once again.

He called up the number for his office assistant, whom he had woken fifteen minutes earlier to make flight arrangements.

"What do you have for me?"

"Sir, there's a six-oh-five A.M. flight on Czech Air into Tel Aviv. You would arrive at eleven-thirty A.M. local."

"Do they even have First Class on those flights?"

"I don't know, but your next options don't arrive until late afternoon. I'll look into it if you want more comfortable arrangements."

"No, book me on the early one, First Class if they have it."

"Will we need to get your weapon on board?" Even though he asked nonchalantly, a positive answer from Frank would necessitate hours spent getting clearance.

"No, I want to go in under the radar. Just list me as a businessman. I'll pick up firepower on the other end."

"Anything else, sir?"

"That's it for now. I'll check back in after arriving at the airport."

He switched off the phone and settled back to plan his next moves.

What to do about Richards? How best to control her in their next engagement?

Searching for some key to unlock the mystery of Jaime Richards, Frank replayed their encounter in the bell tower once again, this time with focus on her face and voice. And suddenly he remembered a moment of vulnerability, one he could exploit when he next had her in his grasp. He smiled a wicked smile as he flew down the highway toward Paris.

Shortly after the heady victory of supplying the information about what Frank knew and his airline plans out of Paris–Charles de Gaulle Airport, Jaime realized just how much trouble she was in.

Assuming they were in a rental car, Frank would undoubtedly turn it in to the company from which it was rented. Thus he would be there, awaiting his paperwork, when the clerk on duty filled in the miles and checked the backseat and the trunk.

What do I do when they check the trunk at the rental car return? she texted.

Jaime had been riding in the trunk for an hour. Her muscles were cramped and protesting, the motor was loud, and the ride wasn't exactly smooth. The blood on her back was scabbing, and she was fairly certain some of it had melded to the inside of the sweatshirt.

Still . . . there was a great satisfaction to the fact that Frank thought he'd won. He'd caught her and tortured her. He had no idea the roles had reversed and he'd become the prey.

If she could help, even in some small way, to make this into a world where the likes of Frank McMillan did not kill, capture, or torture people, she would rest easier at night. It was worth the risk. Even if they were getting to the danger point.

Jaime had spent the ride in the trunk refusing to let herself think about the evening. About how wonderful it had been, how much she needed a friend like Mark—and how it seemed like whenever she let her guard down something terrible happened.

Jaime, we're following you. If he stops for petrol, we'll bring you in. If he doesn't, we'll have someone there whenever, wherever he stops the car. Are you all right? How can we assist you once you're safe?

Jaime sighed. *Clothes. Shower. Bed,* she typed.

You've got it, came the reply.

And I need Frank not to shoot me between now and then, she thought to herself, and tried to arrange herself more comfortably once again.

The frightening thing was, Jaime couldn't tell where Frank was going once he got to the airport. She knew Eden Operatives were able to track the car—because she had a permanent tracking device in her body and she was in the car—but also knew they didn't want to be close enough that Frank would know they were following.

If he opened the trunk, she would have only a brief moment of surprise. If someone else opened the trunk—such as a car rental agent—she would have a few more valuable seconds to get out before Frank realized what happened. Then what would he do? Shoot her in full view of a rental car agent?

Although—she wouldn't put it past him to shoot her *and* the rental car guy. Remorse didn't seem built into Frank's genes.

Worst case would be if somehow he didn't go to the rental return, pulled into a deserted garage, found her somehow, shot her, and left her in the trunk to be discovered by the scent of her decomposing body. All right, the other Operatives would find her before she decomposed, but the fact that he would think he could get away with it was chilling.

She had to stop running worst-case scenarios in her mind.

The best she could do was be ready to act, to use her moment of surprise.

Jaime knew when they entered the airport roadways because the GPS in her handheld showed her they did. At some point, Frank used his turn indicator and turned into a structure. Probably a parking garage. She didn't know if rental car returns were inside a structure at Charles de Gaulle or not.

She worked to quietly get herself into a position where she could get out—without lying on her back. Every movement in that cramped space was difficult, especially since Frank had turned off the radio and she didn't want him to hear anything.

Then he swerved into a sharp turn, as if pulling into a parking spot.

Jaime stopped breathing.

The engine was cut. Frank punched the front dashboard twice, as if for emphasis. Then he opened his door and stepped out. He hit the "all unlock" button, and the locks on the backseat popped up.

He opened the door to the backseat.

Jaime tried to breathe silently. Her handheld was in her purse, so no light could escape from the trunk between the seats.

Frank grabbed his bag. Jaime strained to hear him talk to someone. Finally he said, "Level H. Space Sixty-seven."

The door slammed. The sound of his footfalls retreated.

He'd obviously given someone else the location of the car.

No sooner had she thought that than the trunk popped up. She sat up quickly, ready to hit someone's solar plexus and jump out.

"Have you journeyed well?" asked the older man who looked down at her. He extended his hand.

"Exceedingly well," she answered with untold relief, returning the Eden password. "Considering," she couldn't help but add.

A small car idled right behind him.

"Your driver's headed for the terminal," said the man as he opened the back door of the Eden car for Jaime and climbed back into the passenger seat. "Let's be gone before someone picks up the Beemer."

Jaime got just a fleeting look at the Frenchwoman driving the car before she lay down on her stomach on the floor of the car as they headed out of the garage.

January 26, 2007, 4:26 A.M.
(1 day, 5 hours, 4 minutes until end of auction)
Aéroport de Paris–Le Bourget
Le Bourget, France

Jaime thought they'd bring her to a safe house. In her mind, she'd pictured a charming old French house with a movable bookcase and a secret apartment, leftover from the days of the French underground. A hot shower. Croissants and fresh-squeezed juice. Hot tea, all on a table with a French country cloth.

But that was what she would henceforth think of as a "trunk fantasy"—something she created in her mind because she had too much time to do nothing but ride in someone's trunk.

Where they did take her was an airplane hangar at Aéroport de Paris–Le Bourget, a general aviation airport eleven kilometers southwest of de Gaulle. The two Operatives who'd retrieved her had pulled up to the hangar, handed her a small suitcase, then handed her over and taken off. Two men in mechanic's jumpsuits greeted her. The hangar itself was not heated and one of the men handed her a coat, but she didn't dare put it on.

The taller gentleman brought her back to an office, which was heated. He nodded back to where there seemed to be a small apartment and took her back inside.

The term "apartment" was too generous. There was a bathroom with a shower, and an outer room with a cot, a table, a hot plate, and a small refrigerator.

He went into the bathroom and turned on the shower, indicating it might take a minute to get hot.

The other man brought her a steaming cup of coffee. Then they each shook her hand, gave a small nod, and left.

Jaime opened the small duffel bag she'd been given. Obviously, no one had time to go shopping in the middle of the night. They had raided some poor woman's closet to get Jaime a few things to wear. The pants were black and tight and the blouse was white and frilly, with a scoop neck.

Jaime didn't know whether to laugh or cry. She was injured; she was exhausted; she had hoped for softer surroundings. She didn't do frilly and she hated coffee.

On the other hand, Frank hadn't killed her.

She was going to let that one win the day.

She went back into the bathroom, into the shower, which was now running warm, heading for hot. She turned down the water pressure so it wouldn't break any scabbing that was starting on her back.

Jaime stepped into the stall and only then let the silent tears run down her face. Could it be true? She didn't want to believe Mark had done that to her—but if he hadn't, how had Frank known that they'd nearly had lunch in Laret but had seemingly spontaneously changed their minds and come to France? Why had neither Mark nor Derrick come to her aid? And who did Frank threaten to hurt to get Mark to agree? What did Frank say? "Something Shepard obviously values more than he values you." Or did he say some*one*?

How can I do this? How can I choose to live in a world in which someone I trusted with every fiber of my being handed me over to Frank McMillan?

She used the trick Yani had taught her and gave herself three minutes to do nothing but mourn for her friendship with Mark. Then she washed her hair, enjoying the warm water running down her face and the front of her body. She turned around gingerly to try to wash away the spilled blood from her back, without breaking open the wounds.

What happens next? she wondered. She needed someone to help her bandage her back. Surely there were medical Operatives who could help? This was nowhere near as urgent as the medical crisis she'd had with Yani, but there had been help in that situation, albeit remotely, right away.

She smiled, imagining going home to her rented house in Hochspeyer and turning up at nearby Landstuhl and trying to explain how a chaplain had been whipped while on leave. "I fell off my bike," wouldn't quite cut it. She sort of wished Jenkins could be there, just so she could show him that the life of a chaplain could offer a few surprises. She hated that he thought he had her pegged.

On the other hand, Jenkins' most likely response could be wishing he'd been there to help Frank with the whip. So never mind.

Jaime had a feeling there would be at least a debriefing from the Frank interlude, and that someone else would be coming to this "safe hangar" to talk to her.

She just didn't have any idea what the person would say.

January 26, 2007, 5:26 A.M.
(1 day, 5 hours, 4 minutes until end of auction)
Judean wilderness west of the Dead Sea
Israel

The two Arabian horses, one white and one black, galloped through the inky darkness of the desert dawn. They knew their footing, as this was a path they'd often run, with these same two riders—the boy on the black and the girl on the white. They wore no saddles, only tasseled bridles.

Safia clung to the mane of Pasha, her horse, as he flew over the sand. She controlled him not with a bit but with the will of the partnership that ran from her shoulders through the hooves of her horse. To Safia this was, without question, the definition of perfect happiness. The wind in her hair, the strength and speed of Pasha beneath her, her cousin Tarif riding beside her.

Tarif's older brother was the horse master. He was a strapping young man with a ready smile and a gentle strength to which all the horses responded. He'd first put Tarif on a horse—the gentlest one, with a lead, of course—when he was barely able to walk. By the time he was nine or ten, Tarif was an accomplished rider.

Safia had been only four when she'd followed Tarif as he had left camp and gone to the horses. When she saw what he was doing, she had forgotten her manners and her shyness and had presented herself to the brothers, pleading to be allowed to ride. Even as a little girl, she knew the boys would be in trouble—especially Suleiman—if he let her. But she wanted it so badly, and she had believed that since her heart was pure and her desire was so intense somehow it would be possible.

They had let her ride.

Suleiman stood guard while Tarif had put her on the gentlest horse, as his brother had once done for him.

Riding that mare had been everything Safia had thought it would be, and more. Riding became an unbreakable bond that she and Tarif shared. She thought of him as the only one in her life who understood her passion—who even knew she had passion. He had not only taught her to ride; he had taught her to track as well. Things that only boys were supposed to know.

During times like these, when they secretly rode to greet the dawn, the pounding of the horses' hooves gave rhythm to the pounding of her blood, and gave her the wonderful knowledge that real joy was possible—and the terrible assurance that all of it would soon be taken from her forever: the nomadic lifestyle, the ability to be with Tarif, the freedom of the horses. It was all going to disappear. Their way of life was going to disappear. They would be relocated to a piece of land no one else wanted and given slabs of concrete on which to build shanties.

These night rides, and the wonderful colors of their tents, the pouring of the tea for important visitors, the days of herding goats and exploring caves, would be nothing more than crazy stories she would tell her grandchildren, and they'd mock her.

Even now she knew she was crying as she rode, half out of happiness, half out of grief, and the tears were taken by the wind, and hidden forever in the desert sands.

Jaime had been correct. There was a woman waiting for her when she dressed and got out of the bathroom. She had pulled back on the jeans and sweatshirt after realizing the folly of trying to wear a tight white blouse under the current circumstances. Instead, she'd turned the Zurich sweatshirt inside out, scraped off most of the dried blood, put it back to the right side, and pulled it on.

In contrast, the woman waiting for her was impeccably groomed. She wore black pants, a white shell, and a black jacket with white scrolling. It looked comfortable but chic. Around her neck was a gold pendant of what looked to be an ancient shield, and she wore matching earrings. Her hair was black and full, pulled back into a barrette, the hair beneath the hair clip flared with a natural curl.

The woman herself was medium height and medium build, but she had an aura about her that made her seem anything but medium. Her face was oval, her eyes blue-gray, her gaze intense. Jaime knew immediately that this was a woman who was kind, who was smart, and with whom you didn't mess.

The woman had put two hot drinks in take-out cups down on the table, and was opening a bag of pastries. She took Jaime's old, cold coffee away. "Your file says you prefer tea," she said with a smile.

"This looks wonderful," said Jaime, wondering who the woman was.

Jaime took the top off her cup of tea and breathed in the aroma. The piquant smell of oranges and black tea vied for supremacy. She removed the tea bag, and took a taste.

She was coming back to life.

The woman put down a paper plate with fresh croissants, adding, "Here's butter, and jam and a banana."

"Bless you," said Jaime.

"Let's sit down."

Jaime sat. The woman spoke. "As you know, protocol dictates that I can tell you either my first name or my Operative ID. I'm TC2."

"Oh—ma'am—very pleased to meet you," said Jaime. She couldn't believe, of all the Operatives in the world, she was sitting at a table with this woman. Back at Mountaintop, they'd made it clear you should not expect to ever meet one of the two Operatives at the TC level.

"First off, I wanted to meet you in person. I've heard so much about you—your courage, your compassion. Second, I wanted to tell you that you've been getting the short end of the stick. Most Operatives are not taken captive once, let alone on an ongoing basis. You have my apology, and my gratitude for the grace with which you've carried on. Not many people— even Operatives—would have had the gumption to put themselves in Frank McMillan's trunk. But it was of great help to us and gave us intelligence we couldn't have gotten any other way. How are you?"

"Still reeling," Jaime answered honestly. She appreciated TC2's words, yet her saying she'd heard about Jaime's "courage" and "compassion" was a two-edged sword. At the completion of her last assignment, Yani had complimented her on the same thing—before adding that Jaime still lacked an Operative's third needed trait: perspective.

At the time, she'd been insulted.

She'd come to see he'd been right.

If this woman had heard Jaime possessed the first two qualities, she'd undoubtedly heard about her weakness with the third.

"I'd be surprised if you weren't reeling. But I don't have time to mince words. I'm here because I have a question for you. And please know you have the option of saying no."

Jaime put down her tea, mid-sip. This should be interesting.

"As I mentioned, Frank McMillan has stumbled onto the current critical. It involves the box in the photograph he showed you. It's a valuable box in any circumstances, to anyone, but it holds special meaning for gardeners. As you know—and as Frank McMillan also knows—it's currently in the possession of a tribe of Bedouin in the hills of Judea. The sheikh of the clan, a man named Omar al-Asim, has put it up for sale. We would like to have it. We would like to make certain that others, such as Frank McMillan, do not have it.

"We currently have our two top male Operatives on the assignment. But in Bedouin culture, men and women are kept strictly separated, even at weddings such as the one the clan is celebrating tomorrow. While there's every likelihood, given the Bedouin culture, the events having to do with the sale of, and possession of, the box will happen among the men, it's become clear we need someone among the women.

"According to your file, while at Mountaintop you had specialized training in the way of Muslim tribes, as well as Middle Eastern languages. Your reentry was through Iranian goatherds. Obviously, the Bedouin in Israel are different in substantial ways, but you have a good base on which to build. We'd have someone meet you in Israel, someone who could fill you in, give you pertinent cultural information, the correct clothing, and take you to the wedding. Chances are you would not be called on to do anything on this assignment other than be our eyes and ears among the women. I can also tell you the assignment will be very short. The auction for the box ends just before tomorrow's wedding."

"What about Frank McMillan? He's heading that way right now. Wouldn't he recognize me right away?"

"As I said, women and men are strictly separated. McMillan's business will be with Omar al-Asim, and him alone.

And, although the women of this tribe don't cover their faces as a matter of course, they do wear veils that can be used for that purpose if they're in proximity to a man outside their immediate family. It would be easy for you to keep your identity from McMillan. And we can say with certainty that he won't be expecting you. If there was any chance I felt he would continue to be a danger to you, I wouldn't allow you to be considered for the assignment.

"Many people will be arriving for the wedding. We could get you there, successfully planted, hours before McMillan would have a chance to arrive on the scene."

Jaime took a croissant, and spread butter with a plastic knife. She tried to think clearly. It was true she had specialized training in Middle Eastern tribes, and under ordinary circumstances she'd love to observe a Bedouin wedding. She'd also do almost anything to make certain that Frank didn't get the box. But to her, the most compelling argument was that TC2 had said the top two male Operatives were already on the assignment. She couldn't say for certain that Yani was one of them. But he'd not only been a top Operative; he'd also been chosen to be a Sword. While he'd resigned from that special designation and gone back to being an Operative, he'd of course be one of the top—wouldn't he?

Jaime knew that, without unusual circumstances such as this, her chances of interacting with Yani again in her lifetime were small to nonexistent.

It could very well be that he was not on this assignment.

But it could be he was.

"All right," she said. "I'll go."

"Great. Thank you. There's a plane taxiing into the hangar for you right now. We can get you to Tel Aviv by dawn, and out to the desert by midday. The festivities began several days ago. Tonight is the bride's henna night; tomorrow is the wedding. It should be quite an experience."

I bet it will, thought Jaime. *I bet it will.*

A waitress approached Frank McMillan with a glass of champagne as he sat working in the Salon 200 VIP lounge. He waved her off dismissively. Leave it to the French to waste all their time on a drink that took years to make, then once the bottle is opened must be drunk immediately or it would go bad.

He read the update on his BlackBerry.

There is a jeweler from South Africa who has been invited to the wedding, wrote the agent in Tel Aviv. *He is one of three craftsmen asked to create a unique gift for the bride. It is a contest of sorts, in which the winning piece will be chosen by the bride. For a fee, the jeweler will let you go in his place. You are of similar height and build, and could pose as his brother, Hans.*

This would be no problem. With his time spent in Europe, Frank could affect a fair German accent.

Set it up, he typed in response. *I will need papers, of course, and a couple weapons. A Beretta Cheetah .380 pistol will do, and a knife I can carry easily. My flight lands at 11:30 A.M. Have someone pick me up."*

January 26, 2007, 8:03 A.M
(1 day, 2 hours, 27 minutes until end of auction)
Judean wilderness west of the Dead Sea
Israel

The women of the clan had been up for hours, some preparing breakfast and some already starting the meals for later in the day. Spicy aromas colored the air, seasoned by the laughter of the women and girls. No matter what they thought of the Hajj's upcoming marriage, they were hosting a festive celebration, and normal work was canceled for the next few days. That alone was enough to put a smile on the face of the dourest old woman.

It was celebration time!

Many of the invited guests from outside the clan had arrived two days ago; the remainder would arrive today. For the Bedouin, the most serious celebrations really began the night before the wedding. In the old days—days Omar himself could still remember—the men and women had mixed on the bride's henna night. The women's dancing had been festive and free, the songs suggestive, the flirtations intense. Women and men had been allowed to mingle, and the men got to see a side of their wives, sisters, and cousins that was shown very rarely: the laughing, sexual side that hinted that the women might actually enjoy the marriage bed.

But then society had changed; the stern Imams had taken over Islam, and now the women danced and teased only for one another.

Not everything in the world changed for the better.

The Hajj looked at the men of his own clan, gathered now in the big tent. They all ate the offered *mensef,* which consisted of fresh goat boiled in *laban,* goat yogurt, and served on *shraak,* a combination of rice and bread. He wondered, as he had many times over the years, if he had known what it meant to be sheikh, all the headaches and troubles that came with it, would he have wished it so sincerely? More than once he had fantasized life as a simple shepherd or businessman. Then *he* could come to the clan meetings and do nothing but complain. He could sit there and care about nothing except the fortunes of his own family. The politics of the clan, the tribe, the Israeli Bedouin, the state of Israel—what would it matter to him?

He studied the faces of the men around him. Although guests had started arriving, so far they were kin: he knew, or at least recognized, all of them. It was when the others, some strangers, arrived that he would worry.

For that was the thought that dogged him, the thought he couldn't get out of his mind, no matter what he did. The auction for the box was ending tomorrow morning. The auctioneer would come, demanding it. The threats of what would happen if the box was not presented thus far had been vague but the tone strident.

The Hajj did not even know what Abihu el-Musaq looked like.

Maybe the Hajj should have sold the box right away, in the early days, when he could have gone to the cobbler shop in Bethlehem and dealt with Kando, instead of it turning into an electronic international event.

He knew el-Musaq was ruthless. He understood he should not make him annoyed, let alone upset. He also knew Abihu el-Musaq had gone past upset, deep into angry.

And he was angry at the Hajj.

Who had taken the damn box?

The Hajj looked at the men who circled the room. In his mind, he could create a reason for any of them to have stolen it.

Farook, his own oldest son, could be using it as a grab for power. In Bedouin society, leadership didn't necessarily stay in the family, or pass to the eldest if it did. He would have a more-than-fair shot at it, but it wasn't a given.

The Hajj's third son seemed eager to have a role of responsibility. He was a vocal advocate of building up their town and staying there all year. Planting more orchards, doing anything that would prove they were planted, so that the Israeli government couldn't up and move them to a garbage dump, as they had the Jahalin. Branching out into more modern jobs. Many of the younger men agreed with him. He wasn't sure how the box would help with that goal, except, perhaps, to be sold and finance the modernization of the town. Or lawyers to help them keep claim to it.

Then there was the old man—well, the same age as the Hajj—who had stood in line to be sheikh, until the Hajj, Omar, had found the box. Perhaps this was his payback, after all this time.

Or perhaps the father of his third wife, Asad, had discovered that the Hajj was planning to spend some of the money from the box on a fabulous piece of jewelry as a wedding gift for his new bride, Yasmin. Perhaps Asad and her father were angry and wanted their share also.

The Hajj's worst fear, however, was that his cousin—the brother of Rashid—suspected the truth, that Rashid had not gone off into the world to find his fortune. If he had, wouldn't he have written? Come back to show off his car, his money, and his wife?

The brother of Rashid was the only one with a true claim to the box.

Had the spirit of Rashid come to him—in a dream, perhaps—and told him what had really happened?

Now the men were all smiling and laughing. Eating the dates and yogurt. In a celebratory mood. They didn't suspect that in a day's time everything could fall apart. The Hajj could be murdered, the box gone, the clan set on a path of revenge that would put them at odds with modern laws and local authorities.

How could he find out who took the box?

The Bedouin had an ancient ceremony called the fire test,

which forced men to tell the truth. The man whose honesty was in question had to lick the bottom of a scalding-hot pan three times. If he was telling the truth, he would not be burned. But if Hajj asked everyone to do this, it would be taken as an outrage. It would strike at the honor of every man in the room to be suspected of being a liar and a thief.

The Hajj tried to look at it another way. Whom did he *trust*?

He should be able to say his own sons. Up until now, he would have.

There were three cousins who had already arrived. He'd always thought them trustworthy allies.

Those cousins had come with several of *their* cousins, also men whom the Hajj had always enjoyed. Especially the tall one, Ahmet. Ahmet was laughing now, at one of the jokes. But he was also a friend, who went out of his way to bring greetings to the Hajj whenever he came, and usually had words of wisdom or understanding.

The Hajj knew he couldn't wait too long to take more decisive action. Up until now, he hadn't told anyone except his oldest son that the box was missing. It was that son, and his sons, who had searched the family tents.

To say the box was gone would be to relinquish power. In the Hajj's own mind, he pictured himself shrinking back into a normal man.

What should he do?

"What's the problem, old man? Are you afraid your new bride will have too much youthful energy?" teased the Hajj's brother.

"I did not know that would be thought a problem!" the Hajj returned jovially. But what he really thought was, *What will Abihu el-Musaq do, slit my throat?*

Omar looked again at Ahmet, thinking of his wise counsel in the past. Perhaps he could share the problem with Ahmet. He also had the goodwill of most of the other men in the camp. Perhaps Ahmet could ask around to see if anyone knew anything—or if anyone would tell him, point-blank, that he had taken the box, and why. If someone had it, there must be something he wanted. He must be looking to make a deal.

Yes, Omar would speak in private to Ahmet. And he would see if, together, they could find out who the thief was, and what he demanded, before nightfall.

January 26, 2007, 12:08 P.M.
(22 hours, 22 minutes until end of auction)
The bride's camp, Judean wilderness
Israel

Shortly after noontime, the women of the clan came to get Yasmin, to bring her to the spacious tent of her maternal grandmother, where the henna night festivities would be held.

All that Yasmin noticed, or cared about, was that the men were gone. Her stepfather and her younger brother had vanished, and would not be seen again by her this day.

Her celebration clothing for the night was already at her grandmother's when the women arrived, singing and laughing, to fetch her and her mother.

Yasmin knew she should be grateful to her grandmother for hosting the celebration. The women from the Hajj's camp would think Yasmin came from a fine, important family. Yet her feelings were ambivalent. Her grandmother was a powerful woman: the mother of the chief. Why hadn't she done more to persuade her oldest son not to let the widow of his brother marry such a man as the Monster?

Undoubtedly, Yasim's grandmother had expressed her disapproval. But couldn't she have tried harder? Did she not love Yasmin and her brother at all?

Then the women and girls were there, and they were laughing and chattering, and remarking about the bride. In her grandmother's tent, she would put on her new dress and have her hair braided and arranged for the celebration that night. The older women smiled and nodded, and talked to her mother about how pretty Yasmin was, how beautiful her long, dark hair.

The girls of the camp crowded around Yasmin. They were smiling, all talking at once. She knew they were each imagining what it would be like when their own time came, their own henna night.

As they prepared to go, playing tambourines and carved flutes, Yasmin turned around, and nearly bumped into Migdim, who had been Yasmin's best friend since birth. They were the same height and coloring, and had often been mistaken for each other. The girls' mothers were also friends and they had been inseparable as far back as they could remember.

Until Yasmin's mother had remarried.

Then Yasmin had begun keeping to herself.

It was too late to turn away. As she found herself face-to-face with Migdim, the two girls studied each other. Even as the maelstrom of activity happened all around them, for that one moment it seemed they were alone.

Neither spoke.

Yasmin gulped. She knew she deserved recriminations from her friend: *Why did you forsake me? Did our friendship mean nothing to you? And now you are leaving as though our years of sisterhood meant nothing.*

Then Migdim reached out and took Yasmin's hand. As they stood connected, the warmth of Migdim's hand said unexpected things: *I remember. I hope you will be happy. I will miss you.*

Good-bye.

Yasmin squeezed Migdim's hand in silent reply: *My heart stays here, with you.*

And what she had never had the occasion to say before: *Good-bye.*

This time both girls knew the good-bye would be forever.

They dropped hands, and Yasmin let herself be led away by the women before she started to cry.

January 26, 2007, 12:30 P.M.
(22 hours, 0 minutes until end of auction)
Alma Beach, Jaffa, Israel

"Try the salmon tartare; it's the best thing on the plate."

The South African jeweler pushed the plate of tapas toward Frank McMillan, who was ripping into fresh homemade bread just brought by the waitress.

The two men sat on the open-air veranda of the Manta Ray restaurant, overlooking the rolling surf of the Mediterranean. It was a nice afternoon, a comfortable sixty-five degrees Fahrenheit, yet both men wore light suit coats. The jeweler was rarely caught without a coat because in his business it always paid to look professional. McMillan, on the other hand, was hiding his Beretta.

Around them, tables were filled with customers grabbing a quick lunch with friends or associates before heading home to celebrate the Sabbath. The crowded tables, crashing surf, and occasional cawing seabird provided a convenient cover for two men who wished not to be overheard.

Frank's Tel Aviv CIA contact had met him at Ben-Gurion Airport an hour earlier and given him the keys to a Jeep that contained all the items he would need for this mission: papers, weapons, maps, and a satellite phone. The agent was then all too happy to direct Frank to the restaurant where he was to meet the jeweler whose brother he would impersonate.

Frank ignored the tapas plate and continued to tear off pieces of the bread as he considered what he had learned so far about his lunch companion. The jeweler, Erich Myndhart, was born in Capetown, South Africa, and had studied the jeweler's trade with his Afrikaner grandfather. With the waning influence of apartheid, he had left his home and moved on in search of greener pastures, but those greener pastures proved elusive. After many years Erich had landed in Tel Aviv, where he created a niche for himself as the man with the ability to obtain rare gems. This was due in no small part to the connections he maintained in Africa, which caused many Israeli jewelers to seek him out when they required rare gems for their creations. And, on occasion, Erich himself would use his not so inconsiderable skills to create a unique piece of his own design.

"Few people here know my family, so a brother operating on my behalf will not arouse suspicion."

Frank glanced at the South African passport open in his lap. Hans Myndhardt was the name he had been given. Looking back up at Erich, he noted enough similarity in the width of his jaw, the eyes, the hair, that he supposed they could pass as kin.

He listened closely to the other man, focusing on the accent. Frank assumed the Bedouin weren't sophisticated enough to recognize a "Cape Dutch" accent.

If I affect a British accent with a few German words thrown in, the Bedouin shouldn't be any the wiser.

Frank had once impersonated a blood diamond trader, in a much more dangerous and challenging setting. . . . This should be a snap.

"Have you dealt with this tribe before? How is it they chose you over all these local artisans?"

"Their leader, al-Asim, likes rare things. He has many wives, and loves to lavish fine jewelry upon them. I can obtain gems no one else can find and have made several special pieces for him. Bracelets. Pendants. Simple things. But this time, it's different. Al-Asim seems to want something grander. He is welcoming a new young bride, and I sense a greater desire to please her than I have seen before."

Frank listened, in silence. Finally, "So, what has the CIA bought from you? What will I bring that may capture her heart?"

"Ah, this is something very special!" The jeweler's eyes glowed as he pulled a flat hinged leather case from inside his jacket. He opened it slowly, dramatically, revealing a silver-colored pendant with two large diamonds, below which hung a deep blue five-sided stone.

"What is it?" asked Frank. He was never impressed by jewelry, but since this was the man's livelihood, he didn't want to seem uninterested.

"It's tanzanite. Very rare. So named because it is found only in Tanzania. The chain is platinum, and the two diamonds are, well, perfect.

"This necklace was my pride and joy, created for a husband wishing to win back the affections of a wife on whom he had cheated. Alas, it seems she was not disposed to forgive him. She did not like the deep blue of the stone, felt it would make her own blue eyes look washed-out. At least, that was her excuse. Sadly, he returned it."

Frank McMillan held out one hand to take the jewel case from his companion, who grudgingly handed it over. Without a second glance at the beautiful pendant in his possession, he flipped the case shut and slipped it into his own jacket pocket.

Myndhart looked almost hurt as he noted the agent's disrespect for the piece.

"You will need to show a passion for gems if you are to convince them you are a jeweler," he scolded.

"Oh I have a passion for gems. Just not these."

Ruby, carnelian, turquoise, lapis, jade, mother-of-pearl. Only then did his eyes glow.

January 26, 2007, 1:23 P.M.
(21 hours, 7 minutes until end of auction)
Judean wilderness west of the Dead Sea
Israel

"You're here!" called a young girl, running toward Jaime's companion. The woman stooped to catch the girls in her arms in an embrace of reunion.

"May I present Rabi and Safia—two of my best students when I taught them, two years ago. How you've grown! Girls, this is my cousin Jami. Her brother is Ahmet. I believe he's already here."

The girls both nodded solemnly, then went back to excited chatter, filling in their former teacher on the details of the wedding and their lives.

Jaime breathed deeply and looked around. Something inside her stirred, responding to being in the Judean hills, with their timeless landscape carved of sand. The fact that she was wearing Bedouin clothing—a beautiful hand-embroidered tunic, soft pants, and a Bedouin-style burqa, which covered the top of her head and the bottom half of her face and was decorated with beads and coins—led her to feel as though she could have been here a hundred years ago, or two. Jaime also carried a special *herga,* which was a wedding shawl, decorated with beads and sequins, edged with multi-colored pompoms. The desert exploded with color when there was a wedding.

Jaime's flight from Paris to Tel Aviv had been uneventful. Since it was a private plane, she'd even managed to get a little sleep. She'd been met by a guide in Tel Aviv and taken to a safe house, where she'd met her current traveling companion, a woman named Johanna Skilling. All former residents of Eden were expected to be agents of change in the world. Some of them, while not being highly trained Operatives, acted as support staff as they were needed—flying planes, piloting boats, introducing Operatives into closed societies such as the Bedouin. That was Johanna's current task with Jaime.

There had been a range of colorful but modest Bedouin clothes from which Jaime could choose. She'd been happy to take the first galabia that fit, as well as sandals, a selection of dangling bracelets, and some half-moon earrings.

Johanna, although raised in the United States, was gardener support staff who specialized in this section of the world. At five foot four she was three inches shorter than Jaime, with auburn hair and green eyes. She was quick, bright, and compassionate, and apparently had entrée into several hard-to-breach groups. She'd spent two years teaching early elementary school for Bedouin girls, including those of the tribe where the box was being sold. Johanna explained that this tribe was one of the very last that was still semi-nomadic, which meant the children boarded at the schools when they attended.

Johanna told her that "Jami"—a version of her name spelled only slightly differently—was an acceptable female Bedouin name. She'd done Jaime's hair in a braided bun that denoted she was a married—albeit widowed—woman.

And they'd met Johanna's male "cousin"—Jaime's second guide—whose mission name was Alim. Together they climbed into a white flatbed truck. It would cause far more consternation than it was worth if the two women had turned up at the Bedouin camp unescorted, driving themselves. The truck had a bench seat, which, thankfully, had enough room for three. Although she'd managed to hide it from Johanna, Jaime's back was still extremely sore. She was more than grateful that Johanna was willing to ride in the middle.

The asphalt ribbon that wound through the desert seemed like an odd umbilical cord, attaching the desert nomads to culture, whether they wanted to be born into the twenty-first century or not.

It was hard to tell how big the camp normally was. Its population had swelled exponentially for the wedding. The "big tent," which would be the purview of the Hajj, the men, and the elders, was long and rectangular; the goat-hair tenting seemed bright beige in the dazzling sun. Other families' tents, with small pens for goats, dotted the landscape. A white tent sat off by itself: what those in the West might call the honeymoon tent—soon to be occupied only by the bride and groom.

The succulent aromas of cooking were pervasive. Dill and tarragon were the first herbs Jaime could identify.

"You must have coffee!" the little girl identified as Rabi said, pulling on Johanna's hand.

Jaime had been warned that cardamom coffee and mint tea—and lots of it—were the traditional way of welcoming guests. The Bedouin were known for their hospitality. Once a guest arrived, the person was honored and under Bedouin protection, not only for the length of their stay but also for three days after they'd left. The flip side was also true: if anyone hurt a tribe member or guest, the Bedouin's revenge was known to be ruthless.

"We will feast also!" young Rabi continued. "There is mutton, and lamb, and goat—miles and miles of food!" She was a short girl, with a wide face and a grin that currently sported several missing teeth.

"I guess we'd best come along, then," said Johanna. The women followed behind her, Johanna greeting other women she passed along the way.

"He must go in to join the men's feast," Rabi whispered to Johanna, pointing at Alim as they neared the big tent. One flap was fastened open to the *ma'gad*—the men's sitting place—so that the young men could enter easily with the platters of food. Alim gave Rabi a small bow followed by a smile, then entered the tent, bowing his greetings to the others already gathered. Multiple calls of welcome urged him inside.

Jaime knew she shouldn't even glance inside the tent, but as Alim moved from the doorway she could see about half the men who sat on the long cushions surrounding the communal serving dishes in the center. One dish had obviously just been brought in: it was heaped with steaming portions of lamb and grape leaves, with chickpeas prepared into something like a ragout.

Each man had a small plate in front of him, from which he would eat—only from the part of the plate closest to him, and only with three fingers of his right hand. Jaime was fascinated observing these customs that, until now, she'd only studied. So much so that there was a delayed moment of shock when she realized that one of the men talking, laughing, and eating . . . was Yani.

The kaffiyeh on his head was white with an intricate black design; the double *'agal*-rope surrounding it, which signified manhood and the bearing of responsibility, was also black. He was talking in fluent Arabic, and she knew the accent he used would be exactly that of this local tribe. He looked very much like he had when she'd first met him in the ruins of Ur, in Iraq. Only then his kaffiyeh had been white and red.

There was a catch in her chest as she recognized him, as if someone had hit her with a small blade that sliced easily through all her defenses and lodged steel in her heart.

He hadn't seen her. Even if he'd noticed that two women had walked past, half her face was veiled.

"Come in; come in—*'Ahlan wa Sahlan!*" was the excited greeting as Jaime and Johanna entered the *maharama,* the place of women, the section of the large tent divided off from the men by a *ma'nad,* a colorful woven rug, this one in reds and blues.

Jaime cleared her mind. She was here because of the box. TC2 had explained that their first plan was simply to be the high bidder in the auction. A gardener in England, one positioned as a purchaser of fine art, was bidding. But, given the value of the box and the notoriety of those who were after it, clearly it was best to have people in place at the scene. If Frank McMillan knew who currently owned it and where they were, certainly others did as well.

Then the cup was in Jaime's hand, and the hot, bitter coffee was in her cup, and she called on what Arabic she knew to pay attention to the strains of conversation she could hear, hoping more than anything to become another anonymous, welcome member of the celebratory group.

January 26, 2007, 1:30 P.M.
(21 hours, 0 minutes until end of auction)
Judean wilderness west of the Dead Sea
Israel

Abihu el-Musaq sat quietly as the flurry of wedding revelry swirled around him. He had wrapped his red and white kaffiyeh around his face in such a way that his unique facial features were, for the most part, obscured and he could observe the other men with few of the curious glances he often experienced in public.

These barbarians know nothing of music. El-Musaq found the incessant noise from the *rababa* guitar an annoyance, especially when accompanied by the meaningless whiny chanting the Bedouin called singing.

And what did they have against chairs? The body was not meant to sit on the floor like this, at least not anymore. *We have evolved beyond this. We have tools, so make a stool or a table!*

Did my mother truly live this way as a child? This is such a hard life. But the people do seem relatively happy. At least they enjoy a good party.

Young men brought in extra helpings of *mensef,* and those who were not intent on smoking a water pipe reached in to grab more of the meal from the plate. All of the talk, the music, the smoke, could make a person's head spin. But el-Musaq was very focused. He had been intent on watching the

Hajj ever since arriving with his mother late in the morning in a beat-up old Ford Falcon and being welcomed to the celebration as a distant cousin.

For a man preparing to marry a pretty young bride, the Hajj seemed rather subdued. He did not laugh. He did not boast. He did not play the role of the magnanimous host with a tent full of guests.

He seemed, yes, distracted.

Some women passed by the open tent flap, and a young man entered to a great call of greetings.

Everyone except the Hajj was treating this as a normal wedding, a time of celebration. Did the Hajj suspect that el-Musaq was already among them? Did he suspect how much danger his own actions had brought into the camp?

It won't be long now, my friend. It shall come to the ending I desire—or to the ending you fear most.

January 26, 2007, 3:03 P.M.
(19 hours, 27 minutes until end of auction)
Judean wilderness west of the Dead Sea
Israel

Just when it seemed to Jaime that the feasting would never end, Johanna leaned over to the woman sitting next to her and said, "Do you think, since it is such a celebration, that the Hajj will display the box?"

The woman, who had been laughing moments before, was suddenly sober. She said, "I hope he will display it among the family. I'm sorry to say he's never shown it to anyone from another clan. But it is the box that has brought us so much good fortune. The box that has kept us free when all around us tribes are herded into shantytowns," she said. "But the men say the Hajj has spoken of selling it." She was quiet. "We choose to believe that's not true. He would not do such a thing!"

"So we might be able to see it? The children have talked about it in such glowing terms when they were in school."

"You never know. Perhaps the Hajj will bring out the box tomorrow, since it is his own wedding!"

Jaime looked around the tent to see if anyone registered anything more than normal interest in the conversation.

"What other kind of good fortune has it brought?" Johanna quietly asked the two girls who had been her pupils.

"It made us rich," Rabi said, as if by rote.

But it was Safia's eyes that shone. "It brought us horses," she whispered. A smile crept across her face and she looked down, as if she'd shown more emotion than she ought.

January 26, 2007, 5:25 P.M.
(17 hours, 5 minutes until end of auction)
Judean wilderness west of the Dead Sea
Israel

Will I ever be rid of this smell of goat?

Frank McMillan sat on a goat-hair mat, having waded through a sea of goats to enter this tent, and was now reaching into the community food pot to retrieve a helping of fresh goat boiled in goat yogurt.

Yum. I can't wait to see what's for dessert!

Well, at least their hands were probably clean. That was the tradition, wasn't it? But not being willing to take any chances, Frank had brought medicine to make sure the food and drink did not make him sick.

McMillan had driven his Jeep over many kilometers of dusty, desolate road to reach the Bedouin camp. Barren, rocky plateaus jutted up from the soil, and he wondered if the moon could be any less inviting.

He was, however, warmly welcomed by the Hajj and his kin when he pulled into the camp. "Mr. Hans Myndhart" was invited to join the men for dinner, and promised a private meeting with their leader following the meal.

These people think they live like kings. . . . Compared to some other Bedouin tribes, maybe they do. The men around him seemed to be boasting, telling great fish tales about brave conquests and slick deals.

McMillan could not understand most of what they were saying, but the man next to him, tall, with dark, curly hair flowing
beneath a black and white kaffiyeh, was translating for him into
passable English.

What would be the fate of the tribe now that they were to sell
the box? This seemed to be the main topic of discussion. One
old man made a sign against the evil djinn. Another called the
old man superstitious, claiming the income from the sale would
help the tribe to fight off their enemies.

"I have heard of this jeweled box that brings the tribe such
good fortune." Frank leaned toward the man who had been so
helpful in translating for him. "As a jeweler, I am naturally curious. Do you suppose I can see it?"

The man stared intently at him, turned his head slightly,
and said, "Perhaps, if Allah smiles upon you."

Feeling a hand upon his shoulder, Frank looked up to find
the Hajj standing above him, beckoning for him to follow. He
stood and pushed his way between two colorful hanging rugs
into a private meeting place. It looked to be the Hajj's own
sleep quarters. By Bedouin standards it was lavish, boasting a
number of plush rugs, even a small dresser and a desk with
chair.

The Bedouin leader lowered himself to the floor and sat
cross-legged on a thick blue mat. Frank sat down facing him.

"Mr. Myndhart. You are the third jeweler to arrive and
show me your wares. The others have produced some fantastic
pieces. Yours will have to excel to be chosen."

Thinking of his visit with Erich Myndhart, Frank put on an
air of great pride as he slowly removed the jewel box and
opened it dramatically before al-Asim.

"Imagine this around your lovely young bride's neck. . . ."

Frank watched as a look of surprise and great longing
passed across the other man's face; then the look was quickly
wiped away as the Bedouin attempted to affect a bored "been
there, seen that" expression.

"Well, it might be acceptable, but it will be hard for this
trinket to surpass the others I have already seen."

McMillan was certain the man had wanted it, badly, and

was now playing coy in order to bring the price down. Frank would have to play along and work the angles until he knew how to get his hands on the box.

"Certainly this rare blue tanzanite could not be matched by any of my competitors?"

"I will give your bauble all the consideration it is due and then let you know my decision by tomorrow. You are staying for the wedding, I hope?"

Frank stood to leave as the Hajj, obviously finished with this audience, dismissed him with a wave of the hand.

"I wouldn't miss it."

January 26, 2007, 7:14 P.M.
(15 hours, 16 minutes until end of auction)
Judean wilderness west of the Dead Sea
Israel

Safia sat among the laughing, clapping women and tried to join in the song.

"Who shall be the favored one today?" the lead singer asked. "Is it the skinny one?"

"No, no! It is not the skinny one!" the other women laughed.

The singer pulled a thin cousin of the bride to her feet. The girl blushed but sang, "No! I am not the favored one today!"

"Is it the old one?" the song continued. The singer chose from the crowd a grandmother, then an ample woman to pose the question to before she came to the verse: "Who shall be the favored one today? Is it the little girl?"

As she asked that question, she pulled Safia to her feet.

Laughing and clapping, the women all cried, "No, no, it is not the little girl!"

Safia knew she was supposed to sing, but every word burned as it crept out of her throat: "No! I am not the favored one today!"

She hoped the others did not see her scowl as she sunk back to the ground. She was not a little girl!

She had a new dress; she had even worn a kerchief. Why were they making fun of her?

Everyone else seemed to have thrown care to the wind. Everyone else seemed to have forgotten the precarious position they were in—that all Israeli Bedouin were in. But Safia's talks with Tarif had a sobering effect on her. All of this—their home, their way of life—could be about to change. The Hajj himself was willing to let things change, to sell the box. Why?

Safia did not ask much of life. She wanted nothing more than for Tarif to be the next sheikh. He would be a fine leader; surely everyone could see it. He was from a good family, a family that had produced many leaders. He could trace his ancestors back to princes and holy men. He was not the oldest son, but then, neither was the Hajj.

How could Tarif himself be challenging the old ways? He wanted to build a town of buildings that looked like flowing tents. Buildings that *looked like* tents. Fakes.

Tarif wanted her to stay in school. What was he thinking? She didn't need school to be first wife. The women who were allowed to demonstrate power were the ones with powerful husbands. And powerful men didn't marry girls who bought into Western ideals—such as mixed classes of boy and girls—once the girls were of marriageable age.

Now the women were clapping as the singer asked, "Who shall be the favored one today? Is it the fair one?"

"Yes, yes!" the women replied. "It is the fair one!"

The singer took the hands of the bride and brought her to her feet. Her hands were covered with intricate geometric designs, painstakingly painted on by the women who were closest relatives to the bride, as well as others who were known to be the best henna artists.

The bride, Yasmin, stood up. She wasn't smiling. She seemed like this was all her due, like she was barely willing to grace their clan by marrying their Hajj. She seemed like a haughty, spoiled girl. Everyone could see she was after the Hajj's money, nothing else. Was the Hajj blind, foolish, or merely overcome by desire? The men were never supposed to be overcome by desire. It was not *hasham*.

Somehow the other women were dancing and celebrating like they didn't mind, like this was any ordinary wedding. So why was it bothering Safia so much? She couldn't explain it to herself. Yes, this arrogant girl would soon be living with their clan, but she and Safia would seldom cross paths.

And then the terrible, uncomfortable knowledge came: Safia was jealous. Not of this conceited girl marrying the ancient, overweight Hajj. But of this girl marrying the sheikh of the big tent, having such a huge bride-price, having a henna night and a wedding with days and days of feasting. What if all of this went away before Safia's own wedding? She wanted it so badly. She wanted to be "the fair one," the one everyone crowded around, painted, sang to. She wanted it to be her.

It had not yet been officially explained to her by the women about what happened in your husband's tent during the wedding, with all the men present. Not officially explained, but she had certainly gotten the gist of it from the whispers of the girls. How three of your closest female relatives—married female relatives—brought you into the tent. You were supposed to act frightened and unwilling. Everyone was there except your bridegroom and his father. The bridegroom would be the last to enter. (His father would not come; it was thought to be too embarrassing for the bridegroom to have his father present.)

Your bridegroom would come in, and the women who had come with you would hold you down. You were supposed to struggle and object, to show your father had raised you with modesty. Then your bridegroom came to you with the cloth of honor. He would come and put his hand up under your dress, up inside your female part. He would twist hard. If you had honor, there would be blood. The cloth would be shown to the men, then taken outside and shown to the women.

Then the bride would be a wife, and the celebration would move on to a new level.

The girls said it hurt when the groom did that. They said the good thing about becoming a second or third wife was that the groom would know what to do and where and how to do it. They said sometimes the young grooms were too frightened or too shy to do it right.

The idea of anyone doing that to her, in front of all the men, was enough to make Safia queasy. Anyone but Tarif, that is. When she thought of Tarif doing it, she knew he would be noble and kind—and quick. She would not mind. She would be embarrassed, but she would also be proud. It would be something they had gone through together.

What would the future bring? What would happen when it was her time to be married? She would do what she could to bring the best events to pass. But in the end, it was *gismih o naseeb*.

Fate and destiny.

It was in God's hands.

But wasn't it God who had given her hands of her own?

January 26, 2007, 8:14 P.M.
(14 hours, 16 minutes until end of auction)
Judean wilderness west of the Dead Sea
Israel

It had been years since McMillan had worked as a mere CIA operative, but time had not dulled his senses, nor had he lost his touch at stealth. He had dared to venture into the Hajj's private quarters, daring to search the man's room even as he and his guests partied only ten feet away.

There were very few places to hide anything, regardless of size, and nowhere big enough for the Eden box.

I doubt it's here.

McMillan held a tiny penlight in his teeth to keep his hands free. He had always enjoyed searching through other people's things, learning the dirty little secrets they thought were hidden from the rest of the world.

Maybe that was why he never kept a girlfriend very long. Oh, not because they ever caught him snooping. He was too good for that! After one date with a woman he knew the contents of her diary and whether she carried a spare condom in her purse. And she was never the wiser.

No, the problem was he so quickly learned everything there was to know about his conquests that he became bored. No spice. No surprises. So move on.

But Richards . . . that woman was a challenge. Every time

he thought he had her figured out, *wham,* something new. How the hell had she been equipped to drop a tail, as she had in Tallil? How had she known how to escape from handcuffs in an ancient brick tower that was three stories tall?

I wonder what she's doing right now? He imagined her topless, sponging off the crusted blood on her back, and cringing as the soapy water slid across the wounds. What a shame he wasn't there to help her. He chuckled silently.

Frank opened the top desk drawer, and his light fell upon two small folders that looked interesting. He picked up the first one so he could hold it close enough to the light to read the small print inside.

It was an airline ticket. *Omar al-Asim, destination, San Francisco.*

He thumbed through the ticket. *No return flight.*

He reached down to pick up the second folder, also a ticket.

Yasmin al-Asim. Again, San Francisco, one-way.

This is no honeymoon trip.

Interesting. The man planned to leave the tribe. Probably run off with the money from the box and start a new life. Did he really think he could leave them like that without consequences? There was no talk of this among the men, so they did not suspect. At least not yet.

Frank scanned his penlight one more time across the room as he pondered the various advantages of keeping or revealing the Hajj's plan. Nothing more to search, it was time to move on.

For a brief moment Frank allowed the circle of his light to illuminate the Hajj's bed. As he did, he noticed a movement in the back of the tent—a secret opening. He decided to leave that way, which should take him out to the privacy of the back of the tent. Perhaps this was the Hajj's private way to leave and relieve himself in the middle of the night.

Frank found the place where the flaps overlapped, and crouched down to step outside through them. As he stood up in the chilly night air, he found that someone else was standing there in the dark.

Frank flicked his penlight up, illuminating the livid form of the Hajj. The portly man had obviously been standing there, quietly in the dark, for the length of Frank's search.

January 26, 2007, 8:14 P.M.
(14 hours, 16 minutes until end of auction)
Judean wilderness west of the Dead Sea
Israel

Jaime's primary task during the celebrations was to discover which women were more open to talking to her, an *ajnebiya*, an outsider—to whom she could go if she needed further information, or to follow up on something.

Johanna and Alim had left shortly after the first feast. Unlike Operatives, they were expressly not to be on hand should something go wrong. Should the situation blow up, they needed to be apart from any controversy, removed from suspicion, so they could continue to operate in the region.

Jaime had ridden over to the bride's camp in the back of a white Toyota pickup, and that bumpy ride in itself had engendered tentative smiles shared with several of her cobumpees. Now, as the celebrating progressed, she was trying her best to join in the songs and celebration, but she was becoming increasingly distracted by the pain of her back. Her galabia was as loose as she'd dared wear, but the material still rubbed against her wounds when she moved.

She finally worked her way to a back row of women, sitting along the tent walls. They were women who were too old to dance or needed to sit things out for one reason or another. Jaime gave a small smile and sat down to join those from the

Hajj's camp. She put her hand to her head to demonstrate she didn't feel well—had a headache.

The women nodded. She realized as she sat among them that these were the women who watched from the sidelines—who likely had a greater view of the whole picture than those in the midst of the dance. They had become momentarily quiet when she sat down, but after a few minutes one of them brought up the bride-price and they all began to chat again.

Jaime wondered who all these women were—was one the Hajj's mother? The bride's great-grandmother? Jaime tried to memorize their faces as she sat, thinking she'd give her own kingdom for anything that would bring pain relief. Even though Yani was indeed here, in the middle of this assignment, he was with the men. He might as well be a thousand miles away.

Jaime knew then that it had been a risk—a stupid risk—to come here without first getting medical attention. She didn't know how she was going to stand the ride back to camp in the back of the pickup.

She didn't know how she was going to make it through the night.

January 26, 2007, 8:22 P.M.
(14 hours, 8 minutes until end of auction)
Judean wilderness west of the Dead Sea
Israel

"Hajj al-Asim, I'm afraid I have not been totally honest with you."

Frank McMillan knew the importance of taking control of the conversation and the situation. The sheikh had caught Frank searching his private quarters—a very serious offense. Frank had to talk fast, and talk convincingly. One call out from the Hajj, and Frank would be hopelessly outnumbered—gun or no gun.

The face of the Bedouin leader darkened. "I have offered you the hospitality of my tent, and now you say you have robbed and deceived me?"

"No, on my honor as a man, I have not stolen anything. Please forgive me. I misrepresented myself, but only in order to gain audience with you. No harm was intended. I am not a jeweler. I am an agent with the American CIA."

Frank showed his credentials to the perplexed Bedouin.

"I want to make a bid on the box."

Hajj was no longer perplexed; he looked angry.

"Then use the same means as all the other bidders. It gives you no right to trespass, no right to steal my privacy!"

The fact that the Hajj didn't immediately call for help led

Frank to believe that something else was going on here—something the Hajj wasn't willing to explain to the rest of his family, let alone the rest of the tribe.

"I prefer face-to-face negotiations," Frank said. "I can offer you more money than the highest bidder on eBay. And, one other thing they will not give you. An escape."

The Hajj's answer was careful. Calculated. "I need no escape. I sell the box for the good of the tribe."

"We both know that's not true. You plan to take off with the money and your new bride and never come back."

"How dare you!"

"You needn't worry. I'm not going to tell anyone. I don't care what you do to these people. In fact, I'll even help you, in return for the box. I can offer you a new identity, which will enable you to hide from your tribe and the black-market dealers. And had you thought this through? You have airline tickets, perhaps, but do you have passports? Visas? Do you think a man such as yourself can just waltz into the United States without papers? And with an underage bride? Here again, I can help you in a way no one else will be able to."

Once again, McMillan saw the look of longing, the same longing as when Hajj had viewed the beautiful tanzanite necklace. Then again, as if a door shut, it was gone.

What's holding him back? He should jump at this offer. Unless . . .

"The eBay deal," said the sheikh, almost frantic. "I'm afraid I'll be killed if I do not go through with it."

Frank snorted. "And will your clan not hunt you down as well? Be safe from all of them, and live like a king, with your new young bride. You don't believe I can do this? Here. As a token of my good intent—and of my capabilities—let me present you with the rare necklace I showed you earlier."

Frank handed the hinged box to the old man. The Hajj opened it, and was aghast to see it actually contained the precious gems.

"All you need to do is sell me the box. Of course, I will have to see it to verify you have the real thing."

Now the look of grave concern, followed by hesitation, with that longing mixed in once again.

Why should it bother him that I will need to see the box? Unless . . . he doesn't have it!

Finally, the pieces all fit. Frank understood the fear and concern the man was trying unsuccessfully to hide. He no longer had the box, and desperately needed it for all his dreams to be fulfilled.

Well, this certainly was a setback, but the game was still afoot. The prize could not have gone far, and this man was still the key.

Frank reached over and put his hand on the man's shoulder, saying quietly and confidently, "I won't press you for an answer right now, but promise to think about it, all right?"

The Hajj silently nodded, totally dumbfounded at all he had heard.

Frank McMillan turned back toward the camp, confident his prey had no idea Frank had just placed a tracking device in the collar of his robe.

January 26, 2007, 8:22 P.M.
(14 hours, 8 minutes until end of auction)
Judean wilderness west of the Dead Sea
Israel

Yasmin, the bride-to-be, sat numbly and watched the festivities going on all around her. How could it be that the focus of all this was her? How could it be that she would be leaving her mother's tent forever, tomorrow?

Yasmin knew that it was extremely unlikely, given the circumstances of her life, that things would have a happy ending. She herself had chosen to force the issue, and the timing, just because she could not continue the life she was living. She'd rather die.

And she might.

She might die tomorrow.

Yasmin had promised her mother she would try to be happy, or at least act happy, at her henna night, but she was too weary. No matter what, she was leaving her mother and her brother behind with the Monster. At least Yasmin's mother had spoken up. Perhaps she would go through with her threat.

Yasmin didn't know, but she was almost glad there was something. Was there a way she could save her mother in the future? Would she now have power, as wife of the Hajj, to see that the situation stopped?

Was the Hajj really trying to help her? Had he understood what she'd whispered to him during their meeting? She had decided to tell him then, because if she hadn't, if the un-stained cloth had been a surprise, not even the Hajj could have saved her from the wrath of her own clan.

But she had said it, and it seemed he had heard. He had brought a bride-price, anyway. It seemed they would be married tomorrow.

Still, there was so much that could go wrong. Either he could have misunderstood her situation or she could have mis-understood his intentions. Or someone else could find out the truth of her situation. Perhaps the Monster himself would re-veal her shame.

Yasmin herself put her odds at fifty-fifty of living through the next day.

Even if she did, she would be living away from her family, married to a man four times her age. Her husband would have a right to do with her as he wished. There was no way of knowing what kind of rights he would wish.

Maybe it would be better if she could just die.

How many girls had a grand celebration the night before their shame was revealed? How many girls were sung to and painted with henna the day before their death?

"She is so shy," she heard her mother whisper to a cousin, even though no one had commented in her mother's hearing about how undemonstrative Yasmin was being.

She didn't mean to be. But half of her was bemused by the fuss.

Half of her felt as though she were already dead.

January 26, 2007, 9:22 P.M.
(13 hours, 8 minutes until end of auction)
Judean wilderness west of the Dead Sea
Israel

The Hajj sat among the male friends and relatives who had gathered to celebrate his wedding. He knew them, knew the hard times many of them were facing, knew the problems they had at home, the land disputes, the ambivalence they had about serving in the Israeli Army—which they all did when called—about the new culture shown to them on televisions and radio, about the current state of Islam, which they had always conformed to their own Bedouin beliefs, but it was harder and harder to be allowed to do so.

When had life become so complicated?

He was tired of it.

When he'd found the box those fifty long years ago, he'd thought it would make everything so easy. Instead, it had caused nothing but headaches.

Which was why he'd planned to sell it, take the money, and move away with his new wife.

Now even that simple plan had become so complicated as to seem impossible.

As the CIA man had reminded him, it would be nearly impossible for two Muslims from the Middle East to get permanent visas to live in the United States. In a Western country, it would be illegal for him to claim a fifteen-year-old as his wife.

He had read news stories about the Bedouin from the Khawalid tribe in northern Galilee who was now the Israeli consul in the United States. His office was in San Francisco, California. In his naïveté, the Hajj had planned to move to San Francisco, where it seemed a Bedouin couple could buy a place and be welcomed.

He had never planned past that.

What would he do? What would Yasmin do? Would she be thrilled at their new life? Would she enjoy having a television, running water, a washing machine? Would she enjoy exploring and making friends with the other Arab women? Or would she be lonely and alone, so far from her family, her friends, her way of life?

When he had planned it for her, he had seen only the shiny possibilities. He had seen only all the things they would be escaping.

What would they run to? Even if he had the box, and gave it to Frank, and was moved to Los Angeles, what would they do?

Through the open tent flap the Hajj could see the white honeymoon tent in the moonlight. Instead of staying there for the week they would be granted as newlyweds, he had arranged to leave in the middle of the first night. He had arranged a pickup place with a local Israeli driver who made a living ferrying people from town to town.

It would certainly be several days before anyone realized they were gone.

Then—should he survive the fact that he no longer had the box—what would he do?

He looked at the tent again, and sighed. If he could take it all back, not owe the box to a seller on the black market, would he do so? Would he take Yasmin to their honeymoon tent and stay with her? She had as much as told him that someone was taking advantage of her against her will. What did that mean for him? Would she ever come to the point where she would willingly have relations? Would it be possible for her ever to enjoy it?

Or must their relationship remain purely platonic?

If he allowed that, would she be grateful, still consider him her savior, still think well of him?

Would she perhaps be grateful enough that one day she would come to him?

The Hajj had spoken to his distant cousin Ahmet. Ahmet had agreed to talk with the men he knew, those with whom he felt comfortable, about the whereabouts of the box.

It seemed that God had given the box to Omar those many years ago.

Perhaps now all he could do was pray God would bring it back.

Inshallah, the bridegroom prayed. *If God wills.*

January 26, 2007, 10:14 P.M.
(12 hours, 16 minutes until end of auction)
Judean wilderness west of the Dead Sea
Israel

Everything depended on Jaime choosing correctly.

She was aware, at the edges of her fraying consciousness, that the truck had stopped and women who had journeyed back with her from the henna night at the bride's camp were getting out. They must be back at the Hajj's camp.

The endless desert sky lay over her like a shroud as she crept toward the rear of the vehicle. She slid off the back and tried to keep her balance by holding on to the truck while finding the ground with her feet.

In a moment, all the women would have dispersed, the truck would be gone. At that point she would be left alone and ill in the dark until she was discovered by a passerby, at which point she would become the focus of attention.

She did not want that.

The women were still talking and laughing, albeit quietly, as they congealed into knots of twos and threes and disappeared into the night, most heading back to the side of the big tent where the women would sleep.

She had to guess right.

Give me wisdom, was the length of her prayer.

January 26, 2007, 10:25 P.M.
(12 hours, 5 minutes until end of auction)
Judean wilderness west of the Dead Sea
Israel

"Suleiman," whispered Safia into the darkness outside the horse pen.

"Who's there?" came the startled reply.

"Shhh. It's me: Safia. I need you to take a message to Tarif. It's important."

"Safia, it's late! Why are you up? If anyone sees you here—"

"That's why they must not!" she said. And then, not able to keep from being distracted, she said of the horses, "Which one is going as part of the bride-price?"

"Azul," he said of the stallion, and as he did, he could imagine the catch in the girl's throat. But she was being resolute. She didn't want to get Suleiman in trouble, but she needed him.

"Please tell Tarif to get Ahmet. Ahmet's sister is ill. Ask Tarif to please bring him to the cave where the spotted kids were born last spring."

"What if my brother gets into trouble?"

"Your brother can become almost invisible. You know that. I am hoping that he will try. It is Ahmet he should bring."

Suleiman let his head fall backward. He'd almost thought to himself: *This little girl asks for so little, I may as well do her a favor.* But then he remembered that Safia asked for horses and night rides and secrecy. She asked for friendship with boys. She asked for everything. And now she was asking again.

"Please tell Tarif," she pleaded again. "And then the choice is up to him."

"All right, Safia. You should be running this country. You can talk anyone into anything."

"Only if they have a kind heart," she said simply.

She turned to slip away, but then she stopped. "Do you think they'll give Azul a good home?" she asked.

"*Inshallah*—if it pleases God," was all Suleiman could bring himself to reply, as he headed back toward camp.

January 26, 2007, 10:46 P.M.
(11 hours, 44 minutes until end of auction)
Judean wilderness west of the Dead Sea
Israel

Jaime was in a cave hollowed out of a series of hills of sandstone into which the wind and rain had worn a myriad of nooks, pathways, and caves. The one where Safia had brought her had a wide mouth, then narrowed as it abruptly turned a corner into a hidden alcove.

The girl knew her caves.

Jaime had no idea how long she'd been there, fading in and out of consciousness, when she heard Safia whisper, "She's here. She's hurt. And her head is very hot."

"Thank you," came a man's voice in reply, in local dialect. "You've been very kind. I don't want to get you in trouble. You needn't stay."

And those words, the timbre of that voice, were all it took to bring Jaime back to alertness.

It was Yani.

He had come.

He would help her; she was in capable hands. But, more than that, she would see him; for however brief a time, she would be with him again. She hadn't been sure she'd ever see him again in this lifetime.

It wasn't clear to Jaime whether Safia left her post outside the cave or not. Jaime heard Yani coming forward into the cave, following a small lantern beam around the corner.

He was here.

But when Yani actually stalked into the cave hidden in the hillside, it was nothing at all like the scene Jaime had imagined when Frank was whipping her and she turned to Yani in her mind for strength. The irony was strong: she had imagined him coming to her in a secret cave, and now he was doing just that.

When he came into the cave where she was hidden half a mile from the Bedouin camp, there were no soft pillows, no music, no kind goatherd, no fragrance of tuberose.

And Yani was angry as hell.

As he entered her alcove and knelt down beside her, Jaime expelled her breath. For that one moment, she was relieved. Yani was here. She'd be all right.

"What are you doing?" he hissed at her through gritted teeth. "Do you understand that if anyone finds us here, the entire mission is compromised?"

Jaime had never heard him so irate. She opened her eyes and saw him: the sun-bronzed skin, the quick, assessing brown eyes, the thick black hair beneath his kaffiyeh.

"I'm sorry. I was about to pass out. I didn't know what else to do."

"What is it?" he asked. "What's wrong?"

"My back," she said. "Frank McMillan. Kidnapped me. Whipped me. Not good."

Yani put a hand to his head, like this was too much, she was really causing trouble now. "Take off your galabia and let me see." He silently crept back to the mouth of the cave, making sure the coast was clear. Then he came back.

Jaime was sitting up. She tried to pull her Bedouin dress off, but she couldn't manage. She'd fallen back against the side of the cave.

He didn't say anything. He came over, and started with the sleeves, tugging them over her head. As he did, his hand touched her skin and he pulled it back like he'd been burned.

He turned her dress inside out, which put all the coins and tassels inside. Then he laid it down on the floor of the cave.

He didn't have to tell her to lie down. Her head swam when she sat up. There was nothing else she could do.

He held the lantern aloft and inspected her naked back.

"Dear God," he said. "How did a doctor see this and let you go out on assignment?"

"No one saw it, exactly," she managed.

"You didn't show anyone? How could you have done this?" he asked. And again: "This could compromise the whole mission."

Again: "I'm sorry," she whispered.

"It's becoming infected," he said, flinging each word with the slap of an accusation.

As if she weren't shaking with fever. As if she didn't know that already.

He had brought a camel's hair bag with him, and from the bottom of it he withdrew what she recognized to be an Eden medical kit. She usually carried one herself.

Yani didn't use "the tone," the reassuring voice she'd heard from him when he was comforting someone in difficult circumstances. He didn't talk at all. He worked quickly.

First he injected two different medications into her shoulder. Gardener injections no longer involved needles, but she could feel a prickly warmth as the solutions themselves dispersed into her muscle.

Then he brought out some kind of disinfectant and began to clean the stripes on her back. Each one burned with such intensity that she wondered if it didn't hurt more than the original lash.

Jaime wanted to scream with pain, but she knew she couldn't. Finally, she couldn't help moaning, and when she did—when she got too loud—Yani didn't stop, or give her some pain medication, or pat her hand. He reached into his kit and pulled out a roll of bandages.

"Here," he said. And he went back to work.

It took her a minute to figure out he meant her to bite on it, to keep her quiet.

So she did.

* * *

She thought she may have passed out for a while. Her mind was so foggy it was hard to tell. When she came to, she felt him coating the lashes with some kind of cream. She felt much more clearheaded. Perhaps the medication had broken the fever already.

Jaime knew it was very likely, as the auction was ending the next morning, she might not speak to Yani again on this mission. In fact, in the world in which he traveled she might never speak to him again. But they had unfinished business, and as aggravated as he was, he was here now.

"Ten down?" she asked. That was Operative code for the request to take time to discuss non-mission topics.

"No time," he said. He had something clamped in his mouth. She looked over to find it was the roll of bandages, which must have fallen from her mouth. He was tearing them with his teeth and fitting them across her back.

"Oh, for God's sake," she said. She could only take so much of his king-of-all-Operatives attitude. "Then you can frigging listen while *I* talk. And when you're done, you can leave. That way I won't waste any precious seconds of your time."

He didn't answer, but he didn't stop her, either.

"All I wanted to say was . . ." The anger seeped out, and the words got harder to say. "All I wanted to say was I'm sorry. The last time I saw you . . . I'm sorry for the things I said. You have to understand. Well, maybe you don't. But the fact is, I have issues with sudden death." She felt more like herself now, talking to him this way.

"Okay, that's not entirely correct. As a matter of fact, I'm all for sudden death; in fact, that's how I'd like to go. Every time I face my own death, someone seems intent on dragging it out in very unpleasant ways.

"To be more precise, I have issues around sudden *bereavement*. Losing both my parents and my husband has made me a bit skittish in that regard. When we last spoke, I had once again been plunged into a horribly sudden bereavement, which was shared by someone I hold dear. Someone to whom I felt responsible."

"You have issues with sudden bereavement," he said, something obviously still in his mouth. "So you became an Army chaplain." While his words were heavy with irony, they were the first he spoke that weren't spoken in anger.

"Go figure," she said. She had to wait a moment as the pain across her back flared up again and finally settled back down. "What I'm trying to say is, I wasn't at my most rational. So I'm sorry. On reflection, I've come to see that you were right about some things. Most things."

"Is that it? Anything else you need to say?"

He was so infuriating. Keeping himself a step removed, like he was her therapist. She answered, "You could have been a little more understanding, knowing my background like you do. You could have given me a little room, instead of just exiting my life."

"If you recall, *you* quit. And you told me good-bye. It wasn't a tentative conversation. Sit up."

She sat up. He was behind her. "Raise your arms as high as you can."

Jaime tried to raise her arms. She couldn't get very far before the fragile skin on her back began to pull.

"That's fine," he said. He had a roll of wider bandages. "Hold this," he said. He scooted around front, and put the end of the bandage at her mid-chest. She held the end as he began wrapping it around her body, to hold the other bandages in place. He didn't as much as glance at her breasts, or react when he pulled the bandages taut across them. He was all business. Not the merest hint of jollies.

"Tell me what you know about Frank McMillan," Yani said. Obviously, he'd gotten at least some word from TC2 about her previous outing.

"I believe he's on his way here if he's not here already. He's posing as one of the jewelers bringing the Hajj a gift for the bride."

"He is here," Yani said. "Do you know what he knows about the box?"

"He knows it has some connection with Eden. He recognized the Six Sisters."

"That's it? Do you remember anything he asked you about it?"

"I remember everything he asked me about it. He was quite emphatic," she said wryly. "He believes it somehow reveals some important secret. Maybe the location, maybe a code in the gems, maybe a GPS inside, I don't know." Now she was getting testy. "How can we keep the Hajj from selling it to him? Or him from stealing it?"

"The Hajj doesn't have it," Yani said quietly. He'd run out of the wider bandages halfway down her back, but it would have to do.

"He doesn't have it?" Jaime asked.

"He told me he doesn't know who stole it," Yani said. "And, from his nervous state, I'm inclined to believe he's telling the truth."

"So, what does that mean?"

"It means that, unless we can help him find it, it's all going to blow up at some point tomorrow, when the auction ends and no box is produced. Do you need something for the pain?"

The tone in his voice made it sound like a test.

One she was fine with failing.

"Yes. Please."

He took out a small plastic bottle of over-the-counter pain relief pills, and Jaime accepted it gratefully. The ache was still so intense she had no idea how she was going to make it through the night.

"Oh, for pity's sake. Lie down," he said.

She did. He went back to his first-aid kit.

"So, how did Frank kidnap you?" he asked.

That was such a loaded question. And there was the smallest hint of the old Yani as he spoke. Jaime knew he was asking because he was sorry she'd been kidnapped. But he was also asking because she should have known better, should have been able to head Frank off, keep it from happening. If she was a trained Operative worth her salt.

"He . . . ," she started, and her voice broke. "He was working with a partner. An old friend of mine. Someone I trusted."

"Are you talking about Mark Shepard?" As Yani spoke, he gave her a dose of a serious painkiller in her lower back, just above the briefs she'd pulled on in Mark's manor house. Like he couldn't have given it to her when he'd started working on her back twenty minutes earlier, instead of giving her a roll of freaking bandages to bite on?

"If you knew about Shepard, why did you ask?" she said, fighting to keep from revealing to Yani her tears at Mark's profound betrayal.

"Jaime, I don't know what Frank told you. But he wasn't working with Mark Shepard. Shepard was bludgeoned and bound. He's in the hospital with a concussion and internal injuries. He was battered pretty badly, but they think he'll be all right. His security man was killed, though."

Jaime sat up so fast that her bandages pulled tight across her back, but she didn't care. "What?" she said. "The security man was killed? And Mark's in the hospital?" She faced Yani, fully aware that she was staring at him, her mouth agape.

"Oh, dear God, I've got to call him. Right now. What does he think happened to me? Do you have a phone?"

"Shhhh. Jaime. Are you completely insane? You can't call anyone from here. It's way too risky. What are you thinking?"

"But Mark . . . and Derrick . . ."

As awful as the news was, as horrified as she was about Derrick, great buckets of relief were pouring over her.

"He'll be all right? Mark will be all right?"

"He's expected to make a full recovery." Yani quickly replaced the kit in the bottom of his satchel and prepared to leave.

"He wasn't in on it?"

"No. When your effects were picked up, they found a bug on your ski coat—undoubtedly how McMillan got his info. Now. Put your clothes back on. Give me a five-minute headstart. Then go back down to the women's tent with the girl. If anyone asks, you were helping with the girl's goats."

Yani turned back to her at the bend in the cave. "Mark

Shepard is a good man. There's a gardener file on him. He's clean. He is who he says he is."

There was the smallest beat before he added, "He's worthy of you."

And then Yani was gone.

—SATURDAY—

January 27, 2007, 3:48 A.M.
(6 hours, 42 minutes until end of auction)
Judean wilderness west of the Dead Sea
Israel

The Hajj awoke from a violent dream and sat up, panicked, in his bed.

Rashid had come with a knife to taunt him. Had driven the knife into the Hajj's belly and turned it slowly, laughing at the pain, at the grisly death the Hajj was dying.

The Hajj was still gasping for breath, even though he was now awake. The dream had been so real—he was frightened that it was an omen. That today was his day to die.

He heard a noise, felt a scraping of movement, and someone was behind him, arms wrapped around his shoulders, the sharp blade of a real knife at his neck.

"I regret I have no physical wedding gift to give you," said a gravelly voice in the dark, "but I do have a very valuable piece of advice that I offer in its place. Honor the promises you have made, and hand over the jeweled box by the end of the auction, or you will certainly dishonor your family and your tribe."

The Hajj felt the sharp metal of the *shabriya,* as it threatened to slice through the skin of his neck. Somehow this actual threat gave him presence of mind that omens withheld. "If and when I hand it over, it will be the time of my choosing,"

"And if you choose not to hand it over, your life and the lives of those you hold dear will be in grave danger."

"You dare come to my wedding feast and threaten me?"

"I do not waste time on threats. I simply share a fact of life with you. I will have the item by ten-thirty this morning, or another item of equal value is forfeit in its place."

The man, who was dressed all in black, stalked out of the Hajj's private quarters and into the men's tent, where the guests were all asleep. And the Hajj pondered with a chill that he could not identify the man at all. Should he see the man again, he would not know to worry, until it was too late.

January 27, 2007, 10:14 A.M.
(0 hours, 16 minutes until end of auction)
Judean wilderness west of the Dead Sea
Israel

The only physical evidence that the eBay auction was about to end was the extra adrenaline Jaime could feel coursing through her body. What exactly would happen when it did end?

Would the Eden bidders win it?

Would it matter who won it, if the Hajj didn't have it?

How would it all play out? Although some Bedouin towns had electricity, television, and even Internet connections, the desert camp certainly did not. Very few people here even knew there was an auction, or that the Hajj was truly selling the box, let alone when the bidding would be closed.

Jaime had ended up sleeping in a family tent with the girl Safia and her mother. She was grateful to them both. After Yani had tended to her back, she found she was still not thinking clearly. She wasn't sure if it was the infection or the pain medication Yani had given her, but she had needed to collapse somewhere safe. When young Safia saw that Jaime would not be able to make it all the way to the tent where the celebration was occurring, and where the female guests were staying, she led Jaime to her own tent. Safia's mother saw that Jaime was not well and invited her in to sleep.

She felt much better in the early morning when she awoke. The women didn't let Jaime help cook, but the fact that she'd come back over with Safia and her mother had kept there from being questions about her whereabouts during the night.

Jaime also rediscovered the universal truth that if you let someone help you, a connection is developed. Young Safia, with her profusion of black hair and sparkling blue eyes, now seemed to feel protective of Jaime. Safia pointed things out to her, made sure Jaime knew proper protocol for interactions, and treated her as a personal guest.

Jaime appreciated this. As the morning progressed, she casually asked Safia questions about various women, always careful not to get too personal. Jaime sensed Safia had a good take on personalities. Those women Safia dismissed as frivolous Jaime also put at the bottom of her list of people who might know anything relevant about the current mission.

When they were sitting, eating breakfast, Jaime said, "What is the box I heard Johanna ask you about yesterday? Do you think the Hajj will show it to the guests today?"

Safia froze for a moment, then slid back into the guise of answering a simple question. "Surely she told you about the box? It is a jeweled box that has brought us good luck, and has made us so very wealthy, ever since the Hajj found it when he was a boy."

Jaime couldn't help but feel warmly toward the girl. Any outsider would look at the circumstances in which they lived and dispute the idea that this tribe was wealthy at all. The landscape was barren; the tents, small, with no amenities. The desert was completely desolate.

"What is the thing that makes you wealthiest, Safia?" she asked. "What is your tribe's greatest treasure that the box has made possible?"

"Our freedom," she replied simply.

"That is a very great treasure, indeed," Jaime agreed. "Is the box beautiful? Is that why he likes to show it?"

Now Safia was looking away, almost nervously, as she spoke. "The box is very beautiful. I don't know what will happen to us when it is gone. Perhaps our luck will go to another tribe. But no, I don't believe the Hajj will show it today."

"Why?"

"I don't think he can," was her simple answer.

This girl was smart as a whip, and she noticed things. Jaime was grateful that she'd made a good call last night when she'd asked Safia for help.

Help in fetching Yani, whose final words were, "He's worthy of you."

About Mark.

Casually handing her off to another man.

Jaime knew those words would weigh on her until the day she died.

At least it meant Yani thought highly enough of her that someone would need to be "worthy" to be with her. Did Yani think he got points if his final kiss-off was polite on the surface?

As much as she loved Mark, she yearned for Yani. But apparently, during the last year, during which Jaime had come to know that no matter what she did, Yani was lodged inside her, the focus of her existence, he had spent his time distancing himself from her. Withdrawing completely. Jaime thought she had gotten good at reading him, and she had seen nothing there to signal there'd ever been any feelings on his side at all. No second thoughts. No wistfulness. No remorse.

To him, she was now an interesting psychological study at best; an irritatingly inept third Operative on the current critical, at worst.

The entirety of her emotional life had crashed and burned, and she had no time to deal with it.

A great commotion stirred outside the tent. All the women stopped whatever work they were doing, and the guests got to their feet.

"It's the bride," Safia said. "She's here!"

Jaime knew that in the old days the bride would arrive from her own clan on a camel, in a procession of her kinsmen, who would be singing and dancing.

Today, instead, she arrived in the backseat of the first of a parade of pickup trucks that were honking their way into camp.

Jaime followed Safia outside to stand with the women as they watched the vehicles come to a stop.

The men unloaded from the trucks. Only then did the music start up again. In the midst of the jubilation, the other women in the girl's procession stepped out and helped her down.

It was hard to tell anything about her, except that her galabia was well jeweled and that she was heavily veiled.

The women of the Hajj's clan all stayed in a group, not moving from their vantage point outside the women's tent. The men who had come in the bridal procession went into the big tent first, to join the men of the Hajj's clan.

Only after that did the three women who had come with the bride—who were also heavily veiled—take her arms and lead her toward the tent.

"She's about to become a wife," whispered Safia.

January 27, 2007, 10:27 A.M.
(0 hours, 3 minutes until end of auction)
Judean wilderness west of the Dead Sea
Israel

Three minutes until the auction ended.

The Hajj looked at his watch, then closed his eyes and muttered a prayer. He had heard the threat in el-Musaq's voice in his tent the night before. He knew it was serious.

But what could the man do here, in front of the whole clan?

The Bedouin were ruthless in revenge.

Surely the man was not that stupid?

Two minutes.

Maybe it wouldn't happen today. Or perhaps, when he least expected it, the Hajj's throat would be slit. No one would know who. No one would know why.

One minute.

It was time for him to go into the tent. What would this day hold? How had he ever thought he'd be on his way to San Francisco?

Was he about to be married? Or was he about to die?

Or both?

Ten seconds remaining, according to his watch.

Nine. Eight. Seven. Six. Five.

What had he done?

Four. Three. Two. One. . . .

It was done.

The box belonged to someone else.

The Hajj turned and walked into the tent.

January 27, 2007, 10:33 A.M.
(3 minutes since end of auction)
Judean wilderness west of the Dead Sea
Israel

Yasmin didn't feel like a bride. She felt like a sheep being led to the slaughter.

She knew she should be nervous. She knew she needed to act frightened and unwilling. But the truth was, she felt nothing.

She had no control over the events of this day.

She had no control over whether she lived or died.

The women had led Yasmin forward, brought her to the mats, and made her lie down. She was only peripherally aware of the gathered men around her—or when her new husband, Omar, the Hajj, came in, except that the women's hold on her shoulders became tighter.

The Hajj came over. She was sure he held a white cloth, but she didn't look. His hand went up under her robes, and she felt him brush against her thigh. But he didn't go anywhere near her woman's place. He made a sigh, like a release of held breath, which she took as her cue to also cry out and move slightly.

And then his hand was gone from her robes, and "ahhhs" of appreciation were heard from the men around her. One of the women took the cloth. Yasmin looked up in time to see it had a bright red stain on it.

Then the women took it outside, and the men turned away from her, ready to celebrate.

She could imagine the jubilation among the women waiting outside when the cloth of honor—the one that her new husband had obviously prepared in advance—was shown.

But then something happened that she did not expect.

The sound of gunfire came from outside.

At first Yasmin thought it came from some of the Hajj's men, firing their guns in high spirits.

But it was clear from the looks on the faces of the men inside the tent that this was not supposed to happen. This was no one in their clan.

One of the men shouted and ran for the door. Pandemonium ensued, as the rest of them followed him outside.

There were more gunshots, more shouting.

One of the women grabbed her by the shoulder and helped her to her feet. She was led to the other side of the tent, through to the women's side—although no women were there, they were all outside. The heavily veiled woman led her outside, on the side away from all the pandemonium. She had an arm around Yasmin's shoulders, and seemed determined to get her safely out of the way.

It was then that Yasmin looked up. The woman was not her mother, or her aunt, or anyone she knew.

"Where are we going?" the frightened girl asked.

"Quiet," was the terse reply. "It's your only hope to stay alive."

January 27, 2007, 10:48 A.M.
(18 minutes since end of auction)
Judean wilderness west of the Dead Sea
Israel

As all the men rushed from the tent, a motor gunned to life, and a green truck came pulling around from the other side of the big tent. It raced past the tent, and stopped only long enough to pick up the two men who had been shooting their rifles. Then it took off down the dirt road, heading for the highway.

"Who are they?" shouted one of the Hajj's men.

"What did they want?"

"Why did they insult us like this?"

As if in answer, a female scream came from inside the big tent. The Hajj himself turned and went back in. And there, sitting in the middle of the floor alone, was the bride's mother, her dress and veils completely covering her. Even so, the Hajj could tell she was crying.

"Woman, speak," demanded the Hajj.

"She's gone. The bride is gone."

The Hajj's oldest son, Farook, had come in after him.

Before the Hajj could speak, Farook turned and blustered out of the tent, saying, "The bride is taken! To the trucks!"

There was a mad dash as the men ran to their tents for the weapons and then began loading into the available trucks.

Inside the tent, the Hajj said to the mother, "I will do everything I can to bring her home, with her honor intact."

Then he went into his private bedroom. He hadn't consciously been expecting to find something. But there, on one of his pillows, was a note, written with a flourish on a large piece of paper. The Hajj grabbed it up.

All it said was: *The box for your bride.*

He gave a roar, and stalked back out through the tent. He purposely went out the side away from the gathering posse, so that he could plant his feet and cry to heaven. His howl of pain had no words. It was a plea, a confession, a bellow of wrath.

Then he turned and ran to find Farook.

He didn't notice the young girl with fearful blue eyes watching from the otherwise-empty *maharama,* women's section of the tent, who darted out to pick up the paper where he dropped it as he turned to run.

January 27, 2007, 10:54 A.M.
(24 minutes since end of auction)
Judean wilderness west of the Dead Sea
Israel

"Farook, my son," said the Hajj to his firstborn, "they have taken the bride. You ride in the first wave of trucks; I will follow in the second. It should not be hard to follow the tire tracks if we hurry and go now!"

A roar went up from the rest of the men. They were fired up, and ready to go, do some tracking and some catching and some exacting of revenge. It was a terrible thing that had happened. It was a fine thing that had happened. They knew how to handle this. The taste of blood was in their mouths. It was like the old times.

As Farook held his traditional knife, his *shabriya,* he turned toward the trucks.

"My son, listen to me. This is not what you are expecting to hear," the Hajj said under his breath, his hand firmly holding his son back from going just yet.

"The most important thing is the return of my bride, with her honor intact. We will not make this a blood feud, if that can be accomplished. When you catch the men who have her, do not kill them. Say, 'We will give you the item of great value, in return for our item of great value.' If the leader agrees, it shall be so."

Farook was looking at him like he was crazy. "You are letting someone greatly dishonor our tribe, our people? You are asking me not to kill them? To tell them politely we have a trade?"

"Yes. And if you are to be a great leader after me, in this instance you must listen and obey."

Farook was still staring at him, confused, when the men around him surged forward, and Farook came to and led them, with a shout, to the first truck.

January 27, 2007, 10:56 A.M.
(26 minutes since end of auction)
Judean wilderness west of the Dead Sea
Israel

The Hajj had only one thought: to acquire something of enough worth that he could use it as a ransom for Yasmin.

He had only ever been back to the treasure cave once since that fateful day with Rashid. And that had been only a month ago, when he had gone back, first to see if he could still find it, after all these years—and then to see if it was still as full of treasures as he remembered.

If so, certainly there would be something there of as much worth as the box.

Certainly el-Musaq would be willing to talk, to negotiate? For if the Hajj could find several items of value, perhaps el-Musaq could be talked into keeping one for himself and forgetting the lost box?

The problem that haunted the Hajj was that when he had gone back and had finally found the ravine into which Rashid had fallen, and from which he had escaped, he had looked up and seen the small opening to the cave high above him.

And he had known, given his age, and weight and physical shape, that there was no way he could climb up and reach the entrance to the cave.

Yet there was no one else he could trust with such knowledge.

No one.

But el-Musaq had taken Yasmin, and Omar had to go back. By himself. Now. With no possibility of failure.

As the men of the tribe all ran and jumped into the backs of the vehicles with their weapons, the Hajj disappeared.

He went back through the tent, and followed a path behind the plateau on which they'd been camping. He was heading for the horses.

As old as he was, he had to ride, and he had to ride quickly.

He had to return by the time the men did.

He had to have a suitable ransom.

A bride-price meant for a king.

January 27, 2007, 11:02 A.M.
(32 minutes since end of auction)
Judean wilderness west of the Dead Sea
Israel

By the time Jaime caught up with Op 1—Yani—he was prone, hidden on an outcropping of stone, overlooking the horses. The Hajj was inside the makeshift corral. He had just chosen a stallion as Jaime came and lay down beside Yani.

The young man Suleiman helped the Hajj by bridling his mount while the Hajj found his personal saddle and brought it to the horse. The saddle looked like a beautiful blanket with intricate beading in patterns of blue and yellow flowers. Brown leather had been crafted into a Bedouin version of a saddle horn and also a saddle back. The bridle and girth were handmade, with blue and yellow tassels.

Then the Hajj gave some kind of instructions to Suleiman—perhaps to guard the camp and the women in the absence of the other men—for Suleiman nodded solemnly and started up toward the tents.

Yani waited a moment for Suleiman to disappear, started to get up. It seemed clear Yani intended to follow the Hajj.

Jaime reached out and caught Yani's sleeve in time to pull him back down.

For as soon as the Hajj and Suleiman were out of sight, young Safia emerged from a different hidden vantage point and half-ran, half-slid down to the horse corral. One of the horses, an Arabian, trotted over to her, and nudged her in hopes of a treat.

Instead, she hurried to the gear and selected a bridle, this one with fine silver work, as well as black and white tassels.

Then she walked her horse out of the pen, closed the gate, jumped on, bareback, and headed off into the desert, using the same path that the Hajj had used.

At that point, Jaime and Yani stood simultaneously and headed down for the horses.

"Op 2 is staying here, on site?"

"Yes," Yani replied.

They each chose a bridle from the equipment stash and hurried back to the pen to catch horses.

"Help me with this one," Yani said of a large black stallion he had caught but was having trouble bridling.

Jaime came over to calm the horse and hold his neck as Yani then easily slipped the bridle over the stallion's head. The bridle had intricate patterns hammered into nickel; there was no bit.

Once Yani was set, Jaime turned to find the bridle for one of the other mounts. But as she did, both she and Yani stood up quickly. It sounded like two men were talking as they approached the corral on the camp path above them.

Yani had put the matching blanket/saddle onto the stallion and had mounted.

"Come," he said, and he held a hand down to her.

She reached a hand up to him and tried to jump, but as he pulled up on her arm, her entire back pulsed with pain, all the scabbing about to rip open.

"I can't," she said.

"Open the gate. Then climb the fence. Quickly."

She opened the gate, and his mount came out, prancing with eagerness. Jaime balanced herself on a taut wire of the pen, and from there was able to swing up behind Yani as he guided the horse her way.

He turned the horse the way the other two had gone, and they headed off into the desert sands.

January 27, 2007, 11:15 A.M.
(45 minutes since end of auction)
Judean wilderness west of the Dead Sea
Israel

The Hajj hadn't ridden this hard and this long for many years. When he stopped at a hidden spring to water his horse, he was so saddle sore that he could hardly stand. Even if he could scale the cliff to the treasure cave in ordinary circumstances, how could he ever accomplish it in this condition?

He figured the cave was about fifteen miles from where they currently made camp. This was fortunate, because they were at their westernmost campsite—at their eastern site, he would have been nearly forty miles away, with no hope of making it there and back in time, especially on one horse.

The Hajj felt every bone creak. He was too old to be doing this.

But then he thought of Yasmin, of how she was counting on him, and he cooled his horse down with some of the water from the spring, remounted, and continued on his way.

January 27, 2007, 11:24 A.M.
(54 minutes since end of auction)
Judean wilderness west of the Dead Sea
Israel

Jaime understood why Safia's countenance glowed when she talked about riding horses.

The black stallion beneath Jaime and Yani must be at least seventeen hands. He was all muscle and sinew, and it seemed as though he'd been waiting all his life to run this race.

When they had stopped at the spring used by Omar and Safia, their mount had hardly been winded. He did drink but was eager to be pointed in a direction and given his head once more.

Somehow, though, he knew he wasn't to overtake the other riders, which he easily could have done. He understood he was tracking them.

There was a square attachment at the back of the saddle, a piece that was meant to hold a second rider. While Jaime loved riding and would have loved to have her own mount, she was content on this magnificent beast behind Yani, her arms wrapped around him, forced to hold him tight. The joyful gallop of the steed, the vast ocean of sand, the winter sun above them, the closeness of Yani. She knew he wasn't hers, would never be hers, and yet, for these moments, it was as if he were. Jaime held him in her arms, and his strength, his passion, the depth and complexity that made him Sword 23, that made him the stuff of legend—that, at one fleeting moment in time, had made him hers—filled her world.

They were on a mission, of course.

Because of that, the moment this ride ended she would let go.

She would let go.

Yani reined in the stallion and looked at the tracks in the sand in front of them. For the first time, the hoofprints of the two horses diverged. The Hajj, with the larger tracks that went deeper into the sand, had gone to the left; the girl, with the smaller horse and lighter tread, had gone to the right.

"Follow the Hajj?" Yani asked.

"Follow the girl," replied Jaime.

"Why?" Yani's tone was interested rather than demanding.

"She took the box. My guess is she's on her way to get it."

Yani glanced back at Jaime, gave a small smile, and pointed the horse to the right.

January 27, 2007, 12:10 P.M.
(1 hour, 40 minutes since end of auction)
Judean wilderness west of the Dead Sea
Israel

The Hajj stood in the ravine below the treasure cave, trembling. Partly because of the arduous ride. Mostly because he now stood in the place he had last seen Rashid. Where his body had fallen. Where the scavengers had come to pick him apart.

The Hajj now stood in the place from which his cousin's hand had finally disappeared.

In his mind, he was no longer the Hajj. He was Omar. No one, nothing, but Omar.

The boy who was nothing special.

He looked up the sheer cliff to the opening of the cave that had once seemed like a palace of riches.

He tried to remember what he had seen inside that cave. If there was anything that would bring Yasmin back to him, unharmed.

Then he looked at the cliff wall. Here and there he could see indentations that were deep enough to be used as handholds. But there were not nearly enough.

He should have brought someone else along. There must have been *someone* he could trust.

Omar's sons were ambiguous about him, as people had been all his life. He did not trust them. His sons sensed that he was not a great man; he was no one who would have become Hajj under normal circumstances. He belonged with the other unremarkables in the middle of the pack. If Omar had brought his sons here, they may have pushed him from the cave the same way he pushed Rashid.

Was that true? Or was it that the events of that horrible day had given Omar a specific lens, a shattered lens, through which he had viewed the rest of his life?

Omar stood and looked up to the cave once again.

And this time, he saw Rashid. Rashid was in the cave, leaning over the edge, looking at him.

Has he lived here all this time, laughing at me? Omar wondered nonsensically.

"Rashid!" he called. The sun shone in his eyes as he looked up. By the time he raised his hand to block out the blinding beams, the head had disappeared.

And he found resolve he'd never had before as he walked to the rough rock wall and began to climb.

January 27, 2007, 12:10 P.M.
(1 hour, 40 minutes since end of auction)
Judean wilderness west of the Dead Sea
Israel

She never meant to hurt anyone.

Safia had taken the box for safekeeping, so that the Hajj could not sell it—not to cause trouble. She had no reason to like the Hajj's new bride, but she certainly did not mean to ruin her life by causing her to be kidnapped. It had never occurred to Safia that something so terrible could happen.

She had to get the box back and pray nothing had happened to Yasmin, and that Yasmin's honor had not been irrevocably besmirched.

Safia reined in her horse, Pasha, and dismounted. She had been to the treasure cave twice before. The first time had been when she'd followed the Hajj out of curiosity. Even then, he had remained helplessly below in the ravine, but Safia had seen the cave opening he was looking at, and had climbed around until she'd found the way in through the hole in the roof.

She had come back once more, bringing the box. She had thought the djinn might continue to favor them if she brought the box back safely to its point of origin.

Safia hobbled Pasha and pushed away the two flat rocks she'd positioned to partially hide the opening in the cave roof. From beneath one she pulled out a rope that was securely tied around the heavy rock, and dropped it down into the hole.

Then, without hesitation, she sat down and jumped onto the rope, shimmying down.

It was all as she'd left it. The warm, glowing colors on the walls: yellow gold, azure blue, emerald green.

There were the old water jars, empty now but beautifully shaped, with graceful, curving necks and intricately painted sides. There were matching plates and round clay cups.

There were shelves, upon which sat several boxes, a dozen tall jars with lids, and other hinged boxes—although none half as beautiful as the jeweled box the Hajj had brought back.

The Hajj's box was still here on the shelf, exactly where she'd left it. She ran and grabbed it, clutching it tightly to her chest.

Safia had never taken the time to explore the other items. She promised herself that once this was all sorted out, she would bring Tarif back with her and show him the things that were here.

Most of the way here, Safia had been following the Hajj. It seemed he, too, was coming back to the cave. But why? Did he know she'd taken the box? Had he guessed she'd brought it back here? If he had, why didn't he confront her about it? It made no sense.

Furthermore, when he came here, he never actually came to the cave. He only came into the ravine and stood looking up at it.

Perhaps he'd forgotten the way to the top?

Safia couldn't help herself. She walked over to the lower mouth of the cave and peered over into the ravine.

And there, many feet below her, stood the Hajj. Looking up. Directly at her.

She nearly screamed.

She fell back into the cave, pressing herself against the wall.

Then she looked straight ahead, and she did scream.

January 27, 2007, 12:17 P.M.
(1 hour, 47 minutes since end of auction)
Judean wilderness west of the Dead Sea
Israel

One of the men from the wedding was standing behind her.

He must have followed her here. He was very tall, well muscled, and imposing. She had led him here.

Now what? Now everything was ruined.

Certainly he would take the box.

Was he the person who had kidnapped Yasmin?

Safia clutched the box to her chest, and stared at him, wild-eyed.

"Don't be afraid," he said. "I'm here to help."

Then the last thing Safia ever would have expected happened.

The woman Jaime came down the rope behind him.

Safia had liked Jaime. She had trusted her. Was it Jaime who had followed her and had brought the other? She now recognized the man as Jaime's brother, Ahmet, who had come to help Jaime in the other cave.

Why were they here?

"Safia," said Jaime. "Don't be frightened. We want to help get Yasmin back. We really are here to help."

Safia started to cry. "I never meant for any of this to happen!"

"I believe you," said Jaime, coming over to her. She put a hand on Safia's shoulder.

"You won't tell?" the girl asked. "You won't tell anyone about the cave? Or that I took the box?"

Jaime was about to answer when all three of them became aware of a pulsating noise. At the beginning, it was enough to confuse them, to cause them to stop and pay attention, trying to sort out what it was.

The noise got louder. Quickly. And as it began to reverberate off the walls, the entire cave seemed to shake. Small pieces of rock began to break off.

"What is it?" asked Safia.

"It's—a helicopter," answered Jaime. "Safia . . . are you—are we the only ones here, that you know of?"

Safia thought just a moment and shook her head.

"No, the Hajj came, but he doesn't know the way up. He's down there, in the ravine."

She pointed outside. The man Ahmet walked over, hiding carefully along the wall of the opening, and looked down. He looked back at Jaime and nodded. Then he looked up into the sky.

"I can't see anything," he said in English. "It must be coming from a different direction."

The sound was getting so loud that Safia took her free hand to cover one of her ears. She could see, but not hear, Jaime and Ahmet talking to each other.

And then a terrible thing began to happen.

The roof began to cave in.

January 27, 2007, 12:10 P.M.
(1 hour, 40 minutes since end of auction)
Judean wilderness west of the Dead Sea
Israel

The S-70A Black Hawk helicopter sped across the barren desert with a crew of three and one passenger. As the crew chief watched for any impediments that might endanger the aircraft, Frank McMillan scanned the horizon with his binoculars for any sign of the Hajj.

McMillan had watched an hour earlier as the Hajj slipped away from the crowd of searchers and headed for the corral. How could he help rescue his bride by riding off into the desert? Unless . . . he was going to retrieve the box.

But with the sheikh on horseback, there was no way Frank could follow in his Jeep without being seen. Returning to his vehicle, the CIA agent grabbed his satellite phone and made an emergency call back to Tel Aviv. He needed air transport, *now*.

The CIA had nothing, but in the interest of international cooperation the Israeli Army agreed to support with a Black Hawk and crew. So, forty-five minutes later Frank was airborne and following the tracking device he had planted on the Hajj.

For some minutes now the track had stopped moving on Frank's handheld device. That must be it. The Hajj must have reached the location where the box was hidden. Checking his

map, then peering through his binoculars, Frank found a
ravine that seemed to match the correct location.

"Let's take a closer look down there," he said into the aircraft's internal commo system, and pointed toward the ravine.
The pilot nodded, banking the aircraft down and to the right.

The sun was straight up, and there were no shadows to im-
pede their vision. All four men were watching closely for any
signs of life when the copilot suddenly shouted.

"There," he cried, and the pilot banked hard back to the
left, toward a spot where the little valley seemed to dead-end
into a cliff.

McMillan peered through his binoculars. There was something moving—a horse. The horse had a saddle and bridle, so
there must be a rider somewhere! As they swung around from
a different angle, he saw it. The form of a person, laboriously
climbing up the side of the ravine.

"I see him. Land there!"

"I can't, sir," responded the pilot. "The ravine is too narrow; a wind gust could take us right into the cliff."

"Okay, how about that plateau." As he trained his binoculars on the plateau, he was surprised to see two more horses.
"Set down there and I'll take a look and see if there's a way to
get down into the ravine."

The Black Hawk banked one more time, heading for the
flat plateau above the ravine. The noise of their approach was
enough to scare off both horses. Frank didn't see which way
they went. However, the fact that they disappeared implied
there would be a way down.

Hovering over the landing zone, the rotors kicked up a
whirlwind of dust, and the pilot had trouble sensing when they
would touch down. They hit rock before he expected, landing
hard. It was not enough to damage the aircraft, but the jolt made
the ground shake beneath them.

"Whew!" said the crew chief, shaking his helmet as the rotors slowed. "That was close. Much harder and this bird might
have come apart." He waved to catch the attention of the pi-
lots. "I'm gonna check for damage while he," throwing a
thumb in their passenger's direction, "looks for his man."

Frank already had his belt unbuckled and was climbing out the door.

"Chief!" he yelled back as he walked away from the aircraft. "You better be ready for a quick liftoff. This ground doesn't feel too stable."

The man waved acknowledgment as he circled his helicopter, checking struts, rotors, any crucial areas closely for sign of damage from the landing. A crack here, a loose nut there, and the chopper could come apart in midair. Satisfied that all looked okay, he climbed back inside to help prep the bird for liftoff.

McMillan walked to the edge of the cliff and looked over. It was straight down. From this angle, he couldn't see the Hajj making his way up.

Walking back toward the center of the plateau, trying to get his bearings, Frank noticed some rocks piled around a hole in the ground. Was that a rope tied to one of the rocks?

He drew his weapon and crept toward the opening, noting that the rope was taut and swaying as if someone was climbing.

Well, this could certainly be interesting. McMillan waited curiously to see who might emerge.

January 27, 2007, 12:18 P.M.
(1 hour, 48 minutes since end of auction)
Judean wilderness west of the Dead Sea
Israel

Behind them, rocks were showering down as great chunks of the cave roof began to fall in.

"We've got to get out of here!" said Ahmet.

"Hurry!" said Jaime. "Safia, quickly, up the rope!"

"You've got to trust me," Ahmet said to the girl. "Let me hold the box and help you up the rope. You've got to get up and out and run as far in the opposite direction of the helicopter as you can. Give me the box; then once you're standing on my shoulders, I'll hand it up to you!"

"No!" said Safia, clasping the jeweled box to her with all her might.

"Safia, you've got to get out! We might not all make it! If he says he'll hand the box up to you, he will. I promise," Jaime said.

Safia looked at Jaime, and thought she saw truth in her eyes.

"I promise!"

Great slabs of rock were falling now, and Safia knew one could hit and kill any of them at any moment.

She handed the box to the man. Then Jaime cupped her hands together and boosted Safia up to the rope. She pulled herself up, and was bold enough to put one foot, then the other on Ahmet's shoulders.

Then she reached back down for the box.

Ahmet handed it up to her.

Safia reached through the hole in the roof and put it outside on the ground. Then, with a boost from Ahmet, she pulled herself up the rest of the rope, out into the sunlight.

She gasped with the effort as she threw herself prone onto the ground, purposely landing on top of the box, to protect it.

A hand reached down to help her up.

She looked up and saw another man standing there.

This one was not smiling.

This one had a gun pointed at her head.

January 27, 2007, 12:20 P.M.
(1 hour, 50 minutes since end of auction)
Judean wilderness west of the Dead Sea
Israel

Things were happening so fast. Jaime was plunged from won-der at the colors and artistic detail of the cave, to confusion at the falling rock, to purpose in getting Safia safely out of the way.

Jaime was also surprised that Yani had actually given Safia the box—the box that was the focus of this whole mission.

But the main goal was to get the box to safety. They still had another Operative back at camp. And once the girl was out, a whole other section of the roof began to cave in.

Yani was still helping Safia the final distance out of the cave when the sandstone roof above the spot where he'd just stood looking down into the ravine began to collapse.

Jaime saw it coming, and grabbed Yani's hand, pulling him back into the inner recesses of the cave. The thunder of the collapse was almost deafening.

"They landed a helicopter on top of the cave!" Yani was yelling.

"They mustn't have known it was hollow—didn't know it was a cave!" Jaime called back.

Jaime closed her eyes and grabbed her burqa and held it over her nose and mouth, trying to filter out enough debris that she could breathe.

The two of them flattened themselves back against a wall until the din subsided.

When it stopped, the air was filled with sand and rock particles. As the dust began to settle, Jaime opened her eyes. She and Yani were in a space maybe eight foot square, with rock all around them.

Yani was already on his hands and knees, trying to find any weakness in the wall now formed by the fallen slabs. He was working his way along on the side toward the cave entrance where they'd recently stood. Jaime took her cue from him, and started on the other end, working back toward him.

Every now and then she would come to a rock or a pile that she could budge just a little. Once, there had been a small opening in the slide, but when she began to clear it out, the rocks above her, which had been supported by the caved-in rubble, became unstable and she had to back off.

After only a few minutes, there came another crash from above.

It hadn't been caused by the work either she or Yani was doing. But the earthen roof just above where they were working began to shake and crumble.

This time, Yani grabbed her, in the nick of time. He pulled her backward and down.

Jaime's heart revved as the cave once again began collapsing around them.

With only pinpricks of remaining light, Yani had seen a ledge protruding from the back wall. He shoved Jaime behind him, and pulled her into a crouching position. There was a small niche in the cave, and Jaime's back roared with searing pain as she was flung against the wall of it. Yani fell back beside her. She'd always thought him the last one on earth to be sexist, but he instinctively held her head down and positioned his body as a shield for hers.

The collapse only took one, maybe two more minutes, but it seemed as if their whole life had been crouched back in the hollow, trying to breathe, waiting for the noise to stop.

Jaime pulled her newly scraped back away from the wall of the cave, and tentatively leaned forward.

It took a full minute for her to notice there was just the tiniest bit of light coming through here and there, in openings only as big as drill bits. It took a while for her eyes to adjust.

Their world was now about six feet long, five feet high, and six feet wide.

Yani moved before she did.

He carefully inched forward and felt the new wall before them. He pushed at it, then worked his way along the entire length of it. Only once did something move—and it was a rock pile from above that rained down on him. He shook it off and continued down the rock wall. There weren't any large boulders. It was rock and debris. It was packed solid.

Yet Jaime had never known Yani to be defeated.

On the two missions they'd done together before, even when they'd faced likely death, Yani had cheerfully announced that their escape would be "a challenge."

Jaime waited for his pronouncement, for their plan of action.

Instead, Yani sat back down, leaned his head against the back wall, and said in a voice filled with anguish, *"Why are you here?"*

January 27, 2007, 12:22 P.M.
(1 hour, 52 minutes since end of auction)
Judean wilderness west of the Dead Sea
Israel

The last thing Frank McMillan expected to see pop out of the hole was a young Bedouin girl.

And she was carrying, of all things, his box.

Well, this was shaping up to be a very good day. Time to grab the object and be gone. He leveled his pistol at her and waited calmly for her to complete her ascent and turn around.

How gratifying to see the look of shock in her eyes. But give her credit, there was no fear. He would soon fix that. But first, the box.

"Do you speak English?"

She nodded.

"What's your name?" he asked the young girl in a conversational way that belied the fact that he was pointing a gun at her head.

She stood tall as her thin frame would allow, and tucked the box under her arm. She didn't speak but looked at the ground.

How annoying were these customs, that wouldn't allow a female child to talk to him? He proceeded anyway.

"How about we make a deal. You give me the box and I don't kill you. Sound fair?"

She held the box closer, and shook her head as if she was

willing to die rather than give up a piece of wood with a few jewels glued to it. Amazing, such devotion to a piece of old detritus.

Then, scrambling up a path over the back edge of the plateau appeared a teenage male. He was only a couple of inches shorter than Frank, and had deep black hair and a muscular build. Frank was certain he had seen him in the men's tent during the celebration.

The young man seemed to quickly assess the situation, and said something to the girl in their language as he walked toward her and pointed at Frank. The intent was clear: *Give him the box; it's not worth it.*

She was shaking her head, and he continued to approach her, continuing to argue.

Let me help you convince her. McMillan lifted the Beretta and took aim at her head, and loudly flicked off the safety latch.

Now the young man was pleading, and finally the girl seemed to relent, handing the box to him.

Very solemnly, the Bedouin youth walked to Frank, holding the jeweled box in outstretched arms as if making an offering to an idol.

"This box has been the source of great good fortune for our people," he said in English. "I will not have it become, instead, the cause of great sorrow. Take it, but be aware that in the manner of its taking you may discover that what has been a blessing for us might become a curse for you."

Frank laughed out loud, and then motioned to the pilot to start the engine. The rotors began slowly to turn, then picked up speed.

"Superstitious drivel, kid. You look smarter than that."

McMillan stepped back onto the skid of the copter and placed the box carefully inside the door before motioning the pilot to take off. Then McMillan turned to face the two Bedouin children. He hooked his left arm through a strap hanging in the open door and brought up his right hand, which was still holding the Beretta.

"Good riddance!" he yelled, and took aim at the girl. Just

as he was preparing to squeeze off a round, there was a flash
of movement from the boy and a slim silver projectile hurled
in McMillan's direction.

Frank look down to find a knife buried up to the hilt in his
midsection. As the helicopter pulled up and away, he let go of
the strap and the pistol, grabbed his gut with both hands, and
plunged down into the ravine below.

January 27, 2007, 12:32 P.M.
(2 hours, 2 minutes since end of auction)
Judean wilderness west of the Dead Sea
Israel

The tone of Yani's voice chilled Jaime to the core.

He was the top Eden Operative in the world.

He had been Sword 23.

Jaime had never heard him betray an uncalculated emotion while on a mission. Ever.

She did her best to slough it off and instead concentrated on his question.

She said, "What do you mean, why am I here? I came following Safia. I thought she had the box—and she did. That was my mission."

"That's not what I mean." His tone was much more controlled than it had been. "I mean, why are *you* here?"

"I met with TC2. I already knew about the box. I was familiar with Frank McMillan. I understand Arabic fairly well, and I specialized in itinerant tribes. But you know all this."

"Jaime. Don't be difficult." He was sitting down, leaning back against the wall. "You had been kidnapped and tortured. You purposely accepted the assignment and misled others—including TC2—about the extent of your injuries so they would allow you to come, when they easily could have sent someone else. Why?"

"I was mad as hell at Frank—" she started.

"You helped us nail him, told us exactly where he was and where he was going. Certainly you know there are other more experienced Operatives who could have taken over, could have brought it to successful resolution."

Why was Yani doing this? Why did he constantly bring up her inexperience? Did he really hate her so much?

"I found the damn box," she said.

"Yes. And now you're likely going to die."

What?

"The cave-in is severe, and my guess is it's not over. If more sandstone comes down, there won't be much air. If we survive being crushed, we'll die from lack of oxygen."

This wasn't Yani. He didn't talk like this.

There was silence for a minute.

"I knew that something like this would happen to me eventually, and I'm prepared. I'm ready to go home. But not with you. You're not supposed to be here."

"I'm sorry if my death is interfering with yours. I'll try to die quietly in the corner. You can pretend I'm not here." The sarcasm dripped from each word.

"You are so . . . infuriating," he said, and she felt some small pride in that accomplishment.

"It must be hard that not everyone worships at the shrine of Sword 23." Jaime almost drew back. She was close to going too far. Perhaps she already had.

Yani answered, "A year ago when you refused your first assignment ring and quit—quit our relationship, quit being an Operative—at first it was difficult for me to understand. But I came to see that it was for the best. You're young. Go, marry a rock star who promotes sustainable communities. Model what living in the kingdom of God can look like. Become the coolest chaplain in the Army. Help a lot of people. Make the world a better place."

Damn him anyway. Why did she feel like he was dismissing her even when he said nice things?

On the other hand, what he said was correct. He had given up a lot for their relationship. He had shared with her private information he didn't share with everyone. And she had shut him down completely. It couldn't have been easy on his part, any more than this current rejection was for her.

"The reason I'm here," she said through gritted teeth, "is because I thought this assignment might be my one and only chance to see you again. I was willing to come all this way after Frank McMillan split my back open on the small chance you might be here. It was stupid on many levels, I know. And I am sincerely sorry if it might have jeopardized the mission at any point." She was glad they were staring straight ahead, not looking at each other, when she continued.

"But the truth is . . ." Jaime was working hard to retain her anger. "The truth is, there has been nothing in heaven or on earth that I can do to get you out of my mind. You're inside of me. Your courage strengthens me. Your passion drives me. When Frank McMillan kidnapped me at gunpoint; told me a good friend had betrayed me; stripped me; and started flaying me with a bullwhip, you were the person I turned to in my mind. I could stand it because I thought you might be proud of me if I did.

"But, as you said, it was stupid of me on every level. I'll never do it again. If, in fact, I ever do anything again. Bad time to learn my lesson, I realize." She fought to keep control of her voice. "So, here I am, apparently dying when I'm not supposed to, intruding on your preplanned transition. My bad."

"You should have stayed with Mark Shepard. You didn't need to come here to apologize to me. He didn't betray you, Jaime. He's a good man."

"Have you not heard a word I've said? I don't want Mark Shepard. He's the most wonderful guy in the world, a treasured old friend. We shared a great dinner. He showed me his sustainable farm. We shared a hot tub and massages, and we made out by the fire. And all I could think was, he's not you. So what I need from you, even if we're about to die, is for you to tell me it's all over, from your side. You don't love me anymore. You don't want me. Cut me off cleanly, so I can let go."

Yani didn't speak. After the longest minute of Jaime's life, his head jerked up. It was clear he was listening for something. "Look out," he said.

And then Jaime heard it, too. The roof above them began to shake. As it began, the sound of the helicopter became louder. Much louder—and then began to recede.

The helicopter had taken off.

But who had been in it? What had they wanted? What had happened to Safia?

What had happened to the box?

Then the walls started to close in.

The two of them hit the ground, and rolled together back into the farthest reach of the cave as the space where they had just been filled with rock.

And for the first time, Jaime truly understood that it wasn't theoretical this time.

She and Yani were about to die.

January 27, 2007, 12:32 P.M.
(2 hours, 2 minutes since end of auction)
Judean wilderness west of the Dead Sea
Israel

Ever since he had seen his cousin Rashid in the cave above, the Hajj—Omar—had a new sense of purpose.

He was going to climb up, confess his evil thoughts to his cousin, apologize for killing him, and revel together with him in the wonders of their treasure cave.

Omar was going to have another chance at life. He would not be the Hajj, he would be Omar, and he and his cousin would have a secret world of their own. They would be best friends. The years would be kind to them.

It was hard finding handholds in the cliff wall, but sandstone is very porous and sometimes Omar could hollow out enough of a space for his hand, and later his foot, to use as a wedge.

Omar didn't look down, only up. Up toward the cave, up toward his cousin, up toward a different life.

Omar was so far into his own world that he didn't hear the roar of the helicopter. He was confused at first that rocks and pebbles began raining down. But he didn't let them stop him.

Finally, he had to look up when large chunks of cliff began to fall on him. Omar hugged in close to the wall, and most of them fell in a trajectory farther out, away from his precarious hold.

He flattened himself against the cliff wall, and closed his eyes.

Thus he didn't see the large, sharp rock that fell straight down, landing on his head, shattering his skull.

The surprise, more than the pain, caused him to lose his grip. He was still conscious as he began the free fall into the ravine.

He was flying. As he flew, he saw another body dropping beside him.

It was Rashid.

Omar smiled and stretched out his hand to his cousin as they flew together.

And everything was the way Omar knew it should have been, all along.

January 27, 2007, 12:44 P.M.
(2 hours, 14 minutes since end of auction)
Judean wilderness west of the Dead Sea
Israel

They now lay in total darkness. No pinpricks of light, no slight breeze.

Jaime and Yani lay together, prone, in a space that barely contained them. She could easily feel the rock on every side. The space was shaped like a coffin: three feet high by four feet wide by six feet long.

Horror gripped her—they had been buried alive.

Jaime had never thought of herself as either afraid of death or claustrophobic. But the fact that the earth was surrounding her, and pressing down on her, began as a seed of panic in her chest, and it began to spread.

She didn't care if anyone beat her to death with a whip. She didn't care if they shot her in the square at Al Qurnah, or drowned her in the sea under the island of Patmos. But she had to get out of here . . . had to. *Had* to! She couldn't stand this. It was closing in all around her, and with Yani pressed beside her, she almost couldn't breathe.

The panic grew.

She . . . was . . . trapped. In a black, airless space that was smothering her.

Jaime began to hyperventilate.

"I have to get out. Help me get out," was all she could say.

"Jaime." It was Yani's voice. His old, recognizable, strong voice. "It's all right. Don't panic."

"We're . . . buried . . . alive. Help me get out! We can't get out!"

" 'There is nothing either good nor bad, but thinking makes it so.' "

"What a stupid idiot time to quote *Hamlet*!" She couldn't help the rebuke.

"Jaime," he said quietly. "Hush, now. This is perfect. It's dark and quiet—it's like the womb of eternal life. Close your eyes. Breathe slowly." He was stroking her hair. "Remember this one?" he whispered. " 'For I am convinced that there is nothing in death or life, in the realm of spirits or superhuman powers, in the world as it is or the world as it shall be, in the forces of the universe, in heights or depths—nothing in all creation that can separate us from the love of God in Christ Jesus our Lord.' "

She closed her eyes. She knew he was quoting Scripture because it was something familiar to her, something she could wrap her mind around. So that she wouldn't panic and claw him bloody.

Yani said, "You're not afraid to die; I know you're not. We're both waiting—eager—to meet the Boss, face-to-face. And I'm here with you."

Her breathing began to calm.

He spoke again, this time words from Isaiah: " 'Therefore the redeemed of the Lord shall return—' "

It was one of her favorite songs. She finished with him: " '—and come with singing unto Zion. And everlasting joy shall be upon their heads.' "

The panic was receding. Her breathing was regulating. Still, she didn't dare open her eyes. How embarrassing was this? The one person on earth she wanted to have know how strong she was, how capable. And when push came to shove, she'd freaked.

"The first time I knew you were different . . . was the first time I kidnapped you," Yani said. "Here you were, hours after another kidnap attempt, after seeing your friend killed, sitting in a dark earthen room with a man who could have killed you. And you never lost your presence of mind. Or your wit. The second time I realized how different you were was when I let you out of a headlock and you turned around and walloped me." He gave a small chuckle. "Not what I expected from a chaplain."

Jaime's breathing was nearly back to normal. She knew he was doing this to bring her down, to keep her from panicking. But she was willing to go with it. In her mind she was back in Tallil, meeting the mysterious stranger for the first time.

"'*Go, Rams*?' Honestly," was all she could say of the first—truly bad—joke he'd told her.

Yani laughed. Then he was silent for a moment. When he spoke, he said, in a tone of voice Jaime had never heard from him before, "The first time I knew how much I loved you . . . and how deeply I could love you . . . was in the square at Al Qurnah. It wasn't the hand grenade, although the fact that you were willing to risk your life to save that little girl was wonderful. It was when an assassin was stalking over to kill you, point-blank . . . and you were lying there, with an M16 right beside you, and it never even occurred to you to pick it up and shoot back."

"You mean Rodriguez's gun?" Jaime thought back to that moment. Truth was, it had never occurred to her that she could have used his gun, to this very moment. She hadn't been looking to kill anybody. She had been readying herself to die.

If she had done it before, she could obviously do it again.

"The first time I knew I could love you," she said, "was when we were tied together in Satis' re-creation of the Tomb. There was a moment . . . I don't even know if you remember it. A moment, before we tried the escape, when we just sat there. My head was on your chest. In spite of everything, I felt safe."

"I do remember," he said. "Coincidentally, that was the first time I wanted to tear all your clothes off and have my way with you."

Jaime opened her eyes. She still couldn't see anything, but he had certainly jarred her out of her panic.

"Yeah, I noticed," she said. Then she asked, "That was the *first* time?"

"There have been many," Yani answered.

"Coincidentally, I could say the same thing."

Jaime was suddenly very aware of the particulars of her surroundings. There was some kind of wooden board behind her. There were also two or three boxes or ancient containers behind her head, which she easily moved to one side. It seemed like they had taken refuge beneath a shelf.

"Do you think this was some kind of library?" she asked.

"Yes," said Yani, "I do." He shifted, changing his position. Then he reached out to her. "Come here."

Jaime moved closer, and he welcomed her to the strength of his arms. "So . . . ," she said. "Any other firsts you'd care to tell me about?" Jaime was feeling more in control, more like herself.

"The first time it occurred to me I'd like to marry you was that evening in Eden. When the mystery was solved. When you solved it. What a day that had been. And the sky, the sunset . . ."

Jaime didn't hear past the beginning of the sentence. "The first time *what*?"

"I wanted to marry you. Yes. You think I gave up being a Sword for the fun of it? For a change of pace?"

"I . . . didn't know. I thought you and Clement had discussed it. . . ."

"I had many long discussions with my mentor, as well as with Clement. It was a wrenching decision. But I meant it when I told you it had been the right one. Even if there was only a chance, the smallest chance, we could have been a team. Taken on the world."

Jaime felt a tear running down her cheek.

"And I left you. I blew it," she said. "Now, we won't ever have that chance."

Together they lay in the stillness of the earth, entwined in each other's arms.

Yani spoke first. "Jaime. Marry me."

"What?"

"It would mean a lot to me if we were married, in this life, on Earth before we leave. Here. Now. You know a minister we could get on short notice?"

"It wouldn't be legal in any country or state."

"It would be legal for us. God as our witness." He took an impatient breath. "So, would you answer the question?"

"Yani, I . . . I would be honored to marry you. To be your wife. To be a team, to take on the world. For as long as we're here. Although . . ."

"Although what?"

"Well, at least according to Catholic theology, the sacrament isn't complete unless the marriage has been consummated." There was teasing in her voice.

"I did have plans along those lines," said Yani.

"Here?"

"I'd prefer Hawaii, but it doesn't seem to be an option."

"Wouldn't that . . . use up a lot of our oxygen?" Jaime asked.

"Absolutely. Assuming we do it right."

As if, with Yani, there could be any other way. "Do you think we can even get our clothes off?"

"It will be a challenge," said Yani with a smile in his voice. And it was the voice, the attitude—the Yani—she recognized.

"My cloth of honor won't exactly be stained."

"It wouldn't be expected of you," he said. "You've been married before. As have I."

"You have?" Jaime realized how much, how very much, she didn't know about Yani. She didn't care. She knew who he was. That was enough.

"My wife died . . . a long time ago," he said.

"I wish I could have known her," Jaime said. "She must have really been something if you fell for her."

"She was. She was a TC. I was a young Operative."

"So you don't mind strong women."

"Obviously not. Although it did take me a very long time to run into someone else who stubbornly wouldn't get out of my head—or out of my heart. You know, we might not have much time. Is that minister here yet?"

Despite all the wedding services she had done, it had never occurred to Jaime that she might someday perform her own. But she smiled and began, "Dearly beloved, we are gathered here in the presence of God, and this cloud of witnesses—" A strange thought, given that he was tugging off her galabia as she spoke. She felt him kissing her, the skin of her stomach, his strong hands gently removing the cloth over her head, away from her injured back, and she cut to the chase.

"I, Jaime, take you, Yani, to be my husband; and I promise to be your loving and faithful wife, in plenty and in want, in joy and in sorrow; in sickness and in health, as long as we both shall live. And all my fortunes at thy feet I'll lay, and follow thee, my lord, throughout the world."

Yani paused from his task and said, *"Romeo and Juliet?"*

"Hey. You can quote *Hamlet,* I can go for *R and J.* Just always wanted to say that."

"I, Yani, take you, Jaime," this was punctuated by kisses up the center of her breastbone as he unwound the bandages that bound her, "to be my wife. And I promise before God to be your loving and faithful husband," his kisses, following the contours of her breasts, were becoming more urgent and his breathing more shallow, "in joy and in sorrow, in sickness and in health—"

Jaime's own breath was getting ragged, but in a new and different way. She could feel him lighting up every inch of her body; her back was scraping against the back of the cave, and she readjusted with his help, helping dispense with his trousers as he removed hers, and finally rolling on top of him.

"I will be your partner, seeking to live with you in the fullness of the kingdom God means to establish on earth, wherever and however that shall be," he ended.

"I now pronounce us husband and wife . . . may we become one . . . fulfill our promises. And what God has joined, let no one—oh, dear God, Yani—divide . . ."

And they were both naked, and Jaime no longer cared where they were, or the size of the space, or how long they might be there.

January 27, 2007, 1:14 P.M.
(2 hours, 44 minutes since end of auction)
Judean wilderness west of the Dead Sea
Israel

Jaime lay, with her head on her husband's shoulder, in darkness that would never become light. There was less oxygen. It was getting harder to breathe. She was content with this fact. At one point she'd feared it might take them days to die. She would much rather go quickly—or, at least, lose consciousness quickly.

"Can you tell me about the box?" she asked, gently. "As Op 1, I assume you knew much more than I did as Op 3, especially given that Op 3 was such a late arrival. But," she said truthfully, "if you're not supposed to discuss it, that's all right. It doesn't really matter now."

"Ah, but I'm glad you asked."

"I assume you gave it to Safia, in hopes she could get it back to camp, back to Op 2, who is still there?"

"No, I gave it to Safia because the mission was not really about the box."

"What?"

"Two thousand years ago, there were numerous groups of people—religious and otherwise, who found shelter in the caves here in the wilderness outside Jerusalem. Some, like the Essenes, established entire communities. Others had hermit caves, or way stations, or simply shelters. The gardeners had such caves, which were used as libraries, meeting places, places of contemplation and refuge, and as drop points for Messengers. This is one such cave. This one, through severe wind- and dust storms, as well as a political climate that had made it dangerous to come for several years, had been lost. For nearly two thousand years."

Jaime said, "That would explain the way the walls were painted—it was beautiful. It must have been an important cave."

Yani was talking softly, breathing shallowly, trying not to use too much oxygen as he spoke. "Yes, I'm glad we got to see it before it collapsed. In those days, objects left for Messengers were put in a specific kind of box—like the one currently at auction. Records in Eden said that a drop-off was supposed to have been made here, but the windstorms hit before the next Messenger was able to come for it.

"So you see, although the age of the box and the jewels encrusted on it make it valuable to the Terris world at large, the true value is in what the box may have contained."

"But the Hajj had it for years. Certainly he would have found anything that was inside?" Jaime asked.

"Ancient Messenger boxes were built with a false bottom. You have to know where it is, and how to unlatch it."

"This one had—?"

"Yes."

"And while Safia was climbing up, you—?"

"Yes."

"And was there—?"

"Yes. Which reminds me. We'll probably want to put our clothes back on."

"Why?"

"We both have locator devices, my love. Operatives will have to wait until the hoopla over the day's events die down, but once they feel it's safe to spend time digging up the site, they'll come for the contents of the box. Our devices will act as a locator for it. So, officially, our mission was a success." What went without saying was that no one could save their lives, even if they arrived immediately, with digging equipment. The cave-in was too severe, the rock too unstable. It wasn't even a possibility.

Yani kissed her again, deeply, and said, "Whether we get dressed or not is up to us." There was a smile in his voice as he added, "It depends on what kind of legend we want to leave behind."

"I don't care if everyone knows that I love you . . . or what we did in our final hours."

"I don't, either," said Yani. "However, I do know the guys . . . I know the Operatives who will probably be sent out here to find it . . . and us."

"I'm getting dressed," said Jaime.

"Me, too," agreed Yani.

As they took turns helping each other reclothe, Jaime said, "Wait—hadn't you been visiting this tribe for years? Hadn't you seen the box, had time to check it?"

"Over the years, I'd heard Omar—the Hajj—talk about his magical box, but I'd never seen it. I assumed it was an antiquity found in a cave like that of the Essenes. In fact, we Integrators all assumed it came from one of the caves where they found the Dead Sea Scrolls, that the reason he didn't sell it was that he knew the Jordanian government had given exclusive rights of search in that area to the Ta'amireh, so if the Hajj had shown it to anyone outside the tribe, he'd be forced to relinquish it. The chances that he'd found a Messenger box, and yet hadn't disclosed the location of the cave where he'd found it, or any of the other riches therein, seemed too improbable."

"So it was still there, inside the box? Whatever had been hidden for Messenger pickup and delivery to Eden? Did you get a look at it? Any idea of what it is?"

"I have hopes," said Yani. "The Messenger who had next been sent to go to this cave had been told the papers in the box had come from a gardener named Yacov."

"Wait—," Jaime breathed excitedly. "You mean *the* Yacov? The gardener who spent time with Jesus?"

"Then you've heard about him?"

"Yes. Andrea told me that other gardeners, other Integrators, who heard Jesus during his time in the Terris world said

that he had private conversations with a gardener named Yacov. That they were able to talk of things that Terris dwellers
couldn't yet understand."

"Legend has it that Yacov was so well liked by those nearest Jesus that when Mary came to Jesus' tomb, it made sense
that she thought Yacov was there."

Jaime added, "So when the Gospel of John says Mary assumed it was 'the gardener' . . . ?"

"Apparently that's how Yacov was known. And yes, he may
have ended up with his own Scripture reference. Anyway, Yacov thought it of utmost importance to share the content of his
conversations with others. Although he himself felt called to
go on living in the Terris world, he wrote down his conversations to send back into Eden."

"Yani—you really think this might be the box that contains
what Yacov wrote?"

"Whatever was there was in protective layers of a papyrus
sealant, and then in an airtight bag, which will only be opened
back in Eden. But the weight and size of the bag leads me to
believe that the contents are written sheaves. And this is the
cave in which they were to be left."

"That would be wonderful," Jaime breathed. "Can I touch
it?"

Yani kissed her forehead, and handed her the bag. It was
larger than she expected, and in an outer fabric that felt like
velvet.

Jaime handed it back. "Here," she said.

"You can hold it," Yani replied. "It's fine if you have it
when they find us."

"Ah," she said, "but you're Sword 23. You should be the
one who died retrieving the gardener gospel. It's more than
enough for me simply to be here with you."

They both fell silent.

And in the stillness that should have been absolute, they
heard a scraping sound.

January 27, 2007, 1:14 P.M.
(2 hours, 44 minutes since end of auction)
Judean wilderness west of the Dead Sea
Israel

Frank McMillan had requested a small helicopter, a Little
Bird, to take him out into the wilderness. However, he needed
it immediately—"two weeks ago yesterday"—and all that was
available on such short notice was a big old Black Hawk. But
it, along with its three-person crew, had been commandeered
and loaned to him, as a CIA member of the Geneva Terrorism
Task Force, by the Israeli Army.

This particular crew was all male: pilot, copilot, crew
chief. In the short time they had to get to know Frank McMillan, none of them liked him at all. He was arrogant, demanding, and dismissive.

Since he was CIA and terrorism was involved, the crew
knew not to ask questions. But he'd told them he was looking
for a middle-aged man, dressed in Bedouin robes, who was
out in the middle of the wilderness. McMillan had planted a
disk on the man, so it wouldn't be hard to find him.

However, when they got to their destination, things started
going awry. First, McMillan insisted that they make a hard
landing on a plateau that didn't look substantial enough for
the size of the craft. And it wasn't.

Second, instead of dealing with a deadly adversary dressed
in Bedouin robes, McMillan found and attacked a couple of

real-life Bedouin kids. Took a box a little girl was holding, and then aimed his damn Beretta at her, planning to kill her for no reason. No reason at all.

Avi Turrow, the crew chief, was shocked by McMillan's wanton cruelty. Not that Turrow had a particularly soft spot for Bedouin—he understood the problem they posed as well as anyone—but he had a ten-year-old daughter himself. And his little girl also had piercing blue eyes.

Turrow was glad the teenage boy had defended himself and the girl, who was most likely his sister. As far as Avi was concerned, McMillan had lost his footing and plunged to his death.

As crew chief, Avi was the only one who had seen what Frank McMillan had done with the box he'd taken from the child. He'd set it down just inside the open door of the Black Hawk.

As they began to take off, with the ground crumbling beneath them, Avi had a split-second decision to make. As far as he knew, their mission had been about finding terrorists, not stealing from children. He had no idea what this box was, except that it meant a lot to the little girl. And if it got out that an Israeli Army helicopter was involved in trying to murder and steal from Bedouin children, it would easily turn into a national incident.

So as the pilot and copilot concentrated on saving the extremely expensive helicopter—as well as their own lives—Avi picked up the box and gently tossed it out of the chopper to the surprised girl. His aim was good, as were her reflexes.

She caught it, and looked up. Avi gave a brusque wave to the child.

And then they were gone.

January 27, 2007, 1:18 P.M.
(2 hours, 48 minutes since end of auction)
Judean wilderness west of the Dead Sea
Israel

Safia stood, momentarily stunned by the chain of events that had left her alive, the unknown assassin killed by Tarif, and the box back in her possession.

Then she sobered up and got moving.

When the helicopter initially approached, the horses had been smart enough to take off down the path Safia had ridden up, and which the two strangers and Tarif had ridden up behind her.

As the ground crumbled beneath their feet, Safia grabbed Tarif and ran for the same path. It led between the plateau they'd just been standing on and another to the immediate south. Fortunately, since the cave-in was caused by a helicopter and not an earthquake, the plateau next to it stood firm. The path between the two was filling with debris, but the boy and the girl fled down it with maximum speed, preceding most of the damage as it tumbled down behind them.

Even after the path took a hard left turn and falling debris no longer followed them, they continued running. Finally, her legs tired and her mouth filled with the taste of sandstone, Safia stopped, and fell back gratefully against the rock wall behind her.

Tarif threw himself against the wall as well. As she began

to catch her breath, Safia turned and looked at her cousin, where he stood gasping beside her. Something seemed wrong. As she studied him more closely, she saw what it was.

He was crying.

"What? What is it?" she asked. "Are you hurt?"

He looked away from her then, embarrassed to be caught in such an unmanly pursuit.

"What is it?" Safia asked again, frightened by this turn of events. "Are you badly hurt?"

Tarif shook his head. Safia tentatively went to stand in front of him. She took his hand in both of hers. He pulled it back, but she took it again.

"Tell me," she said.

He waited until he had control of his voice. "I killed a man," he said.

Safia hadn't expected this depth of emotion. She somehow thought that since men were handed *shabriya* at a young age they . . . just did things like that.

"You saved my life," she said.

"For that, I'm glad," he said.

Together they stood until the largest part of the collapse seemed to be over.

Tarif looked at the dirt beneath their feet. "The horses came this way," he said.

"They're likely down in the ravine," Safia said. "The cave—do you think it's ruined? Do you think it's all crushed?"

"What cave?" asked Tarif.

"The treasure cave. The Hajj's treasure cave. The helicopter landed on its roof."

"Then yes, it must be gone."

"But—there were people in it," said Safia. "They were there with me. They helped me get out."

"What are you talking about? Safia, tell me what's going on! Why do you have the box? Who was that man? Why did he try to kill you?"

"I don't know. I don't know who that man was. He was probably trying to find the cave. I was going to tell you about the cave, Tarif. I was going to bring you here. Now they've wrecked it. And Ahmet and his sister—I'm afraid they've been crushed."

"Ahmet and his sister? How did they get here?"

Safia stood up and looked back toward the path. "Wait. There is one other way in. It was like a secret escape tunnel. I went through it once to see where it came out. But it's uncomfortable and long."

"It's back there, where everything is caved in?"

"It goes back there. But it starts over here, to the side. As I said, it's very long and dark. But we've got to see if it's still there. They could still be alive!"

"Safia. I don't want to disappoint you, but I don't think anybody is still alive in there."

"I've got to find out. Come on."

Together they left the path and climbed through a V made by the rocks that no one would ever likely try to squeeze through. When they got to the place, which was hidden behind a scraggly old tree and several large rocks, Tarif said, "How did you find this?"

"I found the other end that started in the cave. This is where it came out."

He peered inside. "This part of the tunnel is still intact. But it's awfully small."

"I know," said Safia. "But we've got to try!"

"Do you want me to go?" he asked, expecting her to staunchly stand up for her own right to try to save them.

"All right," she said simply.

"You want me to go?"

"Yes, if you'd like."

As he looked at the small tunnel running into the dark earth, he knew he wouldn't like, but if they had saved his Safia, he would do it.

"Stay there," he instructed her sharply. "In case someone needs to go for help, it must be you."

"Be careful," Safia said, and her mouth moved in a silent prayer.

January 27, 2007, 1:28 P.M.
(2 hours, 58 minutes since end of auction)
Judean wilderness west of the Dead Sea
Israel

The scraping sound had gotten consistently louder for several minutes. It stopped then for a moment, and turned into tapping.

"Hello," Yani said, in Arabic. "Can you hear us?"

"Yes," said a male voice. "Are you in the cave?"

"What's left of it. Where are you?"

"I've come down a long, narrow tunnel, but it's ended. There's wood in front of me. Are you anywhere near wood?"

Jaime could feel Yani moving his arms past her in the dark. "I think so," he said. Then, to Jaime, also in Arabic, "Is that a plank of wood behind your back?"

"Yes," she said. "It feels that way."

"We're by the plank of wood. Is there any way to move it?"

"I can't really see," said the new male voice. "But it seems like a very long, thick plank, and the earth has collapsed on either end of it."

"Jaime, love, switch places with me," Yani murmured to her in English.

She could tell he was feeling the length of the wood. "It's wedged in tight, and I don't think we're going to be able to clear the length of it on either side," Yani said more loudly, again in Arabic.

"I can't, either," said the other person.

"Our only hope is to break it," said Yani. "But there's not much room in here to get a good kick."

"And I don't have room to turn around," said the voice from the other side. "I can go for help."

Yani whispered to Jaime, "I'm not sure we have enough air to make it if he goes for help and comes back—plus, then whoever finds us finds the pouch. I'm going to have to try to break through the board from in here. But that is going to use up our oxygen faster. If I'm not successful, I'll really be . . . not successful."

Jaime almost wished the intruder hadn't found them. She had been centered, calm, and ready. Now, if they didn't make it, it would feel like a failure—adrenaline flowing, hearts pounding, gasping for breath.

But of course, now that they were found, they had to try.

"Go for it," she said.

"Now I *am* going to ask you to wedge yourself in a corner," he said. "I'll try to get a good angle to kick. The wood is very thick, obviously meant to be moved to access the emergency tunnel. Our only hope is that its age has made it weaker." Then he said, more loudly to whoever was outside, "Move back. I'm going to try to kick through."

"I will," said the voice.

Yani began to kick at the wood, just where there was no earth behind it, where the voice in the tunnel had come from.

And finally, just as Jaime was having trouble finding the oxygen she needed to continue breathing shallow breaths, there was a cracking sound.

And another.

And then there was air.

January 27, 2007, 1:48 P.M.
(3 hours, 18 minutes since end of auction)
Judean wilderness west of the Dead Sea
Israel

The four horses—the stallion ridden by Jaime and Yani; Safia's horse, Pasha; Tarif's horse; and the Hajj's own mount—stood huddled together at the entrance to the ravine.

Their first reaction to finding the horses was great relief—and the second, fast on its heels, was the realization that the Hajj had ridden out when they had and they had no idea where he was.

"He was standing below the cave, in the ravine. I saw him," Safia said soberly.

She and Tarif had already told them about the man in the helicopter who had taken the box and tried to kill Safia.

The four of them stood for a moment, wondering if there were two corpses awaiting them in the ravine below the cave.

"Let me go look around," said Yani. "Please hold the horses. I do want us to take the box and be well away from here by the time authorities come looking for Frank's body. But . . . let me take a look." Yani threw his satchel over his shoulder and climbed over the boulders blocking the entrance to the gully before them.

Neither Safia nor Tarif needed a reason to stay behind. It was clear they had no interest in seeing what had become of either man.

Once Jaime was certain the cousins would wait for them, she climbed over to follow Yani.

The corpses of the two men were fairly close together.

Yani moved past Frank, whose body was facedown, to the Hajj, and knelt down beside him. He felt for a pulse at the Hajj's neck, and then said a short prayer. As he carefully lifted the Hajj's head to slide his goatskin rucksack over his neck, Jaime yelled Yani's name.

He hadn't seen that Frank McMillan wasn't dead. Or that Frank McMillan had used the last of his energy to raise his head and his Beretta and aim it squarely at Yani's head.

January 27, 2007, 1:55 P.M.
(3 hours, 25 minutes since end of auction)
Judean wilderness west of the Dead Sea
Israel

Frank McMillan watched quietly as the man in Bedouin clothing climbed through the pass, over the boulders. Frank knew his own legs were broken, his lungs weren't working right, and blood loss had made him slightly dizzy. But he was not done. No, not yet.

The game was not over yet.

During the last half an hour, he had slowly, painfully, crawled to reach his Beretta, which had fallen to the earth near him. Then, after rolling to his stomach, Frank lay prone, and waited. He had his right forearm cupped in his left hand to steady the pistol.

Waiting. Patiently waiting.

He knew someone would come, eventually. And that someone would likely have something to do with the cave, the box. Eden.

And then the tall man came. Frank had seen him at the wedding. If he was here, in the middle of the wilderness, it was for a reason.

Would he be willing to talk?

Or should Frank just shoot him? If he couldn't have the box, he couldn't discover whatever the hell Eden was.

He began to squeeze the trigger.

"No!" came a woman's scream, and then someone was on top of him, the gun still in his hand, but now both gun and hand were flattened on the ground.

For one brief moment, he was so shocked that he forgot his pain.

It was Richards. Jaime Lynn Richards. How she had gotten here he couldn't begin to guess. From Lac-Argent to the Judean wilderness was quite a leap. And she had feigned ignorance of the box. The mere fact that she was here proved that he had been right—she was involved! Score that point for Frank!

It was time to end the game. Frank could feel his life flowing out of him, but his need to vanquish this woman was enough to carry him through his last breath.

"Richards!" he said. "I'm dying. I know I'm dying. Please, help me turn over." He released his hand around the gun.

And Richards was dumb enough to do it.

As she did, he took the knife that he'd brought down with him—the boy's *shabriya*—and brought it up to her neck. And then he whispered, "I want you to look me in the eye when I kill you. I want to see your face as you take your last breath."

To his surprise, Jaime looked steady, calm, and completely unafraid. McMillan saw immediately that he would not defeat her by killing her. But it would sure as hell tie up some loose ends, and cheer him considerably.

"Frank. If you kill me, you never find out what you want to know," she said. "You never find out about Eden."

A wave of pain shot through him and he had to scream. As he did, Richards kneed him in the stomach, which caused his entire insides to revolt. As he screamed again, she wrested the knife from his hand and threw it far away, beyond his reach.

"Ahmet," she said to the other man, "do you have your bag?"

The Bedouin man went to get it. Frank knew then his time was up—her accomplice was undoubtedly going to get his own weapon, to finish Frank off. It didn't matter. Dying like this was not for sissies. The pain was ravaging him, and he gasped and gasped again.

Her accomplice had returned and handed her something. Frank couldn't see what kind of weapon it was.

She carefully unbuttoned the top two buttons of his shirt, and pressed something against the muscle in front of his shoulder. Within moments, the pain began to subside. The damn bitch had given him something for the pain.

"Don't you know who I am?" he asked. "Do you know what I've done to you?"

"I know," she said. "You ambushed me four years ago in Iraq. You helped Gerik kill my friend and you stole what you thought was the Sword of Eden. A day and a half ago, in France, you killed a man, and nearly killed another, and you whipped me. Then you came here and almost murdered a child. You did all of it to get information about a place you'll never go. Even if you got there, there would be nothing of interest to you. The people of Eden would exasperate you. They have nothing for you to conquer. But now, you're dying, Frank. For most people at this stage, I would ask if they wanted me to pray with them."

"If there are 'people of Eden,' then there is Eden," he said. "You've just admitted it does exist!" There was an element of gloating in his voice, as if he were torturing her still and she had finally cracked. "It does exist," he exulted.

She looked sadly into his eyes and said, "Frank. It doesn't matter anymore. It's over."

"It's never over," he whispered. And then he was gone.

January 27, 2007, 3:05 P.M.
(4 hours, 35 minutes since end of auction)
Judean wilderness west of the Dead Sea
Israel

Abihu el-Musaq sat in the corner of the big tent watching the agitated men mill about. It hadn't taken them long to realize the truck they were following, with the men who had shot the guns inside, had been "borrowed" from one of the wedding guests. Or that it had been parked fifteen miles away, by a highway, empty. The men were Bedouin, trackers, and they quickly figured out that the men had had three other vehicles waiting there to take them in three different directions, into three different towns.

They hadn't known what to do. They had come back to rendezvous and get instructions from the Hajj, since it was his bride who had been stolen.

But the Hajj was nowhere to be found. Oddly, his oldest son, who was usually a firebrand, was preaching caution. So they milled, and ate, and swore, and paid no attention to the wedding guest who sat silently in the big tent, watching all of this.

Until a man walked with quiet purpose into the tent and headed straight for el-Musaq. "I need to speak with you outside," the man said.

El-Musaq pointed to himself doubtfully, as if there had been some mistake. But the man didn't engage with the pretense. He unobtrusively exited the tent and waited for el-Musaq to follow.

When he did, the squat man found Ahmet, the much taller cousin of the Hajj, outside waiting for him.

"Let's settle this quickly," Ahmet said. "I have the box. What have you done with the bride?"

"Everyone claims to have the box, but I have never seen it," answered el-Musaq.

The tall man removed it from his bag. It was as beautiful as the photos, as beautiful as el-Musaq had hoped.

"Where is the bride?"

"Give me the box."

This time, Ahmet handed it over to him. And then Ahmet said, quite clearly, in English, "We know the sale price, el-Musaq. We know where you live on Cyprus. Your dealings with us must be honorable if you wish to continue in business."

The next moment, he was back speaking local-dialect Arabic. "Now that we have an understanding, where is she?"

January 27, 2007, 3:05 P.M.
(4 hours, 35 minutes since end of auction)
Judean wilderness west of the Dead Sea
Israel

Of all the things that could have happened on this, her wedding day, being kidnapped was not something Yasmin had foreseen.

Once the shooting had stopped, the burqa-clad older woman had pulled Yasim out of the big tent and had guided her into the honeymoon tent.

Once there, Yasmin had stood, wondering what she should do. The woman's protective arms let her loose, and Yasmin started toward the tent flap to see what was happening. The woman pulled her back into the safety of the tent.

The woman had removed Yasmin's burqa—then she had gone behind her and used both hands to put a wide tape over her mouth. As Yasmin began to struggle, the woman had grabbed one of her hands and put it through a loop of rope. Yasmin cried out behind the tape, and tried to loose herself with her other hand, but the woman hit her, hard, and she fell to the ground. The woman grabbed Yasmin's other hand and pulled the ropes tight.

The woman bound Yasmin's feet, put another length of tape across her mouth, and replaced her burqa and her wedding shawl.

Then the woman dragged Yasmin across the tent, threw a

dark rug over her, so that no one would even see she was in the tent if they looked.

There were more gunshots, and the engine of a car or truck roared to life.

The still-veiled woman looked at Yasmin just before she pulled the rug over her head. She made a sign for silence with her hand. Then she made the motion of a knife slitting a throat.

Then the rug went over Yasmin's head, and the world was dark.

Yasmin didn't cry. Even after the hours went by, and her arms and legs ached from lack of circulation, and she desperately wanted a drink. Her mouth was so dry.

At some point, her eyes adjusted a little, enough for her to notice the few things that were under the rug with her. The largest one was a piece of jewelry. It seemed to be a necklace. And it was lying on a small card that seemed to have her own name written in the Hajj's hand.

That surprised her. It had been a long time since someone had gotten her something nice.

It seemed a long, long time—it seemed forever, before she heard the tent flap open. She tried to kick and move, and it must have worked somewhat, for a woman and a girl who'd entered the tent came back and found her.

They were of the Hajj's tribe. A pleasant-looking woman and her young daughter, called Safia.

"You're here," said the mother. "Allah be praised!

"No one touched you, did they, child? Other than the woman, that evil woman who did this to you?" Safia's mother pulled the tape from Yasmin's mouth in one yank. The pain took a moment to wash over her, and it took a minute before she felt she could speak.

"No," Yasmin agreed, "praise God, no one has touched me."

"We are so sorry this has happened to you, in the protection of our family. Please accept our apologies!" the woman said.

"I would like some water," rasped Yasmin. "Please, some water."

The little girl, Safia, brought her a jug and a cup from across the tent.

"Yasmin," the woman continued. "The men are all meeting in the big tent. There is some very sad news, I'm afraid."

"What is it?"

"The man who masterminded your kidnapping did it because the Hajj owed him a debt. The good news is, the debt has now been paid. The bad news is . . . child, there is no happy way to tell you this. Your husband is dead."

"The Hajj? Oh! I am sorry. I did not know him well, but he was kind to me," Yasmin replied. And her voice sounded like that of a young child.

Yasmin saw the world once again crumble around her, as she had secretly known it would. "Must I then go home?"

By tribal custom, each of the Hajj's surviving wives would become the responsibility of that wife's eldest son. And Yasmin, since she had no child, would return to the tent of her stepfather.

The woman and the girl looked surprised at Yasmin's question, and she realized she had spoken rashly. "I'm sorry. I did not mean to impose," Yasmin said, and she began to cry. "But if there is any chance—" She went across the tent to the rug she had been hidden under. She picked up the beautifully crafted tanzanite necklace that had been left there for her by the Hajj.

"I would gladly give this to help pay my way," she said.

The mother and daughter looked at each other.

Yasmin could see them thinking, the thoughts in their minds running fast. She knew she had taken another chance, admitting to these strangers that there was a reason she did not want to go back.

The mother put a hand on Yasmin's arm. "Let me see what I can do. Safia, run and get Farina; tell her I have women's business to discuss with her. Go quickly, Daughter, so that things may be in place before the men's meeting ends and Yasmin becomes the focus of attention."

"I will," the girl said, and as she left the tent she heard her mother say, "Yasmin, you are the bride, and the necklace was a gift to you from your bridegroom. Tuck it away. It may be you will have need of it some time, but not today. Times have been hard for you, child; the day has been hard. But let me see if things can be made better."

January 27, 2007, 3:42 P.M.
(5 hours, 12 minutes since end of auction)
Judean wilderness west of the Dead Sea
Israel

Jaime found the young girl Safia at the horse corral. Safia hid herself at first, but when she saw who the newcomer was, she came forward.

"Do you know what is happening in the big tent?" the girl asked.

"Not exactly. But Ahmet is there. And Tarif. I'm sure they will guide the others to make wise decisions."

The girl stood by the fence, and her Arabian, Pasha, came over to nuzzle her.

"I hear the bride has been invited to stay here."

"Yes," Safia said, scuffing the ground with her toe. "Farina, the wife of the Hajj's second son, has offered her the hospitality of their tent. She and her husband are both kind. They will see her well married, should the time come again."

"Safia," said Jaime, coming to stand next to her. "You understand that what happened here today—what happened to Yasmin—was not your fault?"

"But I took the box," the girl whispered.

"You hid it for good purpose," Jaime said in Arabic. "The others who sought it—their reasons were not so noble." Safia looked up at her, and Jaime said, "No one will ever know where it was or how you got it back. In fact, Ahmet has told me that he knows who bought the box, who won the auction. He thinks it is very possible that both the money paid for the box *and* the box itself will be returned to your tribe. So you see, it continues to bring good fortune."

"It was kind of Ahmet to give Tarif the second box from the cave, the one covered with gold," Safia said softly. "I know what Tarif wants to do with it." She sighed. "He is probably trying to persuade the men even now. He will want to sell it, to buy land and . . . and design a town . . . a town where the buildings look like flowing tents—"

"I believe Tarif will be a great leader one day," Jaime said to Safia, and for some reason Safia blushed deep red. "And I believe you will be a great leader one day also."

Pasha pushed at the girl's shoulder, still not satisfied that she had no treat for him. "What will become of us?" Safia said sadly. "Will we lose all of this? Will Pasha one day be gone, and the wide-open spaces? Is this the end?"

Jaime looked over the fine, strong horses, including the stallion that had served Yani and her so well earlier in the day.

"I don't know what will happen," Jaime finally answered. "I know that Tarif and Ahmet are giving wise counsel. It seems as though the Hajj's second son will have a large say, and he is a wise and kind man."

Jaime wished she could have given Safia a more definitive answer about the future. Instead, she put her arm around the girl's shoulder and said, "Always remember your courage this day, Safia, and remind Tarif of his courage. I know Ahmet has spoken to him, to help Tarif know that his life is not defined by the fact he killed a man. It is defined by his true heart, and by the bravery he showed."

Safia looked at Jaime then, and said seriously, "Must I continue to go to school?"

"I know it's a hard choice. But it seems to me the men who lead your tribe in the future will need to be educated to deal with the outside world. And it would be good to have women who will be educated as well, who can help bring a good future."

Safia nodded sadly. "I may have to stay in school." She

jumped down, startling her horse, and kicked the ground. "But I don't want to grow up! I don't want to be a woman, who does nothing but sit at home. Life is far too exciting for that!"

This time, the smiled response was from Jaime. "It's not always boring to be a grown woman," she said, and she winked. "Take my word for it."

By early evening, Jaime and Yani had dropped Operative 2 at a safe house in Tel Aviv and returned to the airport for the flight back to Aéroport de Paris–Le Bourget to be debriefed. Their ground crew at Ben-Gurion Airport was preparing their plane for takeoff when Yani strode across the tarmac carrying an English-language newspaper.

"Seen the headlines?" he asked Jaime.

Jaime took the paper, expecting to see more write-ups on Andrea's exploits in Davos. Which there were—but they had fallen below the fold.

Instead, at the top of the paper were photos of Shepard, his home in Lac-Argent, Derrick—and Jaime. "It seems the mystery woman has been identified," Yani said.

"Shit," said Jaime.

"It's all right," Yani said. "The article says you were treated and released."

"Not kidnapped?"

"No. There's only so much gardeners can do—but we can usually do something."

"So, I'm not wanted for questioning by the local authorities? Or the international authorities?"

"Not by the authorities. But popular media outlets—there I'd say you're the number one quarry at the moment."

"That probably means the Army's looking for me, too—at least the Public Affairs Office. I'm almost afraid to turn on my BlackBerry."

But she did.

"Don't worry," he said. "The Army's been told you're going to drop out of sight for the remainder of your leave, and when you resurface, you'll talk to our friends at PAO, first thing."

Meanwhile, her e-mail had come up. "I've got an e-mail from my boss," she said, and opened it—then started laughing.

"You're not going to share?" Yani asked.

She read: " 'Jaime, for some reason I had the camera on my cell phone ready when someone showed the newspaper photo of you and Shepard to Lieutenant Colonel Jenkins. Thought you'd enjoy the result. See you back. CH Sherer.' "

Still laughing, she showed Yani the photo of a very shocked Jenkins.

But she sobered quickly.

"There is one call I have to make," she said.

"I know," Yani said. "Use the secure line. It's not Operative business, but we can't have you traced." He was in Op 1 mode.

"Thanks," she said, and went into the far reaches of the private hangar and dialed Mark Shepard's private cell phone.

Mark's phone was answered by an assistant. "Who's calling?" was all he said.

"It's Jaime Richards," she said. "I was—"

"Hang on," was the reply. Jaime waited for several minutes before the same voice came back on. "What did you have for dinner on Thursday night?" he asked.

"Trout amandine," she said. "And root vegetables."

The phone was handed over, and the next voice was Mark's. "Jaime? My God!"

"Mark, are you all right? Are you still in the hospital?"

"Yes, I'm still in the hospital. Apparently I'll be here for another couple of days. But I'm starting to wean off the morphine drip. Never going back there—but it's kind of nice when it's legal."

"And Derrick, I can't believe it. I'm still in shock."

"I am, too. Awful thing." He paused a moment before blurting, "For God's sake, what happened to you? First they tell me you're kidnapped, your blood is all over the house, next thing I know, they're saying you're fine, you were treated for some mysterious injuries at some mysterious place and released—but they won't tell me where, or let me talk to you. Where the hell are you? Are you all right?"

"I'm okay. There are reasons the whole story can't come out just yet, so please don't repeat this." And Jaime told him as much as she could, including the fact that Frank was dead. "I've got to disappear now, until the end of my leave, so that the press doesn't find me," Jaime said. "But Mark, I still need you to be my friend. A friend of my heart."

"Of course." The words were spoken carefully. There was a beat. "So are you telling me it's best if we're not involved romantically?"

"There isn't a woman in the world who wouldn't be thrilled to be involved with you romantically. Including me. Seriously." Jaime cleared her throat, knowing she had to be honest, but it was not easy. "I know this is going to sound strange, since I just saw you day before yesterday. But back then, someone in my life I thought was gone forever was . . . gone. And now he's back." She took a gulp of air. "And I've married him."

"You've *what*?"

"I've married him. The thing is—I think if Paul met him, he'd approve. And I think you'd approve. I'd really like you to meet him. On Thursday when you talked about what a rare thing our friendship is and you didn't want anything to ruin that—well, I agree ten thousand percent. You're a part of me. A part of my past. And, God willing, of my future."

There was silence on the other end. Jaime closed her eyes and grimaced.

"What are you thinking?" she finally asked.

"I'm thinking, every now and then it's good for the rock star part of me to be put in my place," he said.

"Oh, Mark, no—" she said, but he interrupted.

"And—that it's probably a good thing we didn't go farther than we did. That would have complicated things."

Jaime replied, "It's really hard to be you, to carry off all you do, and I know that. I admire it so much. I believe in everything you're doing. It's so important. We're on the same mission. And I'd feel honored to be counted among your comrades in arms."

"You're there, Jaime. I love you."

"I love you, too," she said.

"So, when do I get to meet this guy?"

"Well, thanks to *your* international celebrity, I can't get near you for a while. But as soon as I get out of Iraq again— I'll find you."

"Hey. Speaking of my celebrity, the one good thing that's come out of all this . . ."

"Yeah?"

"Since the press can't get to me, apparently they're crawling all over Lac-Argent. Which we're completely set up for. They're getting tours of the vineyards, the farms, the wind farms, the whole sustainable outfit. It's getting press even I could never arrange for."

"That is one good thing," Jaime agreed.

"Safe journey, Jaime."

"You, too, Mark. Godspeed, until we meet again."

She pressed the button to disconnect, and looked up to see Yani watching her from across the hangar. The plane was out on the runway, apparently ready to go.

She sat for one moment more, and then gathered herself together, got up, and walked toward Yani.

"So," he said, as they both headed out for the airplane to France.

"So?"

"As you pointed out, we're not yet legally married anywhere in the Terris world," Yani said, looking straight ahead. "Care to make a different choice?"

"So . . . if I decide to take your name as my married name, what am I called? Jaime 23?"

She didn't look over, but she knew he was grinning.

—EPILOGUE—
SUNDAY

Jaime stood, still radiating with amazement at being alive, in the yacht's private dining room. It was an interior compartment, so there were no outside windows. The walls were lined with books, old editions, and there was a self-contained fireplace. It had the feel of an old-world library. She was the first to arrive, and she gave in to the temptation to pull out a copy of *The Misanthrope* and carefully leaf through the brittle pages.

As she was replacing the volume, the dining room door opened and a slender woman walked in. Jaime was thrilled to find it was Andrea Farmer.

"Andrea! I'm so glad you're here safely!" she said.

"I had no idea you were going back so soon!" Andrea responded, and the two women embraced—albeit a bit gingerly on Jaime's side.

"For a short visit," Jaime explained.

In fact, everything about Jaime's upcoming visit to Eden was unusual. TC2 had made special arrangements to allow Jaime to join the group for this door opening—and to allow her to return in a week and a half, in time to report back for duty from her mid-tour leave.

TC2 had made her promise she would return. Jaime had promised—although she knew going from Eden to Iraq would not be an easy transition. TC2 had known that also and had tantalized Jaime with the pendant from Clement that already held her next "juicy" assignment.

The dining room door opened again, and they were joined by two other Operatives Jaime hadn't met, one man, one woman. They each seemed capable yet approachable, physically fit, and mid-fortyish. As they were Eden Operatives, Jaime had no idea of their actual age.

The four of them stood by the fire companionably.

They didn't have long to wait.

When the door opened again, they all turned expectantly.

And in walked two strapping, tall men. They were mid-conversation, and they were laughing.

They were Sword 31, who was overseeing this door opening—and the legendary Sword 23. Jaime saw Andrea gasp.

"Welcome, everyone," said Sword 31. He was perhaps an inch taller than Yani, with sand-colored skin and thick brown hair. But he had nowhere near Sword 23's charisma—or so it seemed to Jaime. "Let's all have a seat, shall we?"

The rectangular table in the middle of the room was masterfully hand carved from olive wood. There were six matching chairs, each intricately worked with a lion climbing the tallest point of each.

The unknown man and woman sat together on one long side of the table, and Andrea joined Jaime on the opposite side. Jaime dared a quick look in the direction of Yani— Sword 23—and was relieved to find he'd chosen the seat at the end of the table, next to her seat.

Jaime didn't dare look at Yani directly. His presence had captured her already, and simply having him in such physical proximity heightened all her senses and revved the blood flow from her heart into high. Even after only hours apart, she was overwhelmed by who he was, what they were to each other, and what he could do to her body—apparently, without even touching it. It was unnerving.

In a wonderful way.

"This is an exceptional door opening," spoke Sword 31. "And not only because everyone gathered here is an Operative, although that does mean we can have a sea start. It also means we may speak more freely."

All eyes were on him. "For one thing," he said, "I feel honored to have Sword 23 in our company today. Although he's now chosen to work as an Operative, he meant a great deal to me in my own training as a Sword."

The other Operatives all turned toward Yani, relieved to have permission to look directly at him. It felt as though they'd like to applaud but settled for a more dignified nod of the head.

"It's good to see each of you again," Yani said simply, "and to meet Dr. Farmer."

Sword 31 gathered their attention again by saying, "You're each here at the successful completion of an assignment. For that I congratulate and thank you on behalf of all the gardeners, and those on whose behalf you intervened." They took a moment to acknowledge one another before turning back to Sword 31.

At the head of the table, he continued, "Sword 23 has two particular pieces of good news, which you will undoubtedly hear more of back in Eden—but he has given me permission to share the news early with the Operatives gathered here."

"First, he shares the good news that he has married—"

Sword 31 had to stop as three of the others each gasped audibly and turned to Yani. "And, I might add, his new wife is returning to Eden with him tonight."

Jaime couldn't help it. She blushed deeply as those at the table played a quick game of elimination and all eyes focused on her.

"My dear girl—!" started Andrea; then she stopped, because she'd run out of words.

"I continue by telling you that Sword 23 and Jaime Ingridsdotter were Operatives together on the current critical, which was brought to conclusion yesterday. It concerned the retrieval of a Messenger box from a lost cave in the Judean wilderness."

The room was so quiet that the spit of the fire had the impact of a firecracker.

"They were able to retrieve both the box and its contents.

Contents which have been lost for two thousand years. We don't know for certain, but we have high hopes—"

"The writings of Yacov?" whispered Andrea.

"We have high hopes. The package returns with us tonight." Yani held up the velvet package.

"Well done," said the male Operative from across the table.

"Indeed," echoed his female counterpart.

"So, we have much to anticipate on our return home," said Sword 31. "Well done, all."

He took out a bottle of red wine and uncorked it.

A silver goblet sat in front of each of them. One of the gems known as the Six Sisters of Eden adorned each cup.

This felt so surreal for Jaime. She'd gone from the Terris world into Eden only once before. And that time she'd sat alone at a small table in a hut at the end of the world. And a mysterious man called Yani had told her of Eden, invited her to come. She had no assurance he wasn't crazy. She had no assurance of anything. He'd poured a cup of wine for her, and spiked it with a liquid drug.

She'd had to choose on faith whether to drink, and risk, and go—or refuse, and stay.

Jaime had bet everything on Yani.

As she had again.

Sword 31 walked behind each chair, his hand resting on the shoulder of the Operative before him, saying a short benediction quietly, for hearing of the person in front of him only, before he poured the specified amount of knockout drug into each cup. He paused an extra moment with Sword 23, and whatever he said caused both men to smile.

Jaime watched as he then poured the drug into the cup of Sword 23, who had become a lowly Operative again—for her.

Then Sword 31 stood behind Jaime; his hand was heavy on her shoulder. "Well done, good and faithful servant," he said simply. "And then he leaned in closer and said, "Well done— on all counts."

Jaime felt warmth pour through her, and she had the courage to look up—at her husband. He was looking at her intently, with a depth of love and passion that she'd never seen before, even from him.

Sword 31 was back at the head of the table. "Let's journey together," he said to Andrea, and poured a draught into her goblet from the bottle of wine. She mixed it with the silver swizzle stick, then took the bottle with a smile before turning to Jaime.

"Let's journey together," she said, and poured Jaime's wine.

Jaime mixed hers as she'd seen Andrea do; then she accepted the bottle.

She turned to Yani. "Let's journey together," she said, and she poured the wine for him. It was the exact opposite of the last time they'd done this, when Yani had poured her two drinks—one spiked, one not—and let her choose.

He mixed his drink, then looked up, and grinned at her.

He took the bottle and poured it for the other male Operative before turning back to Jaime.

Then Yani put his hand on the table, palm up. She took it with hers. As the last two Operatives poured the wine, he breathed for her ears only, "I love you. My wife."

"My husband," she said, "we're alive!" There was wonder in her voice.

"Let's go home," he said. "And continue to journey together."

And then Sword 31 stood at the head of the table and took his own, unspiked, drink. He started, "Let's raise our cups because—"

"Who rules Eden rules the world," they answered together.

Jaime and Yani continued to hold hands as they raised their cups to each other, and together they drank.

ACKNOWLEDGMENTS

What continues to make the Eden Thrillers an adventure for the authors is those who journey with us. Thanks first, as always, to our editor, Jennifer Enderlin, for taking a chance on Eden in the first place, then for her incisive comments and depth of understanding. Sometimes we wonder if she realizes the difference her career has made in the lives of so many. Sara Goodman, for making the road smooth; Susan Cohen, agent and friend; Sarah Silberman, for helpful graphics; John Karle and friends in St. Martin's publicity department; PJ Nunn and the gang at BreakThrough Promotions; Barbara Wild for copyediting expertise; and the fantastic book lovers who own or manage the bookstores we visited across the country. Thanks so much for your knowledge, your welcome, and your enthusiasm. Thanks, too, to Gary Kessler for information hard to come by elsewhere. We'll leave it at that. Our gratitude to Lila Abu-Lughod for her fascinating books, for recording women's voices among Egyptian/Libyan Bedouin with heart and understanding, as well as for timely e-mail dispatches from New York and Cairo. To Xavier and Christine, proprietors and hosts extraordinaire of Manoir de la Semoigne in Villers-Agron . . . just across from the old church with the unused bell tower . . . forgive us for letting an American rock star barge in. As always, we thank our early readers: Robert Owens Scott, Mary Ann O'Roark, William D. Webber, Deb Holton-Smith, Nancy Moore, Lisa Cullen, Stacey Chisholm, Tom Mattingly, and Bill DeSmedt. Your feedback and collective wisdom brought the book into focus.

From Sharon: Thanks to my family who keep the home fires going: Bob, Jonathan, and Linnéa; my parents, Marilynn and Bill Webber; those good friends who keep me sane (well, almost); my godmother, Shirley Nice, for traipsing the hills of San Francisco with me, from signing to signing, in heels that were only for the most intrepid; and, as always, B.K., my invaluable companion for this journey. What a ride it's been! Seriously, what are the odds?

From B.K.: I am so very grateful for the people God has brought into my life at those moments when I most needed a boost. For Peter Jones, whose "spot-on" comments for our manuscripts were equaled only by his Vidor's Toccata on Christmas Eve. For Francis Hanner, my German "mom" and caretaker extraordinaire for Derry, how could I have gotten through the last year without you? For SGT Pamela Atayde, who has continued to serve as my chaplain assistant with zeal despite her horror at the fate of Rodriguez in *Chasing Eden*. For Steve Quigg and Mark Hampton, each of you helped me stay sane during trying times. For the Edens family, once again giving of time and insight to help us connect with readers. For Beth and Ben Sadd, thank you for making sure my New York house remains a warm and welcoming home. And for Carol Lopez, what a truly courageous act to brave the evil neighborhood cats just to bring me croissants. I am blessed to be able to call you and Fred my friends.

Without family I would be truly lost. To my niece Deanna, thanks for the great Italian adventure. Do you think that police officer in San Marino believed our story? To Randy and Lynda, whether we are screaming at the end of the Superbowl or silently watching deer in the snow, I know I am always at home with you. To Linda and Mark, I so appreciated the energy with which you offered input on finance and economics. Suppose I should think about buying some gold, huh?

And finally, to Sharon, who puts up with my predictably unpredictable schedule. Do you think being in the same time zone would make this coauthoring thing any easier? Let's keep this partnership going and hope that maybe one day we can answer that question.

From both of us: Love and thanks to the gang from Springfield, Missouri: Nancy Allen, Susan Welker, Pam Smith, Will and Mary Ellen Nopper, Scott Martin, Donna Sing, and of course the Mercers—what fun to find sometimes you *can* go home again. Or at least return to the scene of the crime.

Most important, as always, thanks to our readers, who give us reason to write. From two simple gardeners, Godspeed.

Please visit us at Eden Thrillers.com